The Lost Glass Plates of Wilfred Eng

The Lost Glass Plates of Wilfred Eng

a novel

Thomas Orton

COUNTERPOINT • WASHINGTON, D.C.

Library of Congress Cataloging-in-Publication Data
Orton, Thomas.
    The lost glass plates of Wilfred Eng : a novel / Thomas Orton.
      p.   cm.
    ISBN 1-58243-023-3 (alk. paper)
    I. Title.
PS3565.R79L67   1999
813'.54—dc21   99-34803
                                                                        CIP

FIRST PRINTING

Book and jacket design by Amy Evans McClure

Printed in the United States of America on acid-free paper that meets the
American National Standards Institute Z39-48 Standard.

COUNTERPOINT
P.O. Box 65793
Washington, D.C. 20035-5793

Counterpoint is a member of the Perseus Books Group.

10 9 8 7 6 5 4 3 2 1

For my family,

and for the memory

of my father

Acknowledgments

I'm indebted more than I can say to Lois and Jim Welch and to Bryan Di Salvatore, dear old friends who not only showed the way, while I wrote this book, but gave me what is no exaggeration to call soul-sustaining friendship. Acts of love like these are impossible to repay except through remembering: I couldn't forget if I tried.

So many other people were unstinting in their offers of friendship, love, enthusiasm, and help while I wrote this book: Bill Kittredge, Ed McClanahan, Ripley Hugo, Tracy and Jonathan Field, Mary Maker, Clay Morgan, Dee McNamer, Marsha and Michael Burns, Randy Hayes and Suzanne James, May and Wah Lui, Walter Parsons, Dorothy Bullitt, Gordon Taylor, Schuyler Ingle, Dianne Hanna, Julie Benezet, Jennifer Seman, Phyllis Hatfield, Sally Anderson, Ivan and Carol Doig, Cindy Burdell, Michael and Sally Carley, Maureen and Ed MacLeod, Maureen and Denny Bekemeyer, Marty Bucher and Jane Lamensdorf, Harry and Anne Kirchner, Ed Marquand, Kate Rogers, Gary Luke, Pam Davick, Barbara Mackoff, Pam Jorgensen, the late Jordan Rand, Carolyn Marr, Diane Jackson, and Deb Evans. Thank you one and all.

I'm also grateful to my agent, Jeff Gerecke, who never lost hope and who couldn't possibly have found a more salubrious and welcoming home for this novel than with Jack Shoemaker, Trish Hoard, and everyone at Counterpoint Press. Thanks also to Connie Oehring for her wonderful copyediting work.

And finally, for the pleasure and the privilege of their company all these years, a special thanks goes out to all my fellow Seattle booksellers, especially my workmates past and present at Beks and Second Story, and to all my friends on the other side of the counter who have shown unceasing loyalty and exercised the questionable judgement of entrusting me to put good books in their hands.

Thomas Orton

We are immortal, I know it sounds like a joke.

Julio Cortazar

1

· · · · · · · · · · · · · · · · · ·

"Lilacs," I said, and offered Judith Lund the loupe. The negative measured 12x15 inches and showed a male figure seated on a divan before a blank wall. The flowers were on a stand in the background over his shoulder. "That means May," I said. "Maybe April."

Judith waved away the eyepiece. "April *when?*"

When she had called me in to appraise this glass plate and four others, I'd warned her that such things usually came to nothing, though clearly Judith was anxious for some more hopeful word. Judith was the scion of Seattle pioneers and a talentless painter of abstracts. I lived just two blocks up the street, and we knew each other better than she liked to admit. For Judith, a photo dealer and historian was a mere accessory to the art world, a necessary evil. But she was an outsider herself—her money impressed people most. From where we stood in the skylit entry hall of her studio I could see the corner of one of her huge, hopeless canvases leaning against the wall. Given her record so far, reflected in cruel jokes circulating around Pioneer Square, it might lean there for some time yet. I told her, "This size plate dates from the 1860s or '70s."

"So they're early."

There were no dates or other markings along the borders, nothing to give the plates a context. In each of the negatives the figure's hair was neatly oiled. In a print the tiny spot on his chest would become the head of a stickpin aslant in his cravat. His eyes, which would be dark in a positive, showed as clear glass, his stare unrevealing, blank as a statue's. "I could make prints if you want," I said. "Something else might show up."

Judith considered this suggestion, probably wondering how much more it would cost and what she would have in the end. Where money was concerned Judith usually took the Lund family line. Her great-great-grandfather Joshua had helped plat the city and had been rewarded with several prime tracts, which he had converted to a modest reserve of cash. From this his heirs had raised an enormous fortune, using financial tactics no more sophisticated than shut-ins saving bits of string.

"Can you tell me any more?" I asked. "Where did you get them?"

"You know what I know," she snapped, impatient that we might have even ignorance in common. Then, in the slightly milder tone of a last-ditch hope, she added, "I found them downstairs in the basement. There's a lot of old family stuff down there."

Members of Judith's family were all notorious pack rats, but it was rare that people's basements and attics yielded anything that had more than sentimental value. "I wish I had better news," I said. "I'm afraid they're probably not worth much."

She grunted, then looked at her watch. "I'm running late," she said. "Thanks for coming, Robert. You can send me your bill."

I set the plate down carefully and cleared my throat. "I wonder if you could pay me now."

She stared at me through the bottoms of her bifocals, magnifying this insolence. "My accountant usually handles these things."

Judith was small but formidable. She was fifty or so, and people who liked her called her handsome. She looked like she took care of herself. Her fine, sandy hair was pulled back tight against her skull, which made her features look sleek, as if she could cut through even the foul weather of failure.

"It's only fifty dollars," I told her reasonably.

Judith parted ways with her skinflint ancestors for one thing only: her luckless art career. She never stinted on it. I'd heard she had trouble even giving away her paintings, but she bought only the finest canvas and paints and had spent a fortune on this state-of-the-art studio. She also kept herself in the picture with well-publicized donations to museums and sponsorship of special events. Every other expense, like paying me, was negligible. I'd been down this road with her once before. Several years ago she'd hired me to negotiate the purchase of a photograph of her infamous, whiskey-drinking great-grandmother. The image was the size and color of an old half dollar and had been exposed on a wafer of treated whale ivory mounted on velvet. The great-grandmother was a favorite among local historians, and since there were few known pictures of her Judith had planned to make a splash by giving this one to the Seattle Historical Society. She was prepared to pay a lot of money for the icon-sized picture.

I managed to get the Minneapolis seller to lower his price and also arranged for shipping, insurance, and the transfer of funds. My own fee came to $200, but I might as well have asked Judith for the moon. Months went by, and my bill went unpaid. I wrote her pleading letters and left her messages. Once when I managed to catch her actually answering her phone, she seemed outraged that I'd even think to ask, then angrily referred me to this same accountant, a man as officious as an IRS agent and whose replies to my entreaties were just as elliptical. Almost a year later a check finally arrived. It was $25 short, a charge meant, I could only guess, as a kind of reverse interest accrued for the insult of my persistence. Between then and now, whenever Judith and I had seen one another she had snubbed me like a faithless lover.

So obviously, when she'd called me the day before about these four negatives, I'd wanted to say no. But business was slow, and I couldn't afford to.

Staring at me now, she left a long silence, then said, "I'm not sure I can find my checkbook."

"I can wait."

She held the look another moment. Her giant leather handbag sat on the floor under the triangular sheet-steel butler's table on which the negatives lay, and when she saw I wasn't going away she picked up the bag and started rummaging. I imagined that paying people also annoyed her because it meant acknowledging that they were professionals, which she wasn't. Also, like her cheapskate forebears, Judith believed paying for advice was like paying for air, and as she punched her hands inside the huge bag it was clear that this waste of good money had worn away the last of her patience. She looked up and sighed.

"Not here." She gave me the same stare, then said, "I wonder if you could do me a favor while I look." She pointed at a carton in a corner of the entryway. A carpenter had just finished building some cabinetry in another part of the studio and had left behind several cans of stain and some scrap wood. "Could you carry that down to the basement? I'll have your check for you when you come back up. It's A-r-m... what?"

"Armour," I said and spelled it while eyeing the box. I could live with this slight if it meant getting paid, though my resentment increased the moment I picked up the carton, which was large and awkward and weighed a ton. "I'll be right back," I told her, then stepped into the hall and headed for the elevator.

Judith's building, called the Glorien, was left over from an uncle's brief return to real estate. The uncle was considered a black sheep by family members who preferred the simple safety of mutual funds and plain old-fashioned savings accounts. Judith had hung on to the Glorien, converting it to upscale condos, and though she didn't live

there herself she had kept the top floor for her studio. Only the basement hadn't been touched.

Pioneer Square basements were at the level of the old city, which
had burned to the ground in 1889. A Victorian town had been built
on top of buttresses and bulwarks set over the ruins, which could still
be viewed on a tour. The Glorien's basement, entered through the
alley, was packed to the ceiling with cartons, crates, furniture, and cu-
rios. Generations of Lunds had left junk here the way dogs buried
bones, forgetting everything but the accumulating comfort.

I set down the heavy box and looked around the dim room. Here
and there narrow paths cut through the junk. Along one wall three re-
frigerators were arranged by age like someone's lifetime allotment. A
grand piano was loaded down like a pack mule: two car batteries and
a leather perambulator sat on its lid along with shoe boxes, cardboard
files, moldering books, and a giant ornate birdcage stuffed with
Liberty magazines from the 1920s. What peace of mind could be
drawn from all of this? The piano had no keys. Under it was an empty
space that seemed to quake with tension from the weight above.

The eccentricity of this room, all its unknowable stories, made me
suddenly curious, so I squatted down and opened the cardboard box.
Inside, along with the paint cans and wood scraps, was a smaller
wooden box that at first appeared to be an old filing case. I lifted it
out. The brass handles on its sides had gone green with age. Two un-
buckled leather straps hung down, still crimped at right angles. They
had left clean stripes on the dusty surface of the lid, which was scribbled over with fingerprints and fitted as tightly as a humidor's. Lifting
it off, I made out a scrolled "WE" painted on the wood. Inside was the
same man.

I smiled. This image was split down the middle, the broken edge an
arabesque so graceful I could almost hear the deep, fracturing chime.
The break was sharp and therefore recent: time wore edges smooth. I
put the halves together and held them to the bare bulb dangling from

the ceiling. This picture was made later in the day; the lilacs, cropped out of the frame, threw long shadows across the wall behind the head of the man, who, in this closer shot, appeared to be Asian. I noticed the stickpin was missing. Such details hinted in a seductive, tight-lipped way. The half told as much as the whole. It spoke the same non sequitur, the same message of incompleteness. The past could be as unknowable as the future. Whole, this man gazed out, straight-backed, mute as ever.

I slipped the halves back inside and picked up the lid, the inside of which was padded with cotton batting. The case had been made to hold the plates, its inner sides notched so that they could be slipped in and out. Such care was not unusual, especially when cumbersome old photo equipment had to be transported the way Carleton Watkins had carried his, hauling glass, chemicals, and camera into Yosemite on the backs of donkeys. Probably only a photographer would take such precautions. I looked at that "WE" again, licked my fingers and rubbed it clean.

Then the air of the basement seemed to pause. I slid out the halves again and held them to the light.

A certain parity was at work in the world. Disappointment, dis-guised by years of routine humility, was bound to yield singular, pen-etrating fantasies: the iris dilated, the raw world flooded back in. For just a moment these were not portraits but *self*-portraits, and a palpi-tating certainty would not breathe denial or allow that they had been made by anyone but Wilfred Eng.

Eng, the great landscape photographer.

Then the moment passed. I let out a breath and thought, *No way*. Fantasies turned into torture if we took them too seriously. I'd seen later portraits of Eng, and the likeness to the face in this close-up was striking. But the idea was ludicrous. It was true that Eng had lived in Seattle for brief periods, but he hadn't made his first trip here until 1881. By then he was using smaller, 3x5 plates. Most of his larger, older negatives had been destroyed in the 1906 quake and fire in San Francisco, Eng's nominal home. San Francisco was my hometown as well. There, and throughout the world, Eng was revered as one of the fathers of American photography. Biographies had probed his towering dichotomies. No less a figure than Alfred Stieglitz had called him a genius. Jacques-Henri Lartigue, Edward Steichen, Ansel Adams, Paul Caponigro—the list of his artistic heirs was endless. Even painters such as Thomas Hart Benton acknowledged a debt to Eng. It was crazy to think that the work of this giant might end up where I could find it.

Still, Eng had experimented with self-portraiture when he was young, though all early examples were believed lost in the quake. He'd also worn a wispy goatee just like this.

He had died in a fire just blocks from this spot.

Other facts welled up—the shows in Paris and New York; the difficult friendships with Lewis W. Hine, Imogen Cunningham, Asahel Curtis, and Stieglitz himself; the bitter racial politics; the peripatetic life. The landscapes. Many of Wilfred Eng's mysterious *Return* landscapes were considered masterpieces. I had studied them in school, in art survey courses. They were part of every major public and private photography collection from Stockholm to Tokyo to New Orleans, from the prestigious Academie Dageurre in Paris to the Botolph in Calcutta to MOMA and the Whitney. A prickling wave rushed over my scalp, and the cramped space of the basement seemed to tremble. My hands started to sweat. It was possible, wasn't it? I shook my head to clear it. I had learned the hard way that doubt was a scholar's best friend, that it was best to deny until the truth made as straight a line as possible. I held the halves together again and swallowed—Wilfred Eng might have held this very image just like this, looking at his own young face.

I straightened and took a breath. Even if it was a long shot I had to tell Judith. She might know or remember something—a letter, a family yarn that connected these plates to Eng. Once more I put the two halves inside the "WE" box and carried it out to the alley.

Holding what might turn out to be a rare treasure made the world look less ordinary. Light was the mundane miracle that could kindle a genius like Eng's. I couldn't help myself and set the box down on the gritty bricks of the alley, carefully sliding out the halves again and looking at them in the sunlight. The medium was most likely albumen—mostly egg white. But in the daylight the negative looked like crystal and stone, formed by slow pressures and broken along a facet. This was maybe the first time in decades that sunlight had touched the image. I forced myself to think practically. The albumen itself might be unstable. Even simple sun might damage the plate.

Plates.

Sweet Jesus, there were *five* of them! Excitement bore down at my back. I wanted to run, but that was asking for trouble. I felt like an acrobat caught on the tightrope while the big top burned down around him. Back in the lobby, the elevator looked dangerous, so I took the stairs. By the time I reached Judith's door I was dizzy and panting, my heart in a riot. I held the case with both hands and kicked the door. "Judith?" Something pink had been stuck underneath, and I toed it out—my check, unsigned. I ignored it and kicked again. "Judith! Open up, it's important!"

Somewhere deep in the studio Pollock, Judith's Great Dane, answered with a bark. Then I heard his running approach, a wild scrabbling like hail. Pollock, who had been absent during the appraisal, now set up deep barks that rattled the door on its hinges. Shocks collided with other shocks. I stepped back, wondering if Judith had left the other four on the table, which Pollock, if riled, might knock over. I thought of the broken plate, the gentle S-shaped break. Judith would have to wait.

....

At my apartment I shut the blinds and turned off the phone. In the spare bedroom, which I used as an office, I set the negative on my desk, then got out my copy of the Aperture volume *Wilfred Eng*.

It was definitely Eng in the negatives. A later portrait in *Wilfred Eng* showed a large mole on his cheek and another on his neck—both were visible with the loupe. The Aperture portrait showed a serpentine stickpin in his satiny tie. I recalled that Eng, who was something of a dandy, had had a large collection of them.

For much of his life he had operated a commercial portrait studio on Grant Street in San Francisco, which he occasionally closed to indulge his famous wanderlust. Among the Aperture images reprinted from the 1870s was a picture made in that studio of a Chinese woman and her son seated on the same divan as the one in the self-portraits. The pattern of the fabric matched. A small tear appeared in one corner. When I bent over the broken plate with a loupe, I saw the same tear and said, "Holy shit," out loud. The five self-portraits had been made in San Francisco and must have been brought here some time later. Eng must have brought them himself. Given that they were cumbersome and easily broken, I wondered why he'd bothered. Vanity, maybe. "This man loves his mirrors," Alfred Stieglitz had observed when the two first met. In 1912 he had invited Eng to show at his 291 Gallery, which had marked the beginning of their prickly friendship. "Wherever we walked, even along busy streets," Stieglitz wrote, "he was forever giving bird-like twitches of his head in order to catch glimpses of himself in shop windows."

According to the Aperture essay, Eng's greatest work "stood in opposition to his life. Publicly, he dedicated himself to portraying the racial imbalance in America to which the landscapes remained a necessary adjunct." Eng had been the first to photograph Filipinos coming to the United States in the late 1910s after the Spanish-American War. He had followed immigrants to Alaskan canneries, Washington bean fields, and California vineyards, documenting what he enigmatically called "the terrible power of the living poor." *Life* magazine had later used some of these photographs in a piece that downplayed continuing prejudice, instead favoring a whitewashed American Dream and shading Eng's vituperation as false modesty when he said, "The poignancy was there before the shutter opened." At the age of eighty-two he'd had his hand broken when a rally went sour in Monterey. He had met Steinbeck there; some believed Eng to be the model for Lee in *East of Eden*.

Eng's restlessness was legendary. His mother, fleeing poverty in Kowloon, had given birth to him in the ship's hold and named him for the captain. Eng claimed that being born at sea had robbed him of a country, and for most of his life he had traveled up and down the West Coast looking for one. He had met the American pioneer movement coming from the opposite direction. He believed that the country's westernmost shore was "not a promise but an end, breathing disappointment in every ocean wave." This disappointment, he claimed, turned people cruel, made them prone to prejudice. In 1941, at age ninety-one, Eng was living in a Seattle boarding house on Maynard Street that belonged to his cousin. During a sidewalk confrontation the cousin's son was mistaken for one of the Japanese just then being railroaded to camps for the duration of World War II, and a patriotic mob of whites set fire to the house. Eng, reading upstairs, did not escape.

Suddenly it was late afternoon, and I'd missed two appointments. I knew the library would help. I had even put my jacket on but then came back to the desk for another look and didn't think of leaving for many hours. I read through the long essay twice, and when I looked up again it was after midnight. The find had put me in a kind of nervous trance. I knew I wouldn't be able to sleep. So I left my apartment and walked to the Central Tavern for a beer. Not even the loud dance band drowned out the high-voltage hum of excitement. I couldn't stop seeing Eng's face in the plate. He was in his twenties; all the consequences of his long life still lay in front of him. He was not yet suffering from the self-delusion critics and even friends would later accuse him of. For half his career he used his camera as an instrument of social criticism and protested to the end that his finest work took place "in slums, on picket lines, wherever imagination could not add its clutter." However, most scholars and critics agreed that those images were his weakest work. His *Baja Children* came to mind, boys and girls staged in a simple game while their supposedly hopeless fathers looked on. These and other forced ironies were criticized during Eng's lifetime by the likes of Jacob Riis and sometime friend Lewis W. Hine, who called them "vaudevillian and absurd." Eng denied the importance of his landscapes so vehemently that his attitude came to seem less like a pose than something he truly believed. On his coastal trips he revisited sites he wouldn't admit had a near mystical effect on him—rock formations and beaches, hot springs, coastal forests, and villages. Sometimes decades passed between visits. In Clover, Washington, Eng's early images were of a logging town in its heyday. His photograph fifty years later showed tumbled chimneys and faint foundations fading in new growth. Eng photographed Haystack Rock on the Oregon coast a total of twelve times, the last in color in 1933. This image showed the rounded top of the rock projecting through swirls of pink fog like the rings of Saturn. The passage of time told more about Wilfred Eng, who believed these landscapes began only as records and failed when uncontrollable pathos crept in. Still, he couldn't stop. The images were sublime, transcendent. They'd been made with the hunger of a zealot.

I chugged three beers, which washed through without effect. I thought food might help the gnawing in my stomach and ordered two withered hot dogs the bartender warned were left over from lunch. The gnawing only turned jittery. Finally I couldn't sit any longer, so I left the Square and drove to Diane Mays' house.

Halfway up steep Queen Anne Hill a spark appeared in my rearview mirror like a match flame. Turning the corner, I stopped at Kerry Park and got out. From there I could see a warehouse fire in the distance, a deep orange dot boiling in the night. Alarms rang dimly. But at this distance catastrophe was not what it seemed, set like another jewel in the glittering dark. It seemed instead like a sign.

Diane Mays and her young son, Budge, lived in a cozy bungalow with a broad roof and two eyebrow dormers that gave it a look of whimsical surprise. The neighborhood was old, comfortably crowded with grandmothers and civil servants. It was past one, which meant I shouldn't call first or ring the doorbell. Instead I sneaked around to the backyard. Diane kept her plastic recycling bins back here. I emptied two on the lawn and stacked them in the flower bed under her bedroom window, then stood on them and tapped the glass until a dark mouth-shape opened in the blind. The blind shut instantly, and a moment later Diane appeared at the back door.

"Jesus, Robert, you scared the hell out of me. Are you all right?"

Inside, she led me through the kitchen that still smelled comfortably of dinner. Coming down the hall she put her finger to her lips, then looked inside Budge's room. "He's out like a light," she said. In her bedroom she touched my back and I nearly jumped out of my skin. Then she hugged me and said, "You're shaking like a leaf."

I was, and I realized it wasn't just excitement over the discovery. I stumbled at first, telling her about the plates. Altruism had served me faithfully over the past decade. But all at once my idealism sounded thin and forced. Diane may have heard it too. More from a practical standpoint she started taking off my clothes while I went on, and when we were under the covers she whispered, "Did you try calling this Judith?"

"She'd just think I was trying to get her to sign my check."

Diane touched my cheek after a telling pause. "You feel flushed."

"I drank too much beer," I said.

"What are you going to do?"

Many of Eng's surviving negatives and original prints were stored in the archives at San Francisco's DeWitt Museum. The museum was the executor of Eng's estate, so the right thing at this point was to tell Judith, then alert the DeWitt. Judith wasn't the ideal person to tell, yet neither was the pompous, well-endowed DeWitt. Suddenly I bristled at the idea of telling either of them.

"Something this big doesn't happen every day," I said. "They could be worth a fortune."

"Even the broken one?" When I nodded tensely in the dimness, she asked, "How much?"

"The needle could go right off the meter."

She fell silent again, hearing something more in my voice. Cautiously she asked, "How much would *you* ask?"

"It's not up to me," I said and felt myself squirm in her sheets. "Look, I know what you're thinking."

"You have to admit, Robert, it sounds like something you regretted once before."

If old photography taught any lesson it was that no one could live without the past, even if they wanted to. In another life, in California ten years ago, I'd owned a small but highly visible gallery, well reputed in the trade, well reviewed, and persistently if honorably poor. After years just scraping by, I'd thought to broaden business prospects by acquiring a privately commissioned suite of erotica by Edward Weston. The photographs, which I'd begun selling at a considerable profit, turned out to be very creditable fakes. The seller, a man I'd known and trusted, had needed the money for a last-chance cancer treatment in Mexico and had already left the country. Worse, as part of the purchase price I had borrowed $20,000 from a private source at high interest. When the Weston estate saw my clients' suits lining up, it kindly dropped its own. Into that void stepped *Art Forum*, *Darkroom Photography*, and other trade magazines. Scandal-hungry editors phoned at all hours. Selling the gallery had paid the legal fees and kept me out of bankruptcy court. I'd come north for a fresh start. In Pioneer Square, with its layers of old and new, I'd found a welcome illusion of redemption and second chances. I still struggled with poverty. I researched and wrote articles. Besides working for individual collectors, I dealt old photography to several art consultants. When money got tight something usually came up. I sometimes lectured at the Cornish Institute. Two years ago the Boeing company had hired me to catalog its visual library. For a decade now I'd kept my head down, focusing on my first love: the images themselves. Their silence. Their suggestion. The fragmentary proofs they offered of vanished worlds, of people just like us who would never have believed their lives would seem poignant or incomplete.

The past only appeared to be over. I needed little more proof than Weston—and now Eng—that it could turn liquid and volatile. I wondered how long the negatives had been sitting down there in Judith Lund's basement. How many times in the past decade had I walked past the Glorien, reveling in my anonymity, in the moist, forgiving Northwest air, never dreaming that such a treasure lay just below the level of the sidewalk? Maybe I hadn't been living my redemption all these years. Maybe I'd been waiting to stumble over it.

"I'd be on the other side," I told Diane. "With Weston, I got stuck in the middle."

"So what would happen?" she asked. "Would you find a buyer and then tell him not to say where he got them?"

"It's legitimate business. And what choice do I have? This is a great artist's early work. Do I pretend I didn't see it? How responsible is that?" When she didn't answer I added, "I know a man in San Francisco."

"How do you know such a person?"

"Don't say it like that. I know him the same way *you* know people."

Diane was director of a small private foundation dedicated to the environmental ideals of a late and beloved senator. She had a deadly aim when it came to getting donations from some of these same Californians who moved their fortunes north. She never asked where the money came from.

"He's a businessman and an art collector," I said.

The man I meant was Leonard Sills. When I owned my gallery Sills sometimes came to the openings and several times bought out whole shows. I hadn't been in touch for years. But what I'd sold him had appreciated, and whatever else Leonard remembered, he would remember that.

"So," Diane said, "you'd sell him the one you have and ignore the rest of this 'great artist's' work."

"Of course not."

"What about Judith?"

"I already told her they're worthless. If I went back on that she'd know something was up."

"Couldn't you make some kind of deal? A partnership, maybe?"

"Judith's a shark when it comes to money," I said. "She'd find a way to deal me out. I could probably make up some story about an article I was writing about anonymous old plates."

"And let her give them to you?"

"I'd offer to buy them."

"Then she'd *really* know something was up. How much would you offer?"

"*Judith's* the only one who thinks she needs the money."

"What's the difference between a fair price and an unfair one? Isn't it what you say or don't say?"

"I'd literally be doing the *world* a favor," I said. "Don't I deserve something for that, for all the dead time I've been putting in?"

I felt her look at me in the dimness. Quietly she asked, "Has it *all* been dead?"

"No, I didn't mean that."

"You always seemed satisfied with your life," she said and paused to let me agree. When I didn't she asked, "What would you say to her?"

"It's what *you* say that makes you good at your job."

"I'm not cheating someone else."

"I wouldn't be *cheat*ing her."

"*Shhh,*" she said and nodded toward the wall at our heads beyond which Budge slept.

"It's the way I make my living," I whispered. "Am I screwing everyone I deal with?"

"People know you have to make a profit, and they trust you to be fair. Suppose you went back to Judith and just leveled with her."

"She'd ask for the moon," I said. "She's rolling in money, and I'm barely making it most of the time. Maybe this is one of the ways rich and poor get evened out."

"Being poor has never bothered you before," she said. "You're a scholar. You're not cut out for this sort of thing. Look what it cost you before."

"Scholars have to eat. They even have to pick up the check once in a while instead of letting their girlfriends do it."

"You do all right."

"I make less money than a monk," I complained and turned to her. "You're in bed with an errand boy."

"That's ridiculous."

"If I leveled with Judith she'd sell them herself."

"I don't see what choice you have."

"The ogres always win," I said.

"In this case they're entitled to. You have to be honest with her."

I shook my head miserably. "She'll rub it in. Then she'll hire me to sell them *for* her. Afterwards I'll have to sit up and beg for another unsigned check."

"Then tell the DeWitt first. Let *them* deal with her."

"What would I get out of that? The DeWitt might pay me a little finder's fee and pat my back. I'd write a couple articles. I'd be invited to speak at the public library, and the tiny audience would ask if I felt like a sucker."

"You're exaggerating."

"Afterwards I'd be back to square one, scraping up rent and kissing ass."

"Were you so rich in San Francisco? Did you kiss any less ass?"

"No, but I was younger. There has to be a trade-off."

"You'd have to move uptown," she whispered, a grin shaping her words in the darkness. "We'd be able to tell you from the other high rollers only by the barbecue sauce on your shirt."

Then, by way of demonstrating one possible trade-off, she took my hand and pressed it between her thighs.

I could still be surprised by the ease with which Diane fitted her frank, often rollicking passions with being a mom. Somehow she made all the different sides work. If there was no such thing as an undivided soul, I believed Diane Mays at least came close. I had never wanted a woman the way I wanted her, which is to say I continued to want her in spite of the usual distractions—money (or in my case the dogged pursuit of it), career, other women. Now she pressed her mouth to mine, then slipped her thigh between my legs and eased it high until I moaned. I rolled over on top of her, and for a while I forgot all about Eng. Diane made love like someone deprived of sensory experience and anxious for a crash course. She clasped my ribs as if she were blind and my body something new each time. She slipped her fingers along the bones as if reading fleshy braille, pressing, molding my flesh to her consciousness. And this shaping didn't stop when we'd finished, Diane tucking herself tenderly around me, sealing the way with small kisses and caresses. Sleep only slightly loosened her hold. When I heard her breath deepen, Eng came back.

I lay awake for some time, thinking about the plates. Diane was right, of course. I'd tried to become a big shot once, and the attempt had bombed. For years now I'd gotten so used to playing the outsider that I might have trouble with anything else. When we first fell in love and I told her about the Weston trouble, I didn't know what to expect. I hadn't told anyone the whole truth and was surprised when the lurid details lost their pent-up tension while she listened. Diane inspired an atmosphere of mutual trust—I'd reached a point in my life where I wanted that as much as anything. Her sane perspective turned all scheming on its head, and I felt sure now that I'd come here tonight to be talked out of a bad idea. Even if Judith were to part with the plates, the right place for them was not with me or other strangers looking to cut themselves in.

I woke at nine the next morning. Diane and Budge were gone. Out in the kitchen she had left fresh coffee in a thermos and a note along the edge of the morning paper: "Budgie tried to wake you with his feather. Love," and it was signed with a lipstick kiss.

Budge, who was eight, had written something too. His Christian name was also Robert, which, Diane joked, had had her assessing my chances in a more fateful light. She and I had met a year ago at a party given by a wealthy arts patron more interested in Diane than in the good cause she'd already talked him into sponsoring. I ate some toast, studying the detail of her lips, vivid and ghostly as a rubbing. Under them the boy had written, "Can you come again tonight?" His elderly scrawl wandered into the front page photo of that warehouse fire. A man had been trapped and killed in the blaze. So much for signs.

When I first met Diane and Budge their life together had long been set in motion, and I was off the pace. I'd been a bachelor too long, and I was lagging, missing something important that had to be made up. I was encouraged but not forced, given closet space and a drawer in which two pairs of my socks sat rolled up like eggs. I was trusted. Before we met I rarely strayed from downtown. When I took Diane to my apartment on one of our first dates she said, "This could be any-body's mess," only half jokingly, as if I could do with some redefini-tion. When I first came to Seattle I felt fuzzy around the edges, and I stayed that way for a good long time. "It's as if you haven't decided to stay," she observed the same night I told her about Weston. I'd never married and hadn't had a steady girlfriend since my twenties. In Seattle, humbled, hiding out, I chose women who were unavailable for the long haul, in transit between lives, newly divorced, or planning to move away. Diane broke the pattern. She wasn't going anywhere. Her life was a thoughtful balance of work, home, and child, and now I was part of that. She'd opened the door and asked me inside, and I was surprised at what a relief it was. Her Saturday cooking sessions with Budge had become *ours*. Her kitchen was a cozy place where she spent a lot of time. We made puffed pastry appetizers, stuffed pork loins, cakes, tarts, cookies, and salmon mousse. At first she poked fun at my fumbling, and when she told me I neglected myself I wondered if she saw it as a serious obstacle. But she'd given me the first sense of belonging I'd had in years, and along the way I'd managed to make her thankful, which I could do in surprisingly simple ways, by fixing leaks or light sockets or cutting the grass. Diane let none of these small tasks pass without marking them in some way. As a result I looked for ways to perpetuate the upward spiral of gratitude, and so on the newspaper, under Budge's note, I wrote, "Yes." Then I left.

Research was an old soul mate, a steadying influence. In the past, ignoring it had cost me my gallery. Now it might soften the disappointment. When I left Diane's I drove to the University of Washington, where once, for a year, I'd been invited to curate the Northwest Collection, housed in the Suzzallo Library. The materials on Eng were limited. Once there I found a long biographical essay I'd read years before and read it again.

Eng's commercial studio did well enough in time that he was able to travel more and also to "document the poor who are made to pay for the misfortune of their state." In 1874 he took the first of many boat trips up and down the coast. "I have never gotten beyond this shore," Eng said late in his life, "never been allowed *inside*." On some of these early steamer trips he paid his way as cook and later, when photo equipment became more portable, by making portraits in logging and fishing villages. Here too he began the haunting *Return* landscapes. On the first of these boat trips he reached Baja. On the second, in 1881, he came north. In Seattle for the first time, he wrote to his assistant, "I have been led here by the softness of the light, the sweet moisture suspended in air. . . . It is a place to become wonderfully lost." He did not add that part of the allure here was the foment of Chinese riots. During his life Eng became as famous a bastard as a photographer. He had a knack for losing friends. Asahel Curtis claimed that he and Eng "nearly came to blows" and described him "spitting at me like a viper." Eng claimed that such conflicts boiled down to acceptance: even if the work of his peers didn't make the grade, it stood a better chance than his simply because of race. Though many who knew Wilfred Eng acknowledged that this claim was true, they ultimately lost patience with him. He almost seemed to punish himself by picking unwinnable fights with the world. This essay described Eng's often tyrannical rages at his studio help. Once an assistant named Wing quit his job when Eng humiliated him before a white client. In his ledgers Eng noted, "Poor Wing quite rightly points out that I love people something less than I love a fight, that I am unhappy and bored when things are too peaceful."

Down in the library stacks I found a copy of Alfred Stieglitz's correspondence and searched the index for Eng's name. Stieglitz wrote to a friend that he and Eng "fought bitterly the evening of his [1912] show, for I have apparently esteemed his genius for all the wrong reasons. He insists that he cares only for fact. But I believe his disciplined little landscapes are full of Soul." On hearing of Eng's death in 1941, he wrote that "Wilfred Eng was so formed by inevitable bitterness as to leave no record but on glass and celluloid and paper that he understood his own spiritual nature."

A morning spent among these familiar fragments sobered me, and Diane's sensibleness took an even firmer hold. Maybe I'd overreacted to the whole thing. It was possible that the world would never have clamored at my doorstep, or money poured into my bank account. Greedy, thinking myself on the verge of reparation for the Weston disaster, I may have blown this discovery out of proportion. The plates themselves might only make an interesting footnote, the remnant of a great artist's youthful experiment. For a moment I felt a stirring of relief, the return of a familiar quiet. When you thought about it, who *wasn't* an errand boy? Maybe Judith would cave in without a fight for once. Maybe the DeWitt would be generous before consigning these plates to a reverential corner of its archive.

At one I drove home, determined to settle the thing quickly.

I considered the best way to do this: I would tell Judith the truth and also tell her I was contacting the museum. I would not give her time to think or act, and if she balked or threw a fit I'd say, "Tell it to the DeWitt."

Judith wasn't home. In her message she dropped the names of those whose guest she would be for a few days' vacation out of town. Annoyed, I hung up, reasoning that this wasn't the sort of thing you left a message about. I picked up the plate again and leaned back in my office chair for another look. On the way home from the university I'd bought two pieces of clear Plexiglas and clamped the broken plate securely between them, and now I held it up to the daylight, maybe for the last time. The sensation was dizzying, like standing inside Eng's head. I set the plate on the windowsill and looked at the clear holes of Eng's eyes, then let my own eyes slip through his to the real world outside the window—a visual loss of traction. A prod. A dare.

February 27

For the first time I fell asleep in your arms. I woke alone & found
you had tenderly tucked your quilt around me. I heard you moving
in the other room & came out to find you squatting naked near the
windows. We had left our clothes strewn on the floor & you had
gathered them in a heap there & now held a square mirror to them.

I thought I must be dreaming. You stared, seeing something I
was sure no one else would ever see. I asked what you were doing
& you answered, "The light moves like wind." I smiled. You are
sometimes so guileless. Loving you is like loving a child. I am said
to be the one leading the sheltered life—how you would despise
me for thinking otherwise! I walked over to you, bent & put my
arms around your neck. You gazed at the heaped clothes which
looked like our shed skins, our ghost selves who had also embraced & now lay tangled in each other's limbs. Outside the windows the day was dark & the fog thick, yet somehow the mirror
stole a pale light. When you moved the glass, faint shadows
jumped & stretched in the folds & blinked in the lace holes of my
petticoat. I couldn't help but laugh.

Then it was time for me to dress. At the door we exchanged
many kisses & gentle words. Always at this moment you are full of
such tender remorse, your dark eyes gentle & sad. You pressed your
head to my breast & begged that it not be too many days before we
met again. Finally we had to let each other go or I would be late.

As I left your street the fog began to lift & the sun broke
through, but nearing home a deeper shadow fell over my heart.

Light, you have told me, would be nothing without
darkness....

2

. . . .

In the air an hour later I opened my briefcase as if I thought the plate might have disappeared. It was still there, packed carefully in cardboard and bubble wrap. What I might have been looking for instead was some certainty that I knew what I was doing, flying off suddenly like this to California. I hadn't traveled anywhere to speak of in years. I told myself it was strictly research—the DeWitt Museum's new library wing had a mountain of material on Eng. On this trip I would be gathering further proof that the plates were his. But as the plane neared the Bay Area I knew this wasn't the whole story.

I'd come here to get a number with a dollar sign in front of it.

I'd do the right thing when the time came. But if Leonard Sills and I could agree on a price, this broken plate would be my consolation prize. Judith, having heard me kick her door and shout when I'd come back up from the basement, would have assumed I was after her to sign my check. Later, if she confronted me about the missing broken plate, I could claim I'd never seen it, that it was rather a hunch and some subsequent research that had led me to believe the plates were Eng's. She couldn't prove otherwise. The alley behind the Glorien was crawling with winos and drug addicts, and I could suggest to her that one of them had broken in and made off with the plate or just moved it to another part of the basement. There was no way she could find out about Leonard. Everything about this plan was workable, except for Diane. Eventually I'd have to tell her what I'd done, though just now I didn't like to imagine what she would think.

Underneath the plate in the bottom of the briefcase, I found a months-old number of *The Journal of Western Pioneer Studies.* In this scholarly periodical was an article of mine on Francis Alquist Melton, who had made a fortune in stereographs and was hanged for murder in Portland in 1888. I read the first paragraph now and suddenly couldn't recognize it. Was this drivel really mine? How petty it seemed. So meticulous and dull, like something hammered out on an ancient Remington by a leather-faced retiree in rimless glasses and a string tie.

Was this the real Robert Armour staring up at me from the page? Was I meant to spend my whole life in the penny-ante peddling of pictures and ideas about pictures?

The minute the plane touched down in San Francisco I felt a different sort of charge than anyone could get writing scholarly papers. I hadn't set foot here since the Weston trouble. On the way downtown in a rented car I drove up Telegraph Hill to Coit Tower. The view there flung itself wide, a grand welcome home. It was as if I'd never been away. I parked at the top and got out. The weather was miraculous for late March. Maybe the idea of San Francisco gloom made this air seem hung with riches. The view was mesmerizing, a debauchery of detail, a forgotten world of tropical contrasts. The old landmark was suddenly drunk with dimension, clamoring for my eye with its razor-sharp edges. A breeze kicked up, an elbow in the ribs for forgotten days of fun. I felt a sudden pang for the last ten years, for all I'd missed here, the lost opportunities—not even lost but thrown away, squandered. If I'd stayed here I might have weathered my troubles. My life might have come right again in time.

I checked into a hotel on Sutter Street, and when I reached my room I picked up the phone. I'd never forgotten Leonard Sills' number: 555-9010. Other dealers joked that it was code for Leonard's percentage scheme—90 for him, 10 for everyone else. While the number rang my hands started shaking and my mouth went dry.

The woman who answered told me Leonard was about to leave for Italy.

"Does he know you?"

"I'm an old friend," I said. This was not exactly true and sounded it. I was shaky, too long out of the saddle. I tried to calm myself by focusing on the plate, the proof I had that it was Wilfred Eng's.

"He's very busy," she said impatiently. "Can someone else help you?"

I said I didn't think so, and she paused, clearly put out. "I'll try to see he gets the message."

I hung up, my skin clammy and my heart pounding. If I waited by the phone nothing would happen. So I decided on a tour and drove over to Grant Street, where Eng's studio had once stood. An aging hotel now covered the entire block. Eng had opened the studio at twenty-one, and I remembered another later portrait of him posed outside. He looked exotic, like Cathay in a homburg, his face sensuous, almost sleepy, his thumb tucked into the watch pocket of his brocade vest. "If photographs only give us inscrutable pieces of life," he wrote in his later years, "they also show that the past is serious, not the curio it seems, not the accumulation of dates and monarchs, the pointless sum of cause and effect. The past has our glossiness and our blood. It is no longer the dream that has landed us here and counts for nothing more."

I spent an hour walking through Chinatown, then around five called my hotel—no word from Sills. I stopped at a Cantonese restaurant for dinner, tempering the nervous excitement with several Tsing Tao beers. When I'd eaten and was walking back to my car I stopped at a newsstand to read the headlines and remembered Budge's note.

At that very moment I was supposed to be with him and his mother.

Panicked, I ran up the block to a phone booth and called home for messages. Budge's said, "You're busted, dude." I hung up and called back to listen again. He didn't sound all that disappointed, though Diane had probably let him call because she knew it would sting. I wondered if the boy's bravado were all for show. Clearly Budge's cockiness came from being loved. Diane's love made him complete, so much so that at times he didn't seem to need anyone else. I'd never had a sibling or been around kids that much. Sometimes I felt as if Budge understood our relationship better than I did. My moments of affection with him were sometimes forced, where he was all instinct and spontaneity. I envied him that. Diane claimed that a measure of uncertainty in adults gave kids a truer picture of what the world was really like. "You're not his parent," she told me, "you're like a friend. All kids need someone like you, an adult who isn't in their face all the time. You're more like him than you know," she added, which might mean that I hadn't grown up yet myself. This trip proved it.

Coward, I waited until the next morning and called from my hotel when I knew they'd be gone. Leaving my message I stumbled, murmuring my apology. I told them I'd gotten busy but didn't say with what or where I was. "I'll see you tomorrow," I said. Then, thinking of Sills, I panicked in the opposite direction and blurted, "Or Friday." I took a breath and heard the guilty silence widen.

Finally I just hung up. What else could I say? "I love you" would have been an insult, given the deception. If Sills didn't call soon I'd have to get back to Seattle. I waited until noon for his call, then drove out to the DeWitt.

The DeWitts' sumptuous campus looked like an English country estate, though visiting scholars were not exactly treated like guests. I had to leave half my wallet contents at the front desk. Admitted to the airy, vaulted library wing, I found more convincing proof after a re-markably short search—a photo of Eng wearing that same stickpin and cravat. I also researched the museum's copyright policy on Eng. Private individuals still owned many Eng negatives, though most people had long since complied with the photographer's wish that all negatives and original prints be donated to the museum. Technically the DeWitt's authority extended only to the materials in the photog-rapher's possession at the time of his death.

But for some reason all this good news did not cause the surge of excitement it should have, maybe because lies were accumulating alongside the mounting certainty. I decided I had enough to take to Leonard, so I wandered restlessly among the stacks for most of the af-ternoon. Finally, at five, I walked out to the pink stone lobby, where a beefy guard at the exit turnstile had his arm thrust deep in a woman's leather briefcase. Overhead, the smug eyes of security cameras watched all our movements. I found a phone and called my hotel—still nothing from Sills. When I left, the same guard gave me a look as much as to say he'd strip-search me at the drop of a hat.

Now, as I drove out the DeWitt's gates, the city sounded warning notes. Only yesterday it had seemed to open its arms. But there were hidden trip wires for me here, disappointments, portents. I found I was headed toward West Portal and decided to go past my family's old home on Castenada Street.

Winding neighborhood streets here still echoed with the old life. With its tall, peaked roof our house was the silhouette of childhood itself. In anybody's first neighborhood the mundane exploded into myth. Events here still eclipsed events in adulthood. You broke an arm, gazed out a certain window, kissed a girl whose fetching cheek mole you still thought about. Concrete steps led up through over-hanging shrubs that hadn't been there before. The third step had an exact relation to a scar on my forehead. My father caught the fall on his 8mm wind up. I was two and ignored the stairs, plunging into the golden air and smiling like a clown. Going for the lens even then, Dad later suggested. Going for immortality. I fingered the scar, right at the hairline; the stairs, mossless as a bunker, darker, pebbly, indifferent, would probably last longer. This whole city had once seemed pre-scribed for my safety, the launching pad for whatever I chose to do. Until things went wrong I'd never thought I was somehow running a gauntlet between looming calamities. Looking at the house, I won-dered if I should be drawing a far different conclusion about the life I thought I was living. Were our lives always less examined than we liked to think, sticking "kick me" signs on our backs while pretending to give us a congratulatory pat? I'd come here once during the Weston trouble. My parents had long since sold up and moved to the desert. It was a foul June afternoon, gray, cold, windy. I'd walked all the way and rung the doorbell, thinking I could ask the new owners for a tour and gather up leftover solace. When no one had answered I'd gone around to the back door and found it unlocked. Our yellow kitchen had been painted white. The old familiarity was fractured but still there. I'd broken down crying, but even that wouldn't help. *Go,* the house had commanded. *Go easy.* I remembered walking back along Portola Boulevard that day and looking up when wind boiled the leaves of a chestnut tree, which then spat crows.

Driving again, I seemed to smell an old disaster, like an ancient shipwreck floated to the surface.

Detouring down to Chestnut Street, I found that my gallery had been turned into a Japanese restaurant.

....

The next morning—my last in San Francisco, I decided—I called Leonard Sills again, and the impatient woman told me he was gone. I hung up feeling whipped. I kicked myself for rashness, for wasting the plane fare. When deluded enough, as I'd been in the Weston case, im-pulsiveness could come to seem like prudence. There was a flight out in an hour, and I decided I'd try to make it. While I was packing, the phone rang.

"How many Robert Armours can there be?"

"Who is this?" I asked.

But I knew.

Parker Lange was the sort of friend I wouldn't have had at all if we hadn't been in the same business. A Ph.D. dropout from Phoenix, Parker had worked in San Francisco art galleries at the same time I'd owned mine. We used to send each other clients, and these favors turned into a kind of one-upmanship carried on after hours in bars. Parker usually won. He could hold his liquor. He also made it his business to know a lot of wealthy idiots; somehow he could pick their pockets right under their noses and make them think he was doing them a good turn. They followed him around as if he were the Pied Piper.

Parker explained that he was now Leonard Sills' corporate curator. His methods had made him briefly welcome at a number of galleries. In the end Parker always managed to outrage his employers. Still, Sills' operation was large enough that it could nurture Parker's abilities and assimilate his scanty scruples. I used to think he was in the wrong line: Parker could not only sell you land in Florida but convince you that the swamp gases rising from it were friendly UFOs. After I'd left San Francisco he'd gone on to New York, and I'd heard nothing of him since. Maybe for the best.

I had to be out of my mind not to hang up on him now. Still, I believed he had never put anything over on me; I'd always seemed to come out ahead.

"I'm just on my way back to Seattle," I told him.

"What's the rush, Robert? No time for old pals? Let's have lunch," he said, then added dryly, "You like Japanese?"

Parker was not the sort to revisit the sites of his own failures, but he knew I was. Besides, I couldn't refuse without sounding relieved that we had fallen out of touch. Just hearing his voice reminded me that we'd been bad boys together and paid the price. No matter what had happened since, there was still that. Parker was more interested in plowing under his past mistakes as mulch for fresh crops of confidence. Errors of judgment were not to be taken as hard as I had taken mine. The club was still open, Parker implied. I could come back anytime.

"Make reservations," he said, then hung up.

On my way to Miyako, as it was called, I drove down steep Scott Street. One night years ago, after too many hours in a crowded bar, Parker and I had found a decrepit bicycle abandoned in an alley. Drunken dares started flying when this bike was found to have no brakes. With his own brand of leverage, strangely weightless and un-hostile, Parker soon had my glands and my mouth working overtime, and in no time I was wheeling the bike to the top of the hill. The ride down was the sort of total blank only youth could produce: I remem-bered the roar of wind, the front tire shuddering over cracks, and that was it. Somehow I knew that cars, trucks, buses, pedestrians, and traf-fic lights would clear the way. I was seized by a state of mind that reached way beyond calculation; a single thought might have killed me. When I reached the top again I found Parker laid out on some-one's lawn. Without looking up he said, "I was just kidding."

I was early, but Miyako was already jammed. I hardly recognized the place until I looked up. Years ago I'd painted the ceiling black to hide its age, and the owners of the restaurant had left it that way. The hammered boards and swirls of plaster now looked like skid marks where a once familiar motion had come to a halt. Gerald Maas, the man from whom I'd bought the Weston prints, had been trained in Europe and was a trusted dealer through whom I had bought work before. In time the high whine of excitement had come to sound like business as usual. I felt a fatal willingness take hold even though I knew the deal was critical enough not to take one person's word for the pictures' authenticity. I pushed on blindly anyway. Maas said he'd bought the pictures in Germany and trumped up a line of ownership that would have been difficult but not impossible to try to trace to Weston himself. I swallowed it whole. Maas' cancer was spreading; only in hindsight did I see how desperate he was.

At two exactly Parker appeared outside. I recognized him instantly. He squared his shoulders the same way he always had, keeping his upper body motionless so that he seemed to sail. It had taken me a long time to figure out that Parker never gestured. He was never off balance. He was so good at being unsurprised that I used to wonder if he practiced it, and if he did, how—jumping out of airplanes, maybe, or watching snuff flicks.

Even in his leather-jacketed days he was meticulous about his appearance. Parker was by now thirty-nine or forty but still whip-thin and natty. An expensive, billowing shirt, buttoned clear up, gave him a finished, slightly formal look. His hair, once long and flowing, was now neatly trimmed and moussed. He'd also added glasses, which softened his eyes and unfocused any appearance of greed or advantage.

Parker used to promote and defend his artists in a way I never could. His outrageous salesmanship made some of them self-sufficient, including an alarming number of no-talents. Parker was a gifted bully. I remembered him phoning phantom buyers in front of potential ones, explaining to the dead line the delicate matter of a stronger offer. Everyone else became the enemy, a strategy that worked against a number of artists who tried to move elsewhere when Parker's reputation faltered. He overnurtured his artists, made them haughty and helpless. Contemporary photographers wanted coddling, which was why I never dealt their work anymore. Ego was mostly a salve against the idea of oblivion, and over the years I had come to depend on time to decide the question of an artist's immortality. Parker's ideals hinged on money. They were rooted in the present, which he refused to think of as something that would one day be gone.

"Missing the old place?" he asked, drawing up to the table. He never used common greetings. The preciousness, the rarity of the Eng plates drew into sharp focus around Parker's stillness, as cultivated as a monk's. This stillness, I reminded myself, was the springboard for his recklessness. His expectancy was like a counterpuncher's. It urged, *You first.*

"I like what I'm doing now," I said.

A week ago such a statement would not have had this shimmy of doubt. Parker sat in a sudden single motion, a silent folding of his joints. No air moved out of his way. He was wakeless. He looked wrapped tight—he looked, in fact, like a tightass. And yet he was irrepressible in his way. He was like one of those toy men, strung together with elastic, that collapsed when you pressed a button, then snapped upright again the instant you let it go. I always felt that I had to watch him, though physically he never seemed to be doing much. Everything happened in his head. It was pure brain power he now channeled into reading what he had missed in the last decade. He heard my ambivalence and looked at me as if to ask what, then, I was doing back in California calling Leonard Sills. Instead, once we'd ordered, he glanced at a poster on the wall of a neon Tokyo cityscape and asked, "Ever been there?"

"No."

"You love Seattle too much, of course. I like Seattle too."

"I didn't know you'd been up."

"Living in Seattle is like having a roommate who can't stop crying," Parker said. "Everyone is so serious and personal. The men are friends to the whale, and the women are all former dancers who think they'll grow up to be Georgia O'Keeffe. You still in Pioneer Square?"

"How did you know?"

"I looked you up in the phone book."

"You never called," I said and added wryly, "No time for old pals?"

Our miso soup arrived, and Parker gave the waiter a questioning look, possibly for her being white and blond. When he tossed out some Japanese greetings she gave back replies until satisfied that she'd heard all he knew.

"You move so gracefully," he told her. "Do you dance?"

"Not since I hurt my knee," she said.

"Where did you do that?"

"In the NFL, of course."

"All California waitpersons are in show business," Parker said after we'd ordered. "Seattle requires that they have bachelor's degrees. It's everybody's dream town, Robert. You'll be positioned perfectly when the fairy tale ends."

He didn't sound convinced—sounded snide, in fact, but I let it go. "What happened to New York?"

"I got fired," he said. "Fortunately Leonard counts it in my favor." He looked at me. "I hate to admit it, Robert, but I owe that one to you."

"How come?"

"You introduced us way back when. I stayed in touch."

"Which is more than I did."

I left a hopeful pause, thinking he might say whether Sills had said anything about me, which was suddenly important. Parker appeared to shrug with just his eyes.

"Holing up is all right," he said. "After New York I worked in Amsterdam for two years. Then I tried L.A., but that didn't last either."

"It was always fun to go to L.A.," I said. "But every time I drove north it seemed like even the air was more intelligent air."

"You must all be geniuses in Seattle," he said.

Parker had the perfect mouth for his subtle repertoire of sneers and smirks. His lips were wider than normal, sensuous and sharply formed, supported by perfect rows of teeth you almost never saw until feeding time.

"In California anything is possible," he said. "I'm dating twins. They're in their twenties. When they get depressed they jog or fuck or take a seminar that ends by walking over hot coals in their bare feet.

Their old man leers at me like he's jealous. Try inventing propriety around *that* anywhere else."

He looked at me across the table. There was something unproclaimed in this old connection, and I faced it with reluctance. Parker knew I was the sort who would eventually come back to the trough. Now there was a short silence during which his miso was gone so quickly that he might have dumped it under the table. I felt him watching while I sipped.

"You've got something for Leonard," he said.

I shrugged. "I'm coming out of my hole, like you did. I just want to talk."

"About what?"

"No offense, Parker, but how did Leonard Sills ever give you a job?"

I wasn't sure what I meant by this nastiness—maybe to test crucial differences. Did I want to be settled in life with a boy and a wonderful woman? Did such a life necessarily require permanently lowered expectations? Was I more like Parker than I cared to admit?

"Like I say, anything is possible," Parker said. "Especially when you finally realize that groveling is aerobic." He turned to the waitress, who stood nearby eavesdropping. "How about that?" he said.

She winked, firing her finger pistol at him, and said, "It's always worked for me."

"My friend Robert here lives in Seattle."

"Nice town."

"He says you remind him of something from a Georgia O'Keeffe painting."

"Really?" she said, giving me a look. "A lily or the skull of a steer?"

By the time she took away the soup bowls a bantering ease had formed between the two of them, though Parker could focus on nothing else once the platter of raw fish arrived. He had ordered a triple portion of the mackerel. His stillness lent him a predator's patience, but now he ate as if colonizing his insides. It was like witnessing something expansionist done in microcosm, the decimation of a prized landscape. His steady energy left me little place to start. He cleared half the platter, his eyes ranging ahead, his chopsticks snipping at the hot wasabe. My eyes streamed and my skull was shot with fire, with the kind of pain it always baffled me to endure. *Good* pain. I tried to keep up, but I was out of practice. Maybe I'd become too sedentary for this sort of mutual egging-on, no longer in shape for bold moves and risk taking. Here, in this setting, I couldn't deny I'd been robbed. Suddenly my throat closed with anger, an unchewed bite of mackerel reeking in my mouth—the taint of defeat. I had to force myself to swallow. Parker might have known what I was thinking. I felt him looking at me and flushed.

"Don't take this wrong, Robert," he said. "In the old days you could be wild and you could be smart. But you could also be soft." He looked at me with his moist, unfocused eyes. "It's what killed you."

"Gerald Maas is what killed me," I said, but weakly, as if I didn't really believe it myself.

Parker turned back to the fish. "Maas told me how bad he felt."

In everything I had heard about Gerald Maas' last days, my own trouble made me hear a steady strain of unrepentance. The treatment had failed. Maas had fought valiantly, as if there were no consequences to face if he survived. Harboring ill will toward the dead, especially from the vantage of Diane Mays' arms, had come to seem like fighting windmills. Whatever happened to you must be fitted into a larger order; you were always broadening your scope beyond pettiness and grudge-holding. Sitting in the midst of what I believed Maas had stolen from me, I couldn't help myself and looked up at the ceiling again. In its hovering dimness was the ghost of a success that should have been mine. Again the poison spurted through my heart. My eyes boiled, and in my belly I felt the hot stab of indignation. Tight-jawed, I asked, "How bad was that?" When Parker didn't answer I said, "You must have heard from him before he died."

"He called."

"You never mentioned it."

"In fact, Robert, I did. You were buried. It wasn't the sort of thing you wanted to hear. You gave him his last chance," Parker added, though in a tone less of tenderness or respect than of mere declaration. "He said not to tell you he said so. Still, I wondered—a lot of us did—why you went ahead with it, given what you knew."

"Maas was a known quantity," I said. "He was your friend too."

"Money lust smothers the small dichotomies."

"As if you are fucking immune."

I suddenly saw myself as Parker must have—a chump taking his medicine. I wanted to cough it back in his face. Parker downed his tea indifferently, as if immunity were not the point. When he stepped away to the bathroom that black ceiling seemed to close around my head. Crazily I thought, *You didn't come here just to sell a negative, you came to get back what you lost.*...This failure would loom over me forever unless I did something about it. Parker might have sensed that I had something more than I said I did. He might have counted on stirring up old anger—the sort of anger I could feel only here at the source. Maas. The bastard got what he deserved, I thought, then shuddered with shame. Then I thought, *Fuck shame,* which was what dying Gerald Maas must have told himself. Never in my wildest dreams would I have said I shared anything with such a man. But if, as Parker implied, I had been dying a slow death in Seattle, the Eng plates—all five of them—might be a miracle cure. And so when Parker came back from the head I told him, "Let's get the check," then took him to my hotel.

························

"Who took it?" Parker had the presence of mind to ask. I hadn't mentioned Eng by name; Parker recognized his face in the cracked negative. Even in highly charged moments Parker could appear unruffled unless you knew what to look for—in this case the barest twitch of his

Adam's apple. He wasn't even trying to be skeptical. When it came to identifying Eng, Parker trusted his own eyes, but more than that, he trusted me. My certainty had become his certainty. This was almost as exciting as the discovery itself.

He meant that the shutter had not been invented yet, so someone else—probably a studio assistant—had had to remove, then replace the lens cover. Parker's eyes ticked in their sockets, roving the image. I experienced another dizzying moment of certainty, then abject fear when he asked, "Where did you get it?"

I didn't answer, and he glanced up with a suddenly doubtful look.

"I've got proof," I said.

He looked back at the plate. "You wouldn't call Leonard if you didn't need to keep it quiet."

Sweat sprang out on my scalp. As calmly as I could I said, "I'm selling it for the owner."

"The owner being you."

Then Parker did what I never would have expected. He handed the negative back and said, "I don't think so."

At first I was so stunned I couldn't speak. Suddenly I was a renegade, the Robert Armour of old who hadn't learned a thing, who still took foolish risks while Parker had grown staid and sensible under Leonard Sills' wing. Then I bristled. Parker saw the anger but only looked back at me as if there were nothing more to say.

"Look," I said, "I've got all the documentation anyone could want."

"I'm sure you do, Robert."

Irony edged into these words. He looked smug behind his glasses. My guts flared, but I managed to control myself. "Shouldn't you ask Leonard first?"

His only answer was to keep staring, and I felt a deflating panic. Parker was shrewd and knowing. He could fill in your most inscrutable silences. He knew I was holding back—I would have to tell him more or risk getting nowhere. I cleared my throat. "There are four more," I said, barely above a whisper. Then I told him the whole story, adding a little shrilly, "I didn't steal this one." I made sure he understood that Pollock and my unsigned check had prevented me from telling Judith. Then I told him the rest of the story, remembering not to mention her by name.

"This woman has the four but thinks they're worthless," he said. "And you thought you'd pay yourself for your trouble before telling her otherwise."

I blushed deep red, then blanched when Parker once more said, "I don't think this will fly."

"Why not?"

"Think about it, Robert. You're asking Leonard to pay you for something you're planning to give the DeWitt for free."

"But the other four aren't mine."

"Is this one? Anyway, the DeWitt Museum is like the government, they'll suck the life out of you if you let them. You know as well as I do that they'd sell the shit out of something this big and call it revenue enhancement. Exactly two fat guys at the top would make out like bandits. The DeWitt archive is just another basement." He pointed at the broken plate. "And if you were *really* interested in doing the noble thing, you'd give them this one too."

I blushed again but said, "I suppose I could get a ballpark for all five from Leonard, then approach the owner with it."

"Then what?"

"I don't know. Make a deal."

"Or ask for your usual fee? If she's the bitch you say she is she'll agree, then have her attorneys throw you out and deal with Leonard directly."

Parker was repeating something like the same scenario I'd described to Diane. But the difference now was that if anyone could figure a way, Parker could.

"The answer," Parker said, "is to get all five, cut ourselves in, and make everyone happy."

This was a tall order. Still, it thrilled me not just that he showed this spark of interest but that he spoke in a summary way. He had absorbed the whole story and now played with it, homing in on the weaknesses, the telling details. With any luck he would bond himself to the unfolding. The air of the room seemed to shimmer with an even greater excitement. I might have been waiting for this moment for ten years. This was more than a one-shot payday—fate was now at work. After a decade I was finally back on track. Luck had come back to my corner. Parker picked up the negative again and studied it.

"You say this Judith is a rich no-talent."

"Some people think the combination has driven her around the bend."

"Frustration," Parker said. "It makes you do crazy things."

My being here, he implied, was craziness of a similar stripe. I decided to ignore the parallel. "She'd get a little farther if she didn't treat everyone like shit."

"What would make her happiest?" Parker asked.

"She'd be in heaven if some stranger came up to her out of the blue and bought one of her paintings."

"She show much?" Parker asked.

"Almost never."

Once Judith had rented a storefront and hung her paintings there for a month. Few came, and nothing sold. This failure made her even more untouchable and forced her to nurse the humiliation on a world cruise.

These days she spread around enough money that even people she'd screwed over treated her with kid gloves. The idea seemed to be that if she could keep paying rent on her high hopes, time might accidentally fulfill them. It occurred to me now that she might see her nastiness and arrogance as necessities; without them she'd seem merely pathetic.

"She'd kill for a show," I told Parker, then looked at him. "Jesus, you wouldn't."

"Wouldn't what?"

"Give her a show? Are you serious?"

If he hadn't been thinking it, if this ludicrous idea had in fact been mine, his gaze didn't give him away.

"You haven't seen her work," I said. "Besides, can you do that? I mean, do you have the authority?"

"Leonard will see the wisdom."

Parker then explained that his job included arranging shows in the lobbies of the office towers Leonard owned. Judith could take over one of these for a month. Leonard would make sure there were lots of the right people and even a review or two.

"Would we just come right out with it?" I asked. "'Your show for the plates'?"

"Eventually."

"It's extortion. She'd never go for it."

"Would you if you were her?"

"I couldn't lie to her."

"When the time was right we'd tell her it was strictly business, nothing personal. Don't play the innocent, Robert. Shit like this happens every day. Unless she's a total moron she'll go for it. I'm your friend," he went on, explaining our approach. "A hotshot curator from the Bay Area looking to put together shows of Northwest talent. Lots of eyes on Seattle these days. She'll buy it."

"I was there, looking at her negatives. Then you just happen to show up."

"Exactly. You looked at the glass; you noticed the paintings. I was in town and you put two and two together."

I looked at him, I suppose, for some sign that this idea was feasible or even sane. He gazed back, embracing the simplicity with one of those lazy-eyeball shrugs. "There's no way Leonard won't go for it when I show him this plate."

These words made my legs weak with excitement, but I managed to say, "Shouldn't we see him together?"

"He's out of town," Parker said, then paused, staring at me. "I've seen that look before."

"What look?"

"A look like you're going to hemorrhage. Like you want to ask what I'll be getting out of this." He shook his head slowly. "The trust factor already. It's probably no good saying what's good for Leonard is good for me."

I pointed shakily at the plate. "I'm not leaving this behind."

"You'll have to sooner or later," he said. "Would you be whining like this if I was Leonard?"

"You're not, are you."

Now he glared, less at me than at his own slip. A spark of anger shone behind the polished lenses. I wasn't the only errand boy, not the only one whose expectations had fallen short of the mark.

"You've gotten to be an old hen, Robert," he said. "It must be all that genius air. I'll talk to him."

"Good," I said. "You always had a way with talk."

March 5

There is no wall or floor or ceiling, no echoing house, no double life—only this bed afloat in the white air. The clock reads ten of midnight & a perfect moon pours through the window across my bed. I need no other light to write here. I wonder if you are also awake & what you are thinking. I imagine you here, holding me, the two of us silently watching the moonlight slip along the counterpane. The bed is bright as a snowbank....

March 6

This was my day to feed soup to the women & men at Fitzgerald House. I have never done this dismal work with more love in my heart. I'm to see you tomorrow—is it wrong to deepen my pleasure in this way, with those who have no choice in the matter of their happiness or misery? Coming home I passed down your street but didn't dare stop—how angry you would be if you knew, if you had seen me. How you would rage at my carelessness. As I drove on, I paid too little attention & in a busy street collided with a milk wagon. Josh reared & tangled himself in the wagon's traces. As the buggy pitched this way & that I foolishly called your name. A man selling vegetables from a stall stepped into the street & pulled the animals apart, then handed back my reins. His apron was soaked where it brushed the flanks of the lathered horses. I blushed, fumbling in my purse for coins to give him. He stared at me as if he knew the reasons for my carelessness & could read all of my thoughts....

Later. Mrs. Dodd has just gone to bed. I asked her to have dinner with me tonight as I often do when alone, though Joseph disapproves. When I came in this afternoon she exclaimed, "Your dress, it's ruined!" The skirt had torn up the back while the buggy pitched. I told her about the incident, then looked at her & suddenly laughed. Mrs. Dodd looked surprised but then joined in. The poor woman tried to apologize but then she was in stitches all over again. We stood there in the pantry howling until we felt ill. I helped her set our table in the small upstairs parlor. I meant to keep our spirits high. I felt strangely sad, perhaps because I'd spent the day among those whose lives are utterly undone, though in the past this has made me sensible of my own blessings & good luck. At dinner I persuaded Mrs. Dodd to drink a glass of wine & the color soon rose to her cheeks. For a short time this house did not seem to bear its hollowness down upon us. We laughed more about my dress. "I could try to mend it," she said. This wasn't in the least funny but we laughed beyond all hope of stopping, holding our sides & toppling sideways in our chairs. "I'll have such a head in the morning," she said but finished her wine. I truly love this woman & perhaps our hilarity & good cheer seem frail now because I feel I am deceiving her as much as anyone. When the conversation lagged she asked if there were any word from Joseph. I hesitated before answering. The thought of seeing him now fills me with shame & dread. I told her no, no word, hoping my face would not give me away. She sighed. Clearly she also thinks that long absences are not natural behavior for husbands—her own has been dead thirty years & she says not a day passes without her missing him. I stood then & laid another log in the hearth. Then I made her tell me stories of her Scottish girlhood & before the roaring fire she even raised her skirts & danced the "Boatman's Reel" she had danced as a sixteen-year-old bride. She hummed the tune aloud & seemed transported, so light on her feet for a woman

her age who works as she does. The air of the room grew warm as
Christmas, but now that she has gone to bed the chill invades
again....

March 7

Mrs. Dodd is clairvoyant. A message arrived from Joseph, though
not by the morning mail. One of his brash young agents brought
it. This man wore a weathered jacket & heavy, scarred boots. I had
never seen him before & wondered if he will be one of those
whose lives, so Joseph has told me, are so often cut short by dangerous work in the forests. He bore a haughty look of someone
who believed he would live forever. He would not say where my
husband was. It angered me that this man knew something I could
not make him tell. Still, I had my own secrets. I asked him where
the letter was & he tapped his temple. This was not the first time
Joseph had entrusted his news to another. He claims he is too busy
to write. I listened with as much composure as I could & was
thankful the message was brief. I know little of my husband's life
but even the shadows have shadows. Joseph's absence has become
a presence. Gone, he inhabits this house more completely than
when he is here. There is no escaping him anywhere. Is it only ignorance that ever haunts us? He must know how awful this is,
forcing me to listen to this grinning lout. He must see how drawing strangers into our midst belittles everything marriage is supposed to be. Still, I am no longer one to point an accusing finger.
Though you are hardly a stranger, my love, deceit is the point.
There seems no end of it. Indeed, when this stranger told me my
husband would be away longer than expected I felt a welling up of
excitement—you & I would have even more time together. The
man's grin was a sneer. He looked as if he expected something for

his trouble. Money would make such a tame errand worth his
while, though he was probably told not to take any. I got him half
a dollar anyway, though without asking him in from the cold. He
said nothing by way of thanks & I just kept myself from slamming
the door at his back....

3

I flew home late the same afternoon. That evening, back at my apartment, I called Diane's, and Budge answered.

"Is she mad?"

"You want to ask her?"

"Maybe not right now."

"What are you doing tomorrow tonight?" he asked.

In the background I heard Diane say, "We're having dinner with Daddy." I couldn't tell much tonewise from the muffled words and took what reassurance I could from the fact that she spoke at all.

"Robert could come after," Budge said. His voice, aimed out into the echoing kitchen, had a surly edge, as if he expected Diane to resist. But she said fine, and the boy spoke back into the receiver: "You could spend the night again."

I agreed too eagerly and resolved to ignore Eng, at least for a day. At five the next evening I got take-out duck and ribs from Kau Kau, then drove to Diane's.

I parked at the curb and walked up her front stairs. But when I reached the top I came up short with a gasp when the eave over the porch suddenly, whitely exploded.

I didn't know what it was at first, and the image came into my head of a kind of psychic lab experiment in which such light showed up the guilty spots. It was one of those new motion-sensing fixtures—probably a wise thing for a single mother. The light was viscid white; I was bathed in it; if I shook I'd shed it in sheets. I felt caught out, exposed.

Inside I looked for the switch, but after a few minutes the light went off by itself. Diane hadn't warned me about it, and I realized that she was probably being tactful. I was pretty sure whose idea it was.

In the kitchen I got a beer from the refrigerator, then went out to the living room, where I opened the food cartons and turned on the TV. Diane's pillowy sofa faced the old stone fireplace, which she had rescued from layers of paint. Along one wall of this room was an antique sideboard and above it a Jesse L. Givens print I had given her of a smiling Salish woman and her child. There was a nature documentary on PBS, a pastiche on the screen of earthly cataclysm, glacier-cut gorges, and lava boiling up from an ocean crevice. The show's host suggested that if the Eiffel Tower represented the life of the earth, the skin of paint on its highest knob was the history of humankind. I switched channels, ate some ribs, then switched back. The camera banked slowly over solid jungle, then jumped to a dizzying top view of a dinosaur's footprint in a Texas stream bed. I had actually seen this footprint myself once, sneaking away from the sort of fine-art trade show I had since learned to scoff at. Most of these took place in the Southwest, near Santa Fe, where modern-day Medicis showed they were no more than retailers at heart. The Eng discovery, and the flash trip to San Francisco, proved I'd been waiting for another chance—but a chance at what? Did the world need another Medici? Another brand of hustler?

Diane once told me that making more money hadn't made her any happier. "You just move up to a new level of disappointment," she said. Which meant that everyone still had to take a certain amount of shit. Why should that change? Humans' pitiful few eons, the TV host implied, were full to the brim with shit-taking. They were slick with enough gore to make the primordial earth look like a tea dance. *Intent* made all the difference. In another moment this host, a fearless, oddly radiant Englishman, was walking across a snowfield, explaining the grim interlude we humans defined between a decipherable past and an inevitable future.

With that thought I fell sound asleep.

Maybe it was the travel, the excitement, and the guilt. I'd heard it said that criminals needed a nap first thing after the rigors of secrecy and heinous acts. When I woke some time later, the sleep I still needed lay on me like a corpse. Diane was gently lifting the carton of cold ribs from my grasp; a chili-oil thumbprint embossed its side, bright as blood.

Without a word Budge climbed into my lap and took over the remote, changing channels to a kids' network. Diane grinned at my dinner. "A little bachelor heaven right here in my living room," she said. She kicked off her shoes and sat down, curling her feet under her. Then she put her hand on my neck, kissed my temple, and pressed her cheek against mine. She pulled away and looked at me, still grinning. Half asleep, I reached up and touched her face. Diane's skin had a faint olive tint from an Italian grandmother, and her hair, thick and cut short, was a deep, lustrous mahogany that in summer became streaked with tawny highlights. Her face was compact—she thought her dark eyes were too close together. It was true she couldn't help a look of pensive mischief, though her features were spared the chipmunk cuteness of women who weren't nearly so intelligent or graceful. "You look like part of the furniture," she said. It was Diane's mouth, I suddenly realized, that I could never fool—I watched it constantly for signs of my own credibility. Curved lines at the corners told me everything I needed to know. Both vanished when she was passionate; one or the other deepened if she was mocking or mad or not being fooled; both were in evidence now, which meant she was pleased.

The boy turned suddenly, showing his avid profile against the bubbling, fizzing screen. "Feel like a torpedo, big guy?"

"Robert needs time to wake up," Diane said. "Why don't you show him your feather."

Budge didn't need to think twice. He jumped to his feet, agile as a chimp, and disappeared down the hall. Diane took a rib from the smudged carton.

"What did Michael cook?" I asked.

"Hamburgers," she said and sucked hot sauce from her fingers. "We ate on the boat."

Michael, Diane's ex-husband, owned a large cabin cruiser named *Rosanna,* built in the '50s by a Slavic fisherman. Michael kept a small apartment in town but stayed on the boat most weekends, even in winter.

"He knows it's so beautiful on the water no one will notice the food," she said, chewing. Then she added, "He's being so good." She sometimes said this to me: "You're being so good," maybe implying that men usually weren't. "He had the new security light installed outside," Diane said.

"Since when is Michael so worried about burglars?"

"Pretty recently. And just in the nick of time, it seems." A smirk here recalled my late-night visit. "He says these lights are very high tech. They have some sort of special gas inside."

Michael Mays and gas had a certain affinity for one another.

I had trouble getting a fix on Michael. A Tupelo transplant, Michael called himself a "chicken-fried" Westerner and claimed that all the Northwest waters had rinsed his accent. He and Diane had separated before Budge turned one. For a short time afterward he was married to a much older woman with grandchildren. For Michael it didn't matter if you never found the love and maturity you were supposedly looking for as long as you made the symbolic effort. Diane admitted he'd been devious with her. But lately, for some reason, he'd been hanging around, helping out as little as always but coming across with lavish, sometimes even useful gifts. Afterward he'd hang around some more, waiting for reactions that proved something about himself—a fresh resolve, a new leaf.

Budge returned with a giant peacock feather. Before I could think I asked, "Where did that come from?"

"A peacock. The other day when you were asleep, I had it this close."

He demonstrated, dipping the gaudy feather toward my face, its iridescent eye like that of someone screaming. What did peahens think was so great about this? Perhaps females in general reveled in male hysterics. I wondered what Diane would think of mine. She might conclude that the negatives had triggered a major life change that excluded her and Budge. Or she might think Eng only a sign of some more temporary wild hair that required patience—the same limitless patience she used with the boy. In a more immediate vein I wondered if I meant to tell her where I'd been the last few days or concoct some plausible lie. Would I also tell her about scheming with Parker? I shuddered at the thought.

Something about the feather got to Diane. She was beside herself but tried to hide it by lunging for the boy, who sidestepped her, then consulted his phantom wristwatch.

"Are you awake yet?"

Budge Mays had his mother's dark hair and eyes. The boy was never completely still, which both fascinated and exhausted me. If his body came to a stop it was only so his mind could drink something in, a fact that now made me nervous in a way it never had before. His movement was like that of a gyroscope—all his motions contained other motions. So far his fears had not shown him the habit of tension and unease. He could claim an absolute trust in the physical world even when it occasionally went wrong and he tumbled down the back stairs or ran in front of a car that braked just in time.

Savvy in the mold of the day, Budge needed less explanation of why he was not to enter the bedroom without knocking than of how I got

away with living like a slob. My bad example was a steady source of fas-
cination and hope: my name could be invoked, with rectitude, if not
success, when it came time to clean his room. Whenever he and Diane
slept over, usually on Friday nights, Budge felt that he should be given
the same rights. Instead he compromised with the mess he made with
watercolors, setting up Saturday morning while his cartoons chattered.
Budge was adaptable. He didn't appear to be as needy as he might actually be. He liked sleeping on my convertible sofa, which expanded in
a clumsy way that made him gasp with laughter: he imagined the sofa
was a giant mouth that might eat him in the night and laughed freely
at the image of it folded up with him inside. For certain things, fear had
to be learned. Then again, maybe fear had to be ignored. I realized all
at once that I was jealous of the way the boy drank down the world in
easy drafts. And once he'd digested what he'd taken in, he spat it back,
often in the form of antic, adult personas. Now one of these—was it
me?—raised a stern finger, directing me up from the couch.

The "torpedo" had evolved, so Diane surmised, as a kind of physical contact to contrast with her own melting embraces. Here again
she assured me that I was giving Budge what no one else could—
"You're letting him be boss," she said. Still, I used to wonder if the torpedo was something she made him do, holding out a secret reward if
he did this one thing to draw us—all three of us—closer.

Budge, who was small for his age, put his hands to his sides and
went missile-shaped. I picked him up in a rolling motion and hefted
him over my head, and down the hall we went, less like a torpedo than
something T-shaped and two-headed at a gallop. According to
Budge's dictates, I described the action and made bomb-and-water
noises that built in pitch as the "fish" neared the target ship, where the
panicking doomed also cried out. Usually I had enough breath for
about two good runs. But tonight, guilty at having stood the boy up, I
gave him all he wanted. By the fourth pass he had lost none of his appetite, shrieking overhead as I labored up and down the carpeted hall-

way. My arms ached so that I could barely keep him aloft, and in my mouth guilt suddenly gave the cries of the imperiled the metallic tang of reality. I thought of Parker Lange. It occurred to me that I had set a plan in motion that might necessitate telling even more lies to both Budge and his mother.

When I dumped him on his bed for the last time Diane called down the hall that it was time for pj's, and the boy obediently began to change. I thought I'd catch my breath in his overstuffed armchair until I saw another of the giant feathers tucked behind it. He saw me looking and said, "Daddy got them from Mississippi." The feather loomed over the chair like the granddaddy of nightmares glaring through a keyhole. The chair, Diane had told me, was the sort maiden aunts had sat in to read the paper in wartime. Budge mostly threw clothes on it. In Diane's own childhood a similar chair had been a refuge. Now she would be a good enough mother to provide escape from her own shortcomings. We were and were not our parents. And Diane was always careful to point out that it was okay if kids occasionally saw that adults weren't perfect.

I thought of Parker again. He had a fondness for wry euphemism, and he'd talked about "maneuvering" Judith's interest away from the plates. Suddenly I imagined myself explaining Parker and his scheme to Budge, trying to sound reasonable and adult, forcing myself to meet his brown eyes with their frightening absorbency. The boy would have a raft of questions, would listen avidly to the answers, especially if the same arguments could be summoned in defense of freedoms he had been denied until now. "Maneuvering" now seemed like something I'd agreed to when dreaming or drunk out of my mind.

Pajamas on, Budge lay down on his bed, musing, his legs crossed. "Daddy was asking about you again."

"What did he want to know this time?"

He shrugged against the bed, the crossed leg bobbing. "Different stuff. Stuff about your job."

"What do you tell him?"

"I say you sell photographs."

"What does he say?"

"He wants to know how much."

"How much I sell or how much I make?"

"I said I didn't know."

"Diplomat. What else?"

"I told him you have hair on your back."

"Sure you did."

"You do."

He rolled over in his flannel sheets and pointed at his nape. "It's right here," he said.

"Hair is supposed to grow there," I said. "Everybody has hair there."

Still, I reached back and felt a rough patch between my shoulders that hadn't been there before. I sat down on the small bed with my back to him. "How far down does it go?" Budge pulled back my collar, and I felt the interested puffs of his breath on my neck. "Right…*there.*" He put his finger under the first big vertebra, took the few hairs in his fingers and tugged.

Diane interrupted, calling down again, and when Budge had slid his feet under the covers I said, "I'm sorry I didn't come the other night."

"That's okay."

"I got busy and just forgot," I added but didn't need to. The boy would place no demands on me. I leaned down, and we hugged each other, and then he asked for Emerson. I got the bear from the shelves above his desk, where there were also three toy ambulances collected with his boy's relish of catastrophe. Besides these there were monster trucks, dinosaurs, and steroid-plump superheroes, and it came to me that these, along with Emerson, had less to do with loving disaster than surviving fear. I handed him the bear, then kissed his forehead and felt stinging betrayal on my lips. Budge turned and shut his eyes. Stepping into the hall, I left the door ajar as I'd been shown.

Back in the living room Diane had built a fire. She gave me a quick kiss and said, "Don't go away," then went to say good-night herself. I sat down in front of the crackling blaze and thought of Eng, his long, undomestic decades. I doubted Wilfred Eng had ever just passed an evening by a fire. All his life he had felt himself afloat in the pitching misery of prejudice. Creature comforts were anathema to pain-forged visions. He never found a home. He left places, came back, and left again. And now most historians and critics agreed that the landscapes that came out of this restlessness breathed regret.

Diane came back to the living room and slipped a CD Michael had given her into the player. Listening, she stared at the bookcase and smiled. It was Vaughan Williams, ribald Elizabethan verse set to a melancholy tune.

> Love bade me welcome; yet my soul drew back,
> Guilty of dust and sin.
> But quick-eyed Love, observing me grow slack
> From my first entrance in,
> Drew nearer to me, sweetly questioning
> If I lack'd anything.

She took my hand and led me to the sofa, where we lay down. When she lay on her back her face broadened slightly, her eyes slitting sleepily. As she drew my head close I saw the tiny crescent shadows framing her mouth suddenly disappear. Diane's kisses were slow and sinking. She moved under me, fitting us closer, and the kiss made it seem like free fall. A flutter of panic started up in my stomach.

"I thought Emerson was a thing of the past," I said, breaking off. I'd assumed at first that the bear was named for the poet rather than Fittipaldi, an Indy racer and an even more fearless protector against the night.

"Budgie's been asking for him again lately," Diane answered. "Probably just a phase."

"It's those feathers," I said. "You get the feeling they're looking right through you."

Diane laughed, then asked, "Did you ever have a bear?"

"Hoss," I said. "I soaked him with a can of aerosol moth repellent. Then I left him strung up in a hawthorne tree. Mom found him. She was pissed off that I continued to sleep so well."

"Budgie will probably start doing things like that pretty soon."

"What happened to yours?"

"Bah-Ha," Diane said. "My mother washed him once and he fell apart."

"And it was never the same."

"Something was," she said. "I never lynched him. Girls know that the bogeyman is death, and he really is out there."

The fire punctuated this sentence with a sharp crack. I thought of Eng again, the impossible picture of him toasting his soles by the hearth. For Eng, fire was nothing so much as the source of light; it was his angel and, in the end, his bogeyman.

"Budgie says you have hair on your back."

"You never told me."

"I never noticed."

I reached back, and Diane laughed. "God, you should see your face. Can I feel?" I guided her fingers to the spot, and she worked her mouth against a grin. "Pretty soon we'll be looking for you under bridges."

"I thought I'd last forever," I said. "I won't at this rate."

Diane laughed again, then put her arms back around me and squeezed gently, shutting her eyes. "'Let us but anoint each other in veneration, Love, and we will fear no man.'"

"You sound like this filthy music."

"I wrote that when I was seventeen," she said. "I thought it sounded like Shakespeare."

The music built on cue. Diane brought her face close. Against my cheek, her breath warmed and cooled and warmed again.

In the bedroom, moments later, we undressed quickly in the grayish light from the hall. Her flesh felt flushed, rich with its own heat. Easing back on the bed, she opened her legs, her whole self, not at all like someone who knew death was waiting.

When we'd made love and lay under her comforter she said, "Robert, what's wrong? You seem remote tonight."

"I got carried away."

"No, *I* did. You stayed right here. Are you thinking about whatever it is you've been doing the last few days?"

I cleared my throat. "Look, I'm really sorry about that."

"And?"

"And what?"

"You're making me pull teeth. Was it something to do with the negative?"

A telling indecision settled around my silence, and Diane moved close. In her clarifying embrace I felt myself turn to wood.

"I couldn't get hold of Judith," I said. "I was doing research on the plates and got lost in it."

"How lost?" she asked, and it just tumbled out.

"I went to California," I said. "It was a spur-of-the-moment thing."

And a mistake, I felt Diane suddenly urging me to add. She seemed to be counseling herself not to overreact. Then she said, "You talked to the DeWitt," as if to justify the suddenness and secrecy. I answered this with another silence, and she sighed impatiently.

"You said yourself it wasn't mine," I said. "The library there has material no one else has."

"Did you tell anyone?"

I thought of Parker and lied, "I didn't think of it."

"Maybe someone from the museum could reason with Judith,"

Diane said. Then, after a pause, she added, "It feels like you don't trust me."

"Of course I trust you. Look, it was stupid not to tell you, and I'm sorry."

"Were you afraid I'd try to stop you?"

"No, of course not," I said, but she knew better.

"Look, I can't nag or give you ultimatums. When Michael and I were married he'd always accuse me of trying to do this major over-haul on him."

"I thought that's what women wanted."

"That's an effect of chronic bachelorhood," she said. "So is forget-ting how big the little things are when you're eight."

"I told him I was sorry."

"We got worried about you," she said. But she didn't scold beyond that. "Budgie thinks the world of you," she said. Then, easing her thigh over my legs, she added, whispering in my ear, "And so do I. Pay at-tention this time, okay?"

"Okay."

She straddled me and straightened up, the comforter slipping from her shoulders. She arched her back to bring her breasts close to my face, then reached behind her, holding her breath as she slipped me inside. And now I let myself go, let this house and this life enclose me again, and it all seemed enough, so much so that I lost myself as com-pletely as Diane did, far enough gone in the end that my cries seemed to come from the distant place we'd both left. Diane leaned close, get-ting her breath, kissing my cheek with an air of congratulation that was both pleased and amused. I pulled her close, forgetting every-thing but the damp heat of her body. I fell asleep looking past the edge of the bed, where her panties made a pale figure eight on the carpet.

Sometime later I woke with a start, heart pounding. A heavy shower drummed the roof. Diane was up. She moved silently across the carpet, stepped into that eight, and pulled it up. Then she put on her robe, an amoeba shape of darker dark falling silently around her. I almost called out but watched her walk out the door instead. She moved into the hall, and the old house answered each step to the boy's room. Budge slept not ten feet from us. The floor creaked again as she moved toward the wall near my head and curled herself into the armchair. I listened but knew I would hear no more.

·················

In the kitchen the next morning Budge felt under my collar.

"It's like moss," he said.

We were having cereal together while his mother was in the shower. On other days I had joined her there. This morning I was uneasy, having told Diane only half the story. Dishes better answered my ambivalence, though maybe because cleaning them up was itself only an ambivalent act of love. I'd done dishes here before and once made the mistake of turning on the dishwasher when it was only half full. I got no speeches from Diane. Conservation was part of her job, and she only half joked that my effort balanced out a "static personal ecology." Maybe it was too static. Maybe the past had whetted powerful appetites that had too strong a hold. I wondered now if doubt was the cause of Diane's nighttime visit to the boy. Was Budge really getting from me all she said he was? Did she think she had to make up this lack without anyone knowing? I remembered her telling me that though Budge wasn't quite one when his father left, he seemed to know something was wrong, manifesting the loss with minor infections, colic, and fussing. The temptation, she said, was to spoil him and ignore the consequences, though eventually everyone had to think about living normally.

Now she came out to the kitchen in her dark green robe, running a comb through her wet hair. She put her arms around my neck and kissed my head. Budge, watching out of the corner of his eye, repeated some motion of his legs that drummed through the table. When

Diane straightened and went to get her English muffin he asked me to read him the captions under pictures in the newspaper. "*You* read them," she said, which put an end to it. Budge turned to me and asked, "What are you going to do with *your* picture?"

I flushed and glanced at Diane, who stood at the counter with her back to us, innocently waiting for the toaster.

"It's not a picture," I said, enunciating carefully. "It's a negative."

I hoped this would be enough, but the boy asked, "What's it of?"

"A famous photographer," I said,

He paused, unsatisfied, then asked, "Can I see?"

....

"Where did you get it?" Budge asked when, downtown at my apartment, I carefully set the plate in his lap.

"I found it."

"Where?"

"In a basement."

"Yours?"

"No."

"Did you steal it?"

"No. Not exactly. I took it to keep it safe."

The boy thought about this. I opened my mouth to say something more, but nothing came out.

"It's broken," he said. "Why's it such a big deal?"

"Because it's old and he's famous and nobody knew it existed before."

I looked at Diane, who pretended to be engrossed in the Aperture volume, apparently having decided that I needed to do this on my own. She'd only shrugged and said, "Whatever," when I had suggested coming down here, letting it be my decision. We'd already agreed to spend the morning together, after which Budge was off to a friend's and Diane to her office to catch up on work. Saying no to this plan, it was implied, would be like flying off to California.

"Is it worth a lot of money?"

"I don't know," I said uneasily. "It could be."

"Did *you* break it?" one of those haranguing personas asked.

"No," I said, relieved at the unencumbered answer. To head off more questions I carefully slipped the two halves from their Plexiglas splint and had him gently brush his thumb over the old edges and the fresher ones of the break. "The whole thing is liquid," I said. I'd seen vintage plates that had been stored on edge for seventy years, the images badly wrinkled, distorted like faces in a funhouse mirror. "It's like painting on water," I told him preachily. Budge looked as if he didn't understand, so I started telling him about the old picture-making process. A child of his time, he was fascinated by excess and listened closely as I described the enormous trouble early photographers went to, washing, fixing, and varnishing their plates, risking cuts from the glass and burns and lung disease from the chemicals.

"Are you going to give it back?" he asked.

Finally Diane intervened, showing us an image in *Wilfred Eng*. "This soldier looks like he's crying."

"It's the long exposure," I said.

According to the introductory essay, this black World War I infantryman had visited Eng's studio as a young recruit for a fairly standard pose and had come back three years later without one arm. Eng usually couldn't take revealing portraits without forcing a statement. But this one worked. The man had pinned his empty uniform sleeve like a salute across his heart. Normally not a subtle ironist, Eng had cropped the sleeve near the bottom edge. You didn't notice it at first. Instead you saw the eyes and face, the naked human head afloat in a world of light and consequence. The strain of the long exposure drew beads of tear along the soldier's lower lids. The slight movement of his eyes gave them a soft, cataract-like blur that unfocused his anger and his certainties. He beseeched the camera, let it lift away the drapery of propriety and humor and hope, revealing the fatigue that was maybe everyone's final legacy.

"Avedon did the same thing with Borges, Marilyn Monroe, and the Eisenhowers," I said. "Somehow, without saying a word, the subjects agree to let the camera inside. There's this moment of absolute trust."

There was an early Hitchcock film, I remembered all at once, in which a murderess can't stop hearing the word "knife." When I stopped talking now, even the abrupt silence spoke eloquently for what I was trying to keep under wraps. The air percolated with guilt.

"It sounds more like analysis," Diane said after what seemed like a knowing pause. Bending, she lifted the two pieces from Budge's lap and raised them close to her face. "I see how you get so lost."

Something had piqued her interest—the contagion of discovery, the excitement of being at the center of something unexampled. Or maybe she realized the power this glass could have over me, over us. For a moment now she seemed not to be looking at the image but waiting for me to say something, to assure her that bringing her here this morning was not a way of selling her a bill of goods. Budge took his mother's silence as a cue and, perhaps bored as well, ran down the hall to my living room to play. Diane set down the glass and smiled, trying to end the awkward moment. "Budgie and I should get going," she said. She looked ready to say something else but took my hand instead and kissed it. She looked tentative. She must have sensed that I thought so because she grinned and came close for a good-bye kiss. "I love you," she said, then touched my face in such a way that I knew she was especially glad I had decided to spend our morning this way. I was suddenly awash in relief, as if Diane had just assured me that she would love me no matter what. I drew her close and kissed her tenderly. "I'll call you soon," I whispered. Then she went out to get the boy.

When they were gone I sat down at my computer. Like other dealers I had a large mailing list that required constant attention. The work mounted up mercilessly after even a few days' neglect. As I typed, the sweet moment of relief slipped away, replaced by disappointment. Would I sell Diane a bill of goods if I thought I could? Did I think I could somehow win her over to Parker's plan? Writing my letters, I grew impatient, maybe because this work, this skein of inter-connectedness and mutual interest, depended largely on trust. Finally I couldn't concentrate anymore, so I lay down on the couch with *Wilfred Eng*, looking for some reassurance that what had felt so right in California was in fact right. The landscapes stood mutely on the pages, offering no answers. After an hour or so I put the book down and managed to work until six, then took a long walk up the water-front. The violet, melancholy air over the Sound turned the world shapeless. Coming back to the Square I passed the Glorien Building and stopped, looking down into the purplish, grayish gloom of the alley. The blues deepened as I approached Judith's basement door. Sheet tin had been hammered over this door for protection, and now there was a certain petulance in the hundreds of nailheads. All at once I saw this door as the totem of petty resistance, a patchwork of need-less caution hammered shut against golden opportunities just inches away. When I touched it the door swung open lightly on its hinges. Was this another sign? An Eng quotation leaped into my head: "We must take what is truest & protect it with all our might. We must tell no one, we must hide all of it in our darkest heart." It was a gloomy, resentful sentiment spoken by a prickly, aging Eng. Photography scholars assumed he was speaking of his landscapes and his attitude toward them, that he really believed they were his best work but wouldn't admit it. But I was all at once thinking in more concrete terms, my mind seizing on that "all of it."

There might be more.

An entire lost oeuvre might lie hidden down here, waiting to be mined like a vein of ore. I stepped inside, flicked on the light, and went down the stairs. In the empty wooden case I found a revisitation of that first dizzying moment. In this basement, in the harsh bulblight, the idea of personal gain grew suddenly vivid. How many thousands had made money, had even made their livings from Eng? My hands started sweating, and my heart worked in stiff, rapid swallows. How could I ever have kidded myself about the worth of these plates, the scope of this find, the largeness of Eng's vision? Eng's name was known across the globe. He was a compromised, solitary man famous for his flaws and failures as much as for his brilliance. I had knowledge of a precious handful of self-portraits no one had known existed before now.

I felt a soft breeze behind me. I'd left the tin door open, and before I started my search I went back up the stairs to close it. The alley was nearly dark; it would be a relief to shut it out. In its hush I heard a moan and jumped, then stuck my head out to make sure the coast was clear. Pollock spotted me.

At first the giant dog just stared, his eyes glinting like amber balls in the Batman silhouette of his head. Then he shattered the pall with a bone-jarring bark, reared, and fired his body at me.

I slammed the door and an instant later Pollock hit it like a linebacker. His claws raked the tin. There was no inside handle, nothing to hold the door shut with. Then I heard Judith running up, footsteps crunching in the alley's grit.

"Who's in there?" she shouted.

Judith, the model of confident defiance, ignored scoop and leash laws. Evenings, she let Pollock romp along the waterfront and sport with terrified joggers, after which the big dog moved his bowels in the alley. Judith could be awe-inspiring even when wrong. Now she was blind with righteousness and beat the door with her fist. "Get out of my basement, you son of a bitch!" she shouted. Pollock launched barks as if he couldn't get rid of them fast enough, but Judith called him off, and in a split-second's silence I heard the unlikely wind chime tinkling of her keys. Then one of them grated in the lock. Running, trying to hide amid the junk, was as suicidal as facing the two of them with lame excuses. Frozen with terror, with the utter lack of possibilities, I watched my hand reach over and hold down the latch button.

Judith shouted, "Shit!" and sawed at the lock. Through my finger, pressing that steel nipple, I felt her furious twisting, her whole enfeebled might. "Let go, you yellow son of a bitch! Come out here and face me like a man!"

She worked the key, keeping at it for an insanely long stretch. Giddy with fear, I had a sudden thought that Judith's career was hobbled by the failure to bend this same fury to paint and canvas. The enormity of her frustration was clear. The lock seemed to writhe. It felt molten under my fingertip. Judith grunted a mere foot away. Finally she backed off and gave the door a kick that shuddered the jam. "You fucker! Let go, goddamn it!" Then more sawing, kicking, and shouting. She kept it up so long that even Pollock got tired, joining in only with desultory growls. Finally someone up the alley called out, "Hey, shut up."

"Call the cops, I've got a prowler!" Judith hollered back. When no answer came she turned back and gave the door another solid kick.

Then we all endured a period such as swelled tension in horror tales by Poe, the murderer waiting behind a curtain for his victim to fall asleep before tediously carving up his body and entombing the pieces in a brick wall. Judith finally gave in and tried to catch me off guard with sudden wild twisting. She was spookily silent, letting out only involuntary yips. Her other keys jingled with morbid merriment. My fingerbone ached. I felt sick to my stomach. Then she stopped. Silence again. Pollock hadn't bothered to rouse himself. I imagined him adjusting to this, sprawled like a sphinx in the alley until it was time to go. But this nightmare would never end. I began to think about throwing myself on their mercy. I could tell Judith I had found the door open and gone in to investigate. It was probably too late. She would need to show a minion no kindness. Trashing an art outsider like me would make her feel like less of an outsider herself.

"Stay, Pollock. *Stay*, goddamn it."

She whispered these orders. Was she making a move? I strained to hear. She'd crept away—or had she? Judith was sly enough to be waiting me out. But if I were she I'd have gone for some law. I decided to test it, swallowed hard, and hammered on the door.

Pollock had come to believe there was no one inside, and now, alone, he was reborn, starting in at ground zero. He flung himself so hard against the door that he might have broken something. He gulped and gnashed at his barks as if devouring a flayed carcass. He was inches away, sucking breath like a crazed asthmatic. I felt like a diver in a shark cage, fear and too much reality making the world unreal.

I let the button go and hurried back through the piles of cartons and furniture. Near the front of the Glorien was an arch in a wall shared with the building next door, and after moving aside a large, battered chest of drawers I made my way through. The arch was two feet thick and the floor scarred as if by giant claws where heavy objects had been dragged through. The neighbor's basement was nearly empty. Along the street side of this other building I remembered seeing a trap door in a recessed well in the sidewalk. This well collected all manner of trash and was peed in freely by drunks. There would have to be stairs leading up from the inside. There were. When I reached them the smell of piss was overpowering. There was no lock on the inside, only a hasp held shut with a bent nail. I was overjoyed by such good luck until I tried to lift the door. It might have been bolted down. But there was no other way out, so I crouched on the highest step I could, wedging myself in like Houdini. I heaved upward. Nothing. Black panic surged in my limbs. Shaking, I heaved again, and this time the door gave a loud crack. I heaved a third time and lifted it an inch. A tendril of outside air freshened the staleness. I thought I might actually make it. I listened. There were footsteps, voices, but none urgent or angry. I waited there, crouching fetally, thighs and buttocks quaking and the heavy door gnawing my spine.

When it was quiet I pushed up, ignoring the wet that seeped through my shirt as the bottles and food wrappers slid off noisily. The side street was empty for the moment, so I climbed up through the old tube railing and walked as calmly as I could to the corner. Then I broke for home at a dead run.

March 20

Today while you made our tea I wandered into your workroom &
looked at the walls there which are covered with pictures. I had
never stopped to look at them before & yet my eyes seemed to seek
out a picture you had made from the Rialto Bridge in Venice. I
recognized the soothing waters of the Grand Canal—I had stood
in the same spot myself. The waters beyond the bridge were peaceful, the same lapping sound that people have heard there for a
thousand years. The stone of the bridge had the feel of bone from
centuries of hands rubbing over it. It was carved with names &
dates, some a hundred years old & worn nearly to extinction.

   I heard you enter the room behind me with the tea tray & stop
when you looked where I looked. "I was eight when I made that,"
you said. Suddenly I felt such a pang, perhaps that our paths had
crossed when we never knew it, that we had each been part of this
lovely scene in ignorance of one another. When I tried to explain
this you answered, "'Chemicals in a black box.'" I was bewildered
more by your drollness & it took a moment to recognize my own
opinion flung back at me. "Picture-making is such a waste of
time," you said. I flushed & smiled. "It never seems like making
anything!" I protested. You glanced up at the picture & said,
"You're right, it doesn't, until you make one yourself." Then we
both fell silent. I could not turn to face you, could not take my
eyes from the bridge. I remembered listening to the gentle waves
as if to the sound of hope itself. How quickly that hope disappeared. I knew so little of marriage then—the clash of wills, the
deceptions. How quickly I learned. I felt another pang & it came to
me that Joseph had taken us both to this beautiful place, you in his

employ & me years later as his bride. I wondered that you had lived many more years with Joseph than I have. You seemed to know I was about to speak of things we have never spoken of before & so set down the tray & came up behind me.

Then you quickly drew me down the hall.

In time, I think, even oblivion becomes just another dream. It is late now & my bedroom has lost the last of the fire's heat. Just now I got up & drew all the curtains shut. There is no moon, no light from the street. All the windows are black & cold. It is as if someone were staring in, though at each pane I meet only my own uneasy face....

4

Reruns of those hair-raising moments kept me awake most of the night. But as the hours passed and the sky turned from black to violet, I grew less afraid that Judith had recognized me—I was sure, in fact, that she hadn't. Outwitting her, with one finger pressed against a latch button, seemed preordained and had an almost moral clarity, like an Aesop's fable. I hadn't panicked. I'd come out of a potentially bad situation without a scratch. That *meant* something, didn't it? By dawn I was feeling strangely calm and determined to see the plan through. Now, once more, the problem of Diane and Budge shrank into the background. Things with them would sort themselves out in time. Parker Lange tipped the balance even further when he called later that morning.

"I reached him in Modena," he said. "Leonard is into old Ferraris." He milked the moment with a pause. "He's interested."

"How interested?"

"Enough to give Judith a show. I'm going to need the plate."

I'd told Parker $20,000 apiece for the five, assuming we could get our hands on them, and now I asked, "Did you give him my price?"

"What's the rush, Robert? You considering other offers?"

His snideness annoyed me, so I said, "I might be."

"But you aren't. If you make this a bidding war, word is going to get out. Your buyers might get nervous."

"What would I care?" I said, though everything he said was true.

"I don't have to remind you," Parker said, "that the buyer takes all the risk. You might get a little more somewhere else. But Leonard is solid. He protects his sources, so your reputation stays intact."

"What did he say?"

"Nothing. Which means your number is probably not out of line."

Mostly, I realized, I just wanted to feel the scalp-tingling rush when Parker repeated a dollar amount that still seemed like a dream.

"There's nothing like them in the world," I said, hoping this pomposity wouldn't so much justify the price as disguise greed. I could almost hear Parker grin.

"Save it for Leonard," he said.

I blushed deep red and said, "It's not Leonard I'm worried about."

"We could have screwed each other long before now. There's a reason we never did."

"We didn't because we both covered our asses," I said. "In the end you covered yours better."

"If I screwed you, it would reflect badly on Leonard. Why would I want to do that? I've got a sweet deal here, Robert. Lots of leverage, lots of freedom."

"I'd put money on your being a gofer," I said, "just like me."

A silent moment passed, Parker perhaps mastering that rare anger.

"If you're asking whose side I'm on, you know the answer to that," he finally said. "Leonard will slip me a nice finder's fee. If you and I became partners I'd be out of a job. We'd have to take less from someone who didn't know us. Then we'd go halvesies, Robert, and how would you feel about that?"

....

Two evenings later Diane showed up unannounced at my apartment. I was tired and frayed. My confidence surged and ebbed, and I wasn't sleeping all that well. Also, Parker had ended our conversation by telling me he was flying up. He was due the next morning. I couldn't stop him. In truth, I didn't *want* to, so I was not looking forward to seeing Diane. It must have shown in my face, but she didn't notice.

"Uncle Sonny died yesterday," she said.

Her eyes were swollen, and she clearly didn't feel like beating around the bush. She stepped through the door and fell into my arms, sobbing.

Sonny Mays had been Diane's favorite among Michael's relatives. They had kept in touch over the years, phoning each other at birthdays and holidays. I'd heard a lot of Sonny stories, most of them sad. He had lost his wife, his daughter, and his left leg when a bridge he was driving over collapsed into a swamp. Still, all the loss had saved him from any life but that of a dissolute gentleman. He'd never worked a day in his life, selling off pieces of the ancestral land whenever he found himself short of resources. "His real tragedy was laziness," Diane had said. "The old fake. He bred himself pretty carefully that way long before he ever lost anything." On a visit eight years ago she and Michael and Sonny had driven to a favorite spot of Sonny's near Memphis called the Chicken Drop. Twice a night the proprietor chased a chicken out onto the numbered tiles of the dance floor, and all the drunks laid odds on which tile the bird would shit on. Afterward Diane asked Sonny if it really was his favorite place, and he said, "That's all I can say without putting it into words."

Now Diane calmed herself, breathing more steadily and running her hand along my arm.

"You okay?" I asked.

She nodded. "It was so unexpected, is all. It scares me, losing these old family connections. It feels like there's nothing to replace them."

She followed this with what seemed like a purposeful silence. I didn't know what to say next and so asked neutrally, "How's Michael taking it?"

"He's in pretty bad shape. He came for dinner yesterday, and we sat up all night talking."

"Michael spent the night?"

"If something like this had happened when we were together he'd have taken a bottle of bourbon and sat in the bathtub for hours. I've never seen him so—I don't know what, so close to the surface. He's actually talking about his feelings."

"Becky's working miracles," I said and instantly wished I hadn't. Becky was Michael's latest girlfriend. Diane had once sniped that Budge liked her because she was so close to his age. This wasn't the best moment for taking potshots, but the news that Michael was showing his feelings sounded too far-fetched.

"He broke up with her," Diane said. "It's a phase. What is it with you men and your bimbos?"

"It's not just men."

"Women face facts," Diane said. "After that we get fat and depressed."

"We need to find out if we can keep lying to ourselves."

In the next instant it seemed as if I'd shut up too quickly, my silence drawing a sharp outline around the lies I seemed to mean to tell Diane. Tentatively I added, "We're trying to convince ourselves that we're not really going to die."

She laughed. "How do even bimbos fall for it? 'I'm dealing with my mortality, baby, take off all your clothes except the stiletto heels.'" She pulled back and looked at me again. "How about it, have you had it with bimbos?"

"I need more mature company."

"That's what Michael said the second time around."

"He's no fool. He knows what he gave up."

I wondered all at once if I'd also be finding out how that felt. Diane looked at her watch.

"I've got to get home," she said. "I was with Michael tonight at the boat, and I stayed too long."

"I'll drive you," I said.

"It's okay, I've got my car."

"I'll follow you home."

"Really, Robert, it's okay." A smile flickered across her lips. "Your jealousy could go right to my head."

I flushed. "That's crazy. I'm just worried about you."

"I know," she said and gave my cheek a grateful kiss.

But clearly it amused and pleased her to give in. At her house I said I'd drive the babysitter home, and while the girl put her coat on I took Diane aside.

"Why don't I come back and stay the night."

"I'm really tired, Robert; I'm not going to be good for much."

"That's okay," I said.

Budge must have had a field day with the bashful sitter, who seemed to think giving me directions to her house was an imposition. I wanted to get back to Diane, and the girl hesitated so much I finally snapped, "Spit it out, for Christ's sake!" Diane was asleep when I returned. I undressed quietly and lay down beside her, breathless, feeling sheepish. Did I expect to find Michael letting himself in, disarming the security lamp with a remote clicker on his key ring? Diane was right, I was jealous. I was marking turf. But did I have the right? Was I risking it all? I felt like a novelty performer spinning too many platters on the ends of sticks. In the back of my mind I still thought I could make Diane see eye to eye with Sills and Parker. If I couldn't, something might give, something might come crashing down.

Normally these thoughts would have been good for solid hours of insomnia, but I was suddenly out like a light. Then, deep in the night, a downpour hit and I woke with a start. The drumming seemed just inches overhead. A hand touched my shoulder.

"Duff?"

I had my back to Budge but could hear his breath, gasping and uneven, wringing itself around other words his nightmare wouldn't let him speak. I rolled over, my heart heaving against my ribs.

"Are you okay?" Obviously he wasn't, and when he couldn't answer I asked, "Do you want to get in?"

I lifted the blankets, and Budge didn't hesitate. As he climbed over me his feet and hands made icy dabs on my skin. The rest of him was hot with fear. Diane, who had also woken, gave him a pillow, and he buried his face, whimpering syllables like the remnants of a lost argument. I couldn't help myself and whispered, "Who's Duff?"

Still comforting the boy, Diane didn't answer. She didn't have to.

....

Parker had said no delays. He was due in at ten A.M., and when I left Diane's for the airport the next morning it was still pouring.

Over the phone I'd told him it would sound less suspicious if he called Judith from San Francisco to set up their meeting. Parker, who had a sixth sense about such things, disagreed. "It'll look like we're trying to bury you," he said. As much as I disliked Judith, the idea of lying to her made me nervous. Even a friendly-seeming gesture like this would be met with suspicion. I had to chase her down. I phoned her home and studio, leaving detailed messages so she wouldn't think this was about the still unsigned check. By the time I finally got her I was annoyed enough to not be intimidated by her hostile silences. I was angry not at Judith's money and luck but because for a single stinging instant I couldn't help sharing her disdain of people like me. Judith saw my work as something like the art equivalent of the McDonald's take-out window: I had the advanced degrees and the disappointments; all I needed was a paper hat. I asked, "Are you interested?" and bit my tongue before I could add, "you stupid bitch." Judith thought a moment, then agreed to meet Parker at a restaurant for lunch, alone.

Stepping off the plane, Parker looked as relaxed and focused as a hit man. We hardly spoke on the drive in, and after I dropped him off at the restaurant I went home to wait.

Three hours later, when he showed up at my apartment, the slate-green hood of sky had slid eastward and the sun was raising hopeful tufts of steam from the wet streets. Things had gone well—she was going to think over his offer of a show.

"That's like someone stranded in a desert thinking over a glass of water," I said.

"People need their dignity," Parker said, clearly feeling his oats. "You were right; she's not sure why you're doing her this favor. What did you do that annoyed her so much?"

"I asked for my fee."

"You were right about the paintings too," Parker said. "She brought transparencies. They look like garage floors spattered with condor shit. Poor woman. She'd be eaten alive in a real city. It'll be a challenge, Robert—my own personal *Pygmalion*. When I'm done with her, Leonard won't know she was once just a rich little guttersnipe."

"I thought you said Leonard wouldn't be a problem."

"He won't. But he's like everybody else. He likes his turkey dressed."

I looked at him, sitting almost primly in my chair. "Does Leonard let you fly off like this whenever you feel like it?"

"*He* trusts me," Parker said, a more obvious grin melting on his lips. Good spirits drew his stillness into even greater relief. Only his brain twitched back and forth, leaping like a squirrel from branch to branch. The rest of him didn't stir. I remembered him bragging about dating twins and thought he might have trouble with one woman, let alone two, if sexual prospects also had this deadening effect.

"He didn't even ask about the paintings," he added.

At lunch Parker had told Judith her paintings were "massive textural gestures," which he now glibly qualified: "besides being shit, they're so fucking big. Even in the transparencies they looked like botched masonry. Maybe I can talk her into cutting them up. We could sell them as bricks."

Laughter shook him with faint, languid spasms. Done with Judith for the moment, he now took me on. He moved his eye along the walls of my office, transfixed less by all the old photographs hanging there than by his own mirthful armature. He seemed to take in the new Robert Armour and size him up against the old. "The photo hermit of Seattle," he said. "What a sweet life, Robert. The devotion and the study and…what's the word I want? Selflessness." Not surprisingly, he could name many of the photographers and related the frustrating insurance woes of another photo-dealer friend. "An adjuster told this guy that if there's a negative, it can be reproduced. *Ergo,* it's not as valuable."

"Most of these are limited editions or one of a kind," I told him. "I don't bother with insurance. Why think about paying yourself for an irretrievable loss?"

I made myself stop. Parker's seeming passivity encouraged foolish acts. There was the sense of my getting on a high horse when the real reason I had no insurance was also money, the lack of it. Bluntly Parker asked, "How well do you do?" I mentioned a monthly sum I had actually only made once. In all my years in Seattle I had found no way to avoid the self-employment roller coaster that balled up my taxes and raised my overdraft at the bank, which I occasionally reduced by selling off one of these irretrievable images. Parker may have understood this because he asked, "Which one would you give up last?" High on one wall I pointed out a working proof of a gravure by Sullivan Thompson, who was making portraits of Indians around the same time as E. S. Curtis. The proof showed a Hopi woman and the photographer's gruff notes in the margins instructing his printer to remove the flecks of lint that showed in her hair. There were holes in the top margin where a pin had been inserted as if through a pants cuff; also the perfect crown where a drop of ink had fallen near one corner. This particular portrait, I explained to Parker, was sometimes borrowed for shows, most recently in Frankfurt. It bore the mark of a

human hand; it was an object that contained an image. I'd been offered a lot of money for it but couldn't bring myself to sell. Would this
love change if I could suddenly afford any print I wanted? Parker's eye
roved these images as if spotting commercial leaks where the walls
only seemed money-tight. Was he right? Would I come to see all these
pictures as potential cash cows? Near my desk hung a Marsha Burns
silver-print of Diane, Budge, and me. Parker's gaze lingered over it.

"You never mentioned the little family," he said. "Will I get to meet
them?"

The idea made my flesh crawl, especially in view of last night. *Duff.*
I knew Michael Mays hadn't been taking my place in Diane's bed—no
amount of paranoia over Parker and the plates would convince me
otherwise. The boy had been confused, and maybe "Duff" was an
honest slip. But Michael was showing signs of a new intimacy. Did
Budge want someone closer than I could get? Did he think I might
not be around forever? And who did I think I was protecting when I
told Parker, "They're not my family"?

....

Judith invited Parker to participate in a panel series she moderated
once a month at a downtown hotel. Parker himself had once begun
such a series, much maligned but well attended, offered on the
premise that fireworks were the whole point. And Parker would toler-
ate anything, even boredom, if it caused a stir.

Before going I phoned Diane, telling her I had a late-evening ap-
pointment in the neighborhood where Judith lived. On the face of it
this statement was not a lie. But I was beginning to understand that
there was no symmetry between deceit and consequence, that half
truths did not make us feel even half better.

Besides Parker and Judith there were three other panelists, including a conspicuous local sculptor who Judith feared would show
up drunk and provide a pitched, embarrassing moment. Richard

Stanfield, the sculptor, did come late to the panel, but the commotion he caused, walking to the dais, refocused on his rigid silence. Parker tried to incite this man but got nowhere. Judith managed to keep things going with another panelist, a Manhattan poet named James Barry who was on his way home from a refugee camp in Thailand. Barry and Judith lobbed each other bland theses and affirmations about the state of war-ravaged nations. Stanfield, finally coming to life, pointed out loudly that Judith and Barry were both rich. Then he attacked Western art as an extension of capitalist isolation in the guise of what he considered the collusive sin of regionalism.

"No one who's rich can understand the Third World," he said.

"The Third World was always there," Parker put in. "Aren't we trying to regionalize it by calling it that?"

Maybe it was Parker's attitude, but this too got no response except from Stanfield himself, who continued to participate just to prove he wasn't pouting. It was Barry who shut up, isolating himself in the event of a free-for-all. Barry looked better than anyone in the room. His shirt alone must have cost $500. He wore his expensive clothes like the banners of aristocratic sanction.

After the panel Judith hosted a party at her enormous house, which looked, in Parker's words, "like a Cubist refrigerator." The house was surgically spare and bore the brute cantilevering of an academic school of design whose disciples wouldn't think of living that way themselves. Standing at the entrance to the crowded living room, I watched Judith gesturing at Barry, and Barry, who was preparing himself for a reading, not paying much attention. Then Parker appeared at my side, untouched drink in his hand like a prop. Though the evening's shortcomings had left him outwardly calm, Parker was lit up from within, radiating hidden energy like a turbine whirring in the bowels of a dam.

Judith's husband, Ron Rizer, now spotted us and made his way over. During the panel Parker had sought other inflammatory avenues without much success. He had even tried turning the crowd against him by announcing that Seattle's art community had "the temperament of a prairie cow town." No one objected. Or maybe they simply didn't take him seriously. Parker had also proclaimed that kitsch, not serious art, was responsible for extending the life of any culture, and now Ron Rizer, who made an annoying habit of such things, cheerfully begged to disagree.

"What do you want a culture to do?" Parker asked. He fixed Ron with a look, plainly irritated that this objection had not been raised earlier, when it might have caused trouble. "When it's here, all you do is complain about it dying."

"What causes that?" Ron asked earnestly.

"What makes *you* die?"

"I hadn't thought of it that way."

"When does it go?" Parker asked. "Today, when the female weight lifters you saw in *Mad* magazine are serving coffee on airliners, or tomorrow, when the president has a sex change in office?"

"Jude does weights," said Ron, lighting up a sudden sleepy smile. "Is he for real?" he asked when Parker suddenly left us. But Ron didn't wait for an answer. Instead he began telling me about a motivational seminar he had recently attended. Ron and I had met at openings half a dozen times since he and Judith had been married. He was a dwarfish, malleable-looking man with a vacant light in his face. He used any excuse to indulge the latest psychochic and tolerated even rudeness and insults as a springboard. He was also wealthy, and as he went on I wondered how he would apply what he had learned to being a dilettante. He pronounced the phrase "strategies for excellence" with proper reverence, the glow of it all still on him.

"You want to know the most powerful word in any language?" he asked.

"Yes."

He gaped, honestly astonished that someone could know the answer without spending all that money.

"By the way," he said, touching my arm, "that screaming kite was incredible."

"What's that?"

"The screaming kite. Aren't you Alden Pesh?" he asked, and added, "The conceptualist?"

I gave him a look but knew better than to think he was joking.

"Ron, I think Alden Pesh lives in Santa Fe."

He was genuinely sorry to hear this. We stood a moment, adrift in discomfort. Finally he asked, "Who are you?"

I got away as soon as I could and moved into the living room near the wall, carefully skirting a vast canvas of turquoise-and-brow n. I meant to get lost in the crowd but instead moved into the limelight, right next to James Barry, in fact, who fairly vibrated, like an evangelist gearing up to galvanize a crowd. Ron was right on my heels—he would be introducing the poet. He and Judith and Barry were all old friends, as it turned out, though Judith was suddenly nowhere in sight.

I thought Barry might move when Ron finished his remarks. But he meant to use the hideous painting for a backdrop. Most everyone sat on the carpet, and when Barry started I sat there too, close to the poet's feet. Someone dimmed all but the track lights above him, and Barry cleared his throat.

"Certain beliefs have it," he started, "that human beings came into existence because a godhead denied life. That we chose life out of the void before we had it. They contend that we are still doing so," he said, "though some like Mr. Stanfield have obviously shopped the bargain basements."

The laughter was raucous and relieved. Heads swiveled like radar dishes, seeking out Richard Stanfield, who stood near the back gripping a tumbler of scotch while his face boiled. I looked around for Parker to see how he was taking it, Barry having succeeded where he had failed. Parker too had disappeared.

When the room died back down, Barry spoke a few more prefatory words. Then came the verse.

As he read I began to feel sorry for Richard Stanfield. Barry was slick. A savvy performer, he spoke his lines with a slyly cultivated patience. He wanted us to believe he was some kind of Uncle Remus, a humble conduit whose moral conclusions were not his own but the world's. Implicit in his glorification of a devastated people was, I couldn't help thinking, the life he created for them and then stole back. His metaphors were straight from the fashion industry. Jungles were "draped in emerald," a man's scalp "jeweled" with lice. His poem, like a beautiful gown, hinted skillfully at what was underneath, which in the end might be nothing much at all. I had to remind myself that this was a decimated population he was talking about, not Bill Blass–meets–Ulysses. Where *was* all that ancient myth coming from? And how was a designer refugee camp anything like Troy?

When he finished the applause was hearty enough, but a sudden surge toward the bar meant Barry had whetted other appetites. Parker was still missing. I looked all over for him, squeezing through the noisy crowd. He was nowhere. The lines at the bar still hadn't gone down, so I killed twenty minutes waiting for a double bourbon, then continued the search upstairs.

"Upstairs" was a questionable term in a house like this. So was "house." Ron and Judith's place demanded words such as "mezzanine" and "dwelling." Baffled by the eccentric floor plan, I approached what turned out to be the master bedroom and heard muffled laughter. Then a group of strangers burst out the two massive doors and passed around me, bubbling like schoolkids. One of them, wry-looking in tortoise-framed glasses with lenses the size of nickels, laid his hand on my sleeve and asked earnestly, "Do you have your Dramamine?" The others fell apart laughing as they continued down the hall. Scowling, I passed into the bedroom, done exclusively in leather the watery ochre of hemorrhoid ointment. Even the king-sized bed had a leather duvet with a swampy gloss from huge lamps flanking it like centurions.

The bathroom was polished steel. It looked like an autopsy room or an airplane toilet that every few minutes flushed itself with acrid blue detergent. I could have peed anywhere with impunity. Each shining surface distorted my face like a funhouse mirror. On the counter was a hand mirror with leftover flecks and razor crusts of coke. Another door led to a naked hallway. The lights here were recessed, unflinching and bright, staring down with benevolent menace. At the end was the sort of metal door put in grade schools built in the 1960s. It even had that square foot of chicken-wired glass. I should have looked first.

This room was a gym, grim as Calvary, walls the same lobotomized gray as Judith's canvases. Treadmill and stairmaster, weight and rowing machines stood under leatherette covers, all unused for the moment, casting craggy shadows.

Maybe it was the Bach playing at top volume. But seeing Parker and Judith was not the shock it should have been, maybe because their grappling was contained by the gentler swaying. In fact, watching them swing back and forth gave me a weird surge of confidence: Parker obviously wasn't worrying anymore—why should I? Suddenly I felt light as a suicide stepping off the ledge—not even the last blinding instant of pain would matter.

The swing was the sort offered by mail in the backs of porn magazines. Each time the two swept to my side of the room, Parker's flattened buttocks lifted like a cleft upper lip, revealing the word "LoveGlider" along the edge of the foam seat. The software jumble of upper- and lowercase lent it an air of universal endorsement that was strangely reassuring: this was no coital toy but legitimate equipment with every right to unironic self-advertisement. Heavy white ropes led to swiveling eyebolts in the ceiling's single beam, around which the architect had fitted two broad skylights, used less for viewing constellations, I guessed, than for reflecting Gliders. Arcing back and forth, Judith glanced up at herself and Parker, soaring like Wallendas at a Club Med. Their hands and arms flailed, grasping at the ropes and at each other, their legs pumping, then dangling like mud wasps'.

I couldn't tell who was screwing and who was being screwed.

They hadn't seen me. Backing out, I closed the door as gently as if defusing a bomb, then stood there staring at it until shadows climbed up from the floor. I wheeled. It was Ron and James Barry.

"Hi—it's Robert, right?"

"Sorry," I said, "you kind of startled me."

Ron gave an apologetic shrug. We passed another complicated moment, then I pointed my thumb over my shoulder. "You're going in there?"

Anyone else would have seized the awkwardness. Ron nodded thoughtfully. Then he raised his bushy eyebrows, excusing himself to pass by. I stepped in his way. I was frantic, though not for mild Ron— he seemed made for cuckolding, might not even recognize betrayal if it swung its foam-supported ass in his face. Instead I saw the Eng plan blowing sky high in a welter of anger and accusation, confession and threat. Ron's chest actually bumped mine. Behind him Barry was growing impatient, eyes twitching in their sockets. But Ron was not perturbed. You took life as it came, you accommodated. You said *yes*. His blandness was solid, it went clear through. You could cut Ron in half and his insides would have the textural integrity of a vegetable, clean and seedless as a jicama root. He gave me a questioning look that verged on radiance. The light shone in his brow with the faint yellow of a flashlight with low batteries.

"I apologize," I said.

"Hey. *Mi casa, su casa.*"

"That's not what I mean." I cleared my throat. I seemed to be watching myself through the wrong end of a telescope. "I have a confession to make," I said and shivered when a drop of sweat skied down my ribs. Ron encouraged me with those raised eyebrows that seemed to draw their juice from the same weak power source. "I *am* Alden

Pesh," I said. "I wasn't telling you the truth before. It's this thing I'm working through for a new piece. Something completely different— sort of confrontational, you know?"

I was trying to buy time, to think up some way of getting them out of there—but this was absurd. Judith knew who I was. I could only hope Ron would forget the whole thing later, that I would never see him and Judith together until the deal was done.

"You mean like performance art," he said.

I answered, "Sort of," through a rictus of earnest apology. Ron nodded, bearing this down on the lobes of his brain. His hooded eyelids, the only sensuous thing about him, drooped suddenly as if concentration taxed him to the point of unconsciousness. Somehow I suddenly knew he was one of those people who whistled thoughtlessly through their teeth. The lids blinked over his slightly protruding corneas like tongues licking wet lips, their syncopation weirdly deliberate, like something wired and glue-gunned and latex-laminated for an extravagant fantasy film. Ron looked like a fairy tale bumbling awry of its moral. I caught a whiff of something closety: he'd been smoking dope. I wondered why he'd need to. At last he said, "Cool." James Barry had also had a hit or two and blinked like the March Hare, his pupils huge.

Ron asked, "You know what really makes me weep, Alden?"

Onions, I thought but shook my head.

"That so many fine artists can be such dishonest assholes."

He paused again and I swallowed hard, ready to be shown the joker up his sleeve.

"Thank you for saying what you did," Ron said.

Then he raised his papery, pudgy, ET hand and laid it on my shoulder. His other hand, I saw, brushed Barry's. Something clicked and I got out of their way, forcing a smile as they passed. When they shut the door I leaned back against the wall, half wanting the explosion that never came. There was only insinuation and silence except for one sound—a little door slipping shut over the chicken-wire window.

April 7

Our hours together always begin with hope. As I fixed my hair this
morning I imagined you undoing all my careful work.

You did not disappoint me.

After our lovemaking we lay for a time in the pool of our mingled heat. I swore to myself that I could be taken from the earth
at that instant & not regret a life that held such moments.
The love & the short rest invigorated you. You insisted we rise.
You had a surprise, you said, & pulled me by the arms until I re-
lented. Out in the studio was a small table covered by a cloth
which you now removed. On the table you had arranged a simple
still life with bowls, a bottle & a number of winter gourds. My
heart sank.

I was to have a lesson.

You got me a chair & when I sat you turned your back on me
like a conjurer. I sighed. You were twenty minutes fussing with
these simple objects, talking excitedly, then turning for long moments & simply staring out the windows at the daylight. I might
have been a thousand miles away. A silver tray was a problem, you
said, too much reflection. You took my shawl & draped it around
the bowl. You moved the bottle God alone knew what part of an
inch. Finally everything was perfect. "Ready," you said & showed
me what to do. I felt no less like a fool for all your instruction. I
nudged the Box with my elbow. We waited. You had me count off
the seconds, the Box like a square bottle turned on its side, pouring quack potions into the air & stealing time. Our time. I
bumped it again replacing the cap. Then I followed you back to
the work room & while you bent over the table I looked up at the
waters of the Grand Canal. Suddenly I had a wish to live my life

backwards from that point. You said, "Hopeless"—my picture had smeared. "I'm a failure," I said & my throat closed. But you said, "Let's try again," and your voice was so full of excitement & life. Out in the studio again I stood at the windows looking out. Your horse Kate stood in the little enclosure out back. She did not move a muscle. The world had come to a stop & I with it. You had set to work again, talking as if to no one. "Painting, drawing, sculpture—they're all vanity," you said. "If we don't like the way a painter has portrayed us we fire him & burn the canvas. With a photograph everyone must live with the consequence." (Don't photographs burn? I wondered.) "A photograph tells the truth," you said. "It doesn't lie. The subject creates its own life. Even dead objects are what they are & nothing more." Then why must you fuss? And what did you have in the end but shades of gray? The world has never looked worse. Still, maybe these were the colors of our mortality. I thought of my own death & wondered what I would regret most in my last moments. I thought of your death also. Where would we be when there was no time left in our lives & what would have happened to us by then? I must have lost myself in these thoughts for some moments. The room grew still & when I looked up at last you seemed to gaze through me as if I were air.

Secretly you had aimed the Box at me & opened its Eye.

You looked surprised. "You're so beautiful," you said, though it seemed only a way to meet the anger you must have seen in my face. My hair hung down my back, I had covered myself haphazardly at best. I was undone, turned into the dying creature I never believed I could become. I do not want to meet my own eyes in any image, do not want to see myself staring out from a compromised life. I want no image reflecting the sadness of these recent years, the shame in needing to find love as I have found it. I could not help the tears then & wept in a flood. You stepped near & held me close, not as a lover now but as a tender comrade comforting me in some unimaginable trial. Or perhaps you know that death can make us equal when nothing else in the world can....

5

....

Home at one A.M., I started making panic calls to Parker's hotel, leaving messages at the desk. At four I still hadn't heard back. I was frantic and so drove over there but stopped just short of knocking on his door. What if they'd moved the whole circus down here? So I went back home and tried to do some work. It was all a hash, it all seemed like someone else's business. I couldn't make sense of my own motivation, the scope so petty and constricted. Finally, after trying Parker's room three more times, I threw myself down on the couch to stew but fell asleep instead.

When I woke, the sun was up. Parker stood over me. Still half asleep, I asked, "How did you get in?"

Parker's lenses gleamed. When he moved his head and the angle changed I saw his eyes, puffy as a delinquent's. His cheer was even more annoying.

"Your door was open, Robert. I mean *wide* open. Can you still get away with that in Seattle?"

Sitting up, I saw that Parker carried a briefcase as if to balance the debauched mirth with seriousness.

"Ron said he ran into Alden Pesh, who sounded a lot like you."

"I bet you all had a good laugh over that."

"I didn't say a word."

"The foursome your idea, Parker? Or did you honestly think they meant bridge?"

Parker grinned, his puffed eyes slitting. "I take back everything I ever said about Seattle being a backwater for tree-lovers and sappy cooking-show hosts. You've got some sick citizens here, Robert."

"*You* seemed to be enjoying yourself."

"You won't believe it, but I mostly watched. Ron's bi-, or even tri-. He and Pollock are very close. If you're wondering why Judith ever married him, forget it. Ron makes up for *all* his shortcomings."

"I don't want to hear about it, Parker."

"Ever ask yourself what Mr. Ed had to give up so he could talk? God gave him Ron's brain but hung old Ron like a dray horse."

"Parker, shut up *now*."

"What's wrong?"

I shook my head. "I'm trying to keep our asses *out* of the sling. Meantime, you're having a fuckfest with the enemy."

"It wasn't like that, honest, Robert. Otherwise we'd have invited you." He paused. "You're mad."

"I'm up all night trying to run you down, worried out of my mind. When you finally show, all you can talk about is Dopey Rizer's schlong."

"Wait till I get to Barry, that clotheshorse."

Rage boiled over. I was suddenly on my feet, stabbing my finger in Parker's face.

"I've been down this road once before, you fuck!" I shouted. "I'm not going down it again!"

Parker considered my fingertip, inches from his eyes. I lowered my hand and sat.

"Something happened to you overseas," I said. "You took some kind of drug and it pushed you over the edge."

"Are you feeling left out?"

"Not the way you think."

"Aren't you getting any these days?"

"What does that have to do with anything?"

"It's a veiled reference," Parker said. I looked at him, bewildered. "We're talking about your mystery lady friend."

"No, we're not."

"Everybody feels good except you, Robert. Judy's even thinking about flying back to California with me before she says yes. Ron thinks it's a good idea."

"Isn't *that* reassuring."

"You know, I kind of like her."

"How could you? She doesn't have a sister."

"Under all the hard nails and the pathological sex tricks, she's really kind of sweet."

"I want to talk to Sills."

"Before I get totally out of hand?"

"It's too late for that."

"What's changed? So I happened to get a little nooky. What are you so pissed off about?"

"I don't know for a fact that *you've* even talked to Sills."

"What else would I be doing here?"

"Working your own angles is what. Judith's not stupid. If she knew the plates were Eng's, she could figure out what's at stake."

"She wants a show," Parker said reasonably. "Leonard can give her a juicy one. Other galleries will give her shows just because he did, and Leonard will make sure the press all say nice things."

"So much for Judith."

"If it'll help, Robert, I'll pretend I don't want anything. I'll pretend you don't either." He paused, and I assumed an impatient head shake. "The trust thing's got you by the short hairs," he said. "Look. I'm the one coming in at the second act. This has been your gig from the start."

"Meaning I might have more than I say I have."

"I hadn't actually put it to myself that way. But yes. I don't say you're lying to me through your teeth. Just keeping certain things back. Like your little mystery family."

"Forget it, Parker."

"Sorry, I forgot, they're not your family. Who is she anyway?"

"Look, just leave Diane out of it."

"Like you have? Nice name, Diane," he added, when I couldn't answer. "Very solid, very sane."

"Would I be this upset if I was holding out?"

Parker left a pause to let any lies resonate, and I remembered an old saying: Even a hog can find a truffle. Even someone like Parker Lange could recognize the truth when he saw it. He studied me. "I have something to show you," he said finally. "Why don't we get some breakfast."

"Why don't I get a plane ticket?"

"Three's a crowd."

"Like last night?"

He looked at me again. Then he opened his briefcase. The four negatives were inside.

I sat there stunned, gasping like a fish, my head and heart muddied by too much emotion. I seemed cut off from my own reactions. But at the same time I sensed that clarity lay just a little way ahead and that when it finally came it would be sweet. One by one, Parker handed over the plates.

"I didn't even lie," he said matter-of-factly. "They were propped up on a table in her dressing room. I said I admired them, and she said, 'They're yours.' Then she started unbuttoning my shirt."

Each plate had been put inside a plastic produce bag, and though I knew I should be careful I peeled them like a greedy kid at Christmas.

"I could have taken these and not felt bad," Parker said. "Fuck that I am." More than the words themselves, his tone brought me up short, like a parental rebuke. I couldn't quite look at him. "You'd have been none the wiser," he said. "So don't forget your pal Parker when the check clears."

I couldn't look up, as if I thought the plates might vanish if I did.

"I won't," I said.

....

Parker thought it ridiculous but gave in the next morning when I argued that putting the five plates in a safe-deposit box would keep them safe. "Keep *them* safe, or us safe from each other?" he asked. We put the negatives in Eng's wooden "WE" box, which I'd used to bring home the broken negative. Walking around the corner to my bank, I clutched it to my chest, Parker smirking beside me. We each signed a card and took a key; one couldn't get in without the other. We weren't so much ensuring trust as mechanically doing away with it, especially with the side of it that depended on willingness.

That afternoon we were meeting Judith at her studio.

"I told her I wanted you there," he said.

"Why? I won't be able to look her in the eye."

"It gives credence to our story," Parker said. "Also, if something goes wrong I want us to go down together."

His honesty moved me strangely, and I agreed. We arrived at her door at two. The picture of confident charm, Parker put his arm around Judith. She was petite but lean and wiry with big, pugnacious breasts. Usually she had about her a kind of dogged calm, which some construed as mental instability. More often than not she was ready to wear the world down. But for a moment now she was transformed. She touched Parker's chest and in a low voice said, "Hello, you." She wore black ballet slippers and stood on her toes to reach Parker's cheek with a kiss. *Hello, you.* She looked like she'd melt. She almost seemed normal. I could hardly believe it and stared at them like a doe caught in the headlights. Parker's arm tightened tenderly around her slim waist, and for a moment it actually seemed as if something other than personal gain were pressing them together and that they were not each fucking their way up to the next level.

When they parted Judith turned to me, and the warmth cooled somewhat. She reached out to shake. The gesture had a certain leisure, a regal remove. She held my hand for several moments, gazing at me through the upper, weaker halves of those same glasses, smiling silently with a sort of reluctant instructiveness, as if disappointed that I hadn't thought to wed myself to her cause long ago.

Now she took Parker's arm and let me follow them down the bright entryway into the studio's main room. Pollock was waiting there.

Everything blurred. Then the back of my head rapped something hard—the wall, I thought. But it turned out I was on my back on the floor weakly holding Pollock's sinewy forelegs, which straddled my chest. One sniff had told him who I was. His barks ran together so that he seemed to roar. Death's white noise. His stifling, wet breath poured over my face in buckets. All at once I forgot I was about to make more money than I'd ever seen in my life. I felt I could just shut my eyes and take an endless nap. I could retreat into shock, and when Pollock began to feed I'd calmly watch my blood tint the saliva at the corners of his mouth.

Then Parker and Judith appeared above me, pulling the dog off, Judith shouting angrily—at me, it seemed. Only Parker's amused look kept me from confessing. He got me to my feet while Judith maneuvered Pollock backward with more shouts and surprisingly forceful yanks on his studded collar. Struggling, claws scrabbling on the Swedish-finish floors, Pollock managed to dig in every so often and send up single barks that rattled the top of my skull. It terrified me that Judith might let go. Annoyed, she turned to me. "What did you do to upset him?" she asked. "You were here just the other day and he didn't act like this." Schizophrenic, like his namesake, I thought. "He was in the other room," I suggested, but Pollock drowned me out.

Even when Judith put her equally intimidating face in his he went on, a barking bulimic gagging on his own rage.

Then, with a diplomat's aplomb, Parker ushered me out and back down that hall, where he pushed me into another room with sympathetic gentleness. Slowly shutting the door, he looked as if he were sitting on a killer line and winked to keep himself from saying it.

Apparently all Pollock needed was for someone else to be treated like the dog. Suddenly he grew quiet. Through the door I heard Judith tell Parker how Pollock had succumbed to the hectoring of a neighbor's cat by snatching it up in his jaws and snapping its neck. Cornered by Judith and the horrified neighbor, Pollock had resisted their rescue attempts for half an hour, flopping the limp body back and forth and making a bloody drip painting on the sidewalk. Judith had been sued, but of course she'd won.

Then they must have moved off to the far side of the spacious studio because I heard nothing more. I turned to look for a chair. This was Judith's supply room, one wall stacked with enormous blank stretchers. These, I mused nastily, looked more saleable now than they would later on, caked guano-thick with pigment. Not surprisingly the room smelled of paint and oil, so I didn't realize right away that the large storage cabinet at the far end had been recently varnished—was in fact new—and that the box of scraps and half-empty paint cans I'd taken to the basement that distant-seeming afternoon had been left over from its construction. The cabinet had twelve doors. Two of them stood open, and for a moment, while a distant image tried to resolve itself in my mind, my eye settled on the shelves inside, with their boxes of dry pigment and silver tubes of color stacked like rounds of ammunition.

The image that finally came into focus was of the grand residences ancient panjandrums built to house their harems, a hundred windows with a face at each. As I walked forward now the air turned liquid and heavy; it dragged at my limbs like surf. The room itself grew quiet as a tomb, as if sealed hermetically or plunged deep under water. Suddenly I felt I no longer belonged to myself.

Instead of plain glass, a pair of negatives had been fitted into each of the twelve doors. These plates were also Wilfred Eng's, I was sure of that. But that wasn't all.

A woman was pictured in all twenty-four. Her name was Ellen Danforth McFarland, and she was the young second wife of Wilfred Eng's early benefactor and employer, Joseph McFarland. For eight decades now her brief love affair with Eng had been thought to be a fiction, in part because the images before me now were themselves only rumors, objects of myth, faded as a legend. In one of the images she wore the same necklace and earrings I had seen in a more formal pose in the Aperture *Wilfred Eng*. As I reached out to touch one of them my arm felt weak—it was Robert Armour who lacked reality and substance, his fingers translucent and milky as an X ray, his body and his deeds sketchy, his stabs at fame and humility and love all the products of hearsay. I couldn't think. My mind reeled, searching for a clear space, a way to start making sense of so much raw certainty. Ellen was a New Yorker. She and Eng fell in love a year or so after McFarland brought her out to San Francisco to live in his immense Stockton Street mansion. Eng's mother had worked as a scullery maid in this house and had died when Eng was five. McFarland had seen to the boy's care. He was taken with young Wilfred's intelligence and stately bearing and later trained him as his houseboy and gave him books and free time to read. Eng remained McFarland's employee until he was seventeen and opened his portrait studio on Grant Street. Though he and McFarland remained close, Eng was always uneasy about the nature of their relationship. Joseph McFarland was not the wealthiest man in San Francisco, but he was one of the shrewdest. He had made most of his money selling lumber to gold and silver mines. Semiretired at forty-four, he kept his fortune intact through cycles of boom and bust by means of the modern concept of diversity, some of it illegal. He was an inveterate faddist and gadgeteer and in 1859 sent away for a box camera. When the camera arrived, Eng admitted, his life changed forever. McFarland dressed Eng in a swallow-tailed coat and had him make portraits of his houseguests, and when he and his first wife traveled to Europe he even took Eng along. On the way back, stopping at the Manhattan home of a friend, McFarland met Ellen Danforth for the first time.

At that time Ellen was a radiant, headstrong ten-year-old who loved books. McFarland, whose wife would die two years later, fell in love with her instantly. He postponed sailing home for two months. He drove Ellen out daily in a hired carriage, buying her dresses, ribbons, and baubles and taking her for elaborate luncheons at New York restaurants. An only child, Ellen lived with her widower father, Thompson Danforth. Danforth had lost his family's inheritance and struggled to maintain an appearance of ease and wealth. McFarland supported some of his mostly shaky business ventures and even bailed him out when they failed. When McFarland's first wife, Helene, died, Danforth promised Ellen in marriage to his friend when she came of age. In the intervening decade McFarland visited New York once a year, keeping an eye on his prize.

Though Ellen had described Eng in convincing detail in her diaries, scholars had dismissed the notion that it was Eng whom she addressed as "you" in these entries. She and Eng had known one another, had maybe been friends. But anything more was sheer fantasy and invention. Skeptics pointed out that Eng was a misogynist, that for most of his life he had had little to do with women, certainly nothing that reached the passionate intensity Ellen attributed to her lover. Also, Eng never mentioned a love affair in his ledgers of that period, nor did he catalogue the pictures Ellen described him as making. No such pictures or plates had been found to exist—until now.

Besides that, Ellen herself had said that she'd made the whole thing up.

And now a revered fiction had come to life. For a long moment I lost my grip every bit as much as if Santa Claus himself had appeared before me, hypertensive, smiling wearily and redolent of soot and pipe smoke. This was no longer a matter of belief or disbelief. These plates, I suddenly realized, were a monument to the loss of innocence. A living presence seemed suspended in the door frames. I was one among maybe a handful of people who had ever laid eyes on these images, maybe only the third, after Ellen and Eng themselves, who knew what they were. I brought my head close to one, a full-length image of Ellen in a turban-shaped hat and veil. A satin skirt flared out from her narrow waist in glossy vertical stripes. Shadows from a mullioned window made the skirt look like a textured cage. I remembered Eng somewhere describing his first memory, waking up in his mother's arms and blinking his eyelashes against the rough cloth of her shirt-waist.

In another negative Ellen was nude.

Nudity, the ultimate sign of a lover's trust. What a chance they had taken! I couldn't make out her expression, but the way she held her body spoke of a kind of informed courage. She would do this for her lover, she would take this risk. Her breasts were small and lovely, with tiny, delicate nipples. A sheet was draped over her shoulders, a fold falling across her pubis and one well-rounded hip. The plate itself was forbiddingly dark: she was draped in medium, though a positive would surround her in bright light. As a boy with McFarland in Europe, Eng had seen the paintings of Rembrandt. He'd been taken with the light and shadow and in his ledgers admitted doctoring early plates to imitate these effects. When I opened the door and looked at the back of this one I could make out faint strokes on the glass where emulsion had been brushed in. The door swung with a solemn weight. The paired plates rattled gently. The negatives were not exactly square and fitted loosely in the routed frames, held in place with metal glazier's points pushed into the wood. I closed the door carefully, and it met the stop with a deep wooden thump that echoed faintly. The room was quiet as a church, and I experienced another moment of my own insignificance, of my self passing through the world like vision through glass. If I never did anything else I could do nothing better than to rescue these precious plates right now. Steal the lot and to hell with Parker and Leonard Sills and the DeWitt and Judith.

Then reverence gave ground suddenly to a kind of mercenary clarity. I looked at my watch. Half an hour had passed in the space of what seemed a minute. Parker had said he didn't want to spend all day looking at Judith's paintings. I didn't have much time and didn't really know what I meant to do. At one end of this room was another hallway, and when I hurried down it I came to a smaller room with a daybed. A window here gave onto the alley fire escape. I looked down through the crisscrossed iron bars and in the midst of a kind of wonderful dread an idea took shape—more like a sensation, an instinct like the one that had saved me down in the basement. I unlocked the window, then hurried back up the hall. I took one last look at the doors. Moments later Parker called, "All ye, all ye out in free."

Mindful of Pollock, I opened the door just a crack, composing my face with a kind of bruised dignity. Parker himself had hold of the animal, who did not pull or strain, as if he knew who the real boss was. Parker gave Pollock some leash, and the dog aimed his snout at the narrow opening for a reassuring sniff. Judith stood behind Parker, looking dangerously flattered. At the front door she gave Parker another melting kiss but ignored me.

As we walked down the stairs Parker asked, "Does Diane know about you and Pollock?" Out in the street I grabbed his shirt, and for once he looked genuinely worried. "I'm on your side," he reminded me, and I fairly dragged him back up the street to my apartment.

Once there I slammed the door. By now Parker looked more curious than scared; he might have shown this same face to Judith when she had suggested group sex. "Are you going to beat me up?" he asked.

I could barely get wind to say what I needed to. I was dizzy and beside myself. As I spoke I felt like Pollock, gagging on words that bristled with urgency even if they made no sense. Still, Parker pieced them together. His eyes blinked behind his lenses. The truth of this discovery gathered in his face and bled it of all irony. For once he couldn't fake a response and sat down heavily on my couch. "Are you sure?" he asked, almost like a scared kid. I couldn't remember seeing him this shaken. I got out the Aperture *Wilfred Eng* and showed him a formal photo Eng had made of McFarland and Ellen, pointing out the necklace and earrings.

"Her hair is even done the same way," I said. I pointed with a trembling finger. "She's even wearing this same silver comb. I've seen other pictures of her. It's obviously her."

Then I filled him in with as much as I could remember. When Ellen and McFarland married they spent two years abroad. When they returned, Thompson Danforth accompanied them back to San Francisco, Ellen recording all of these events in her diaries. By the time she settled in McFarland's house on Stockton Street she was already experiencing trouble in her marriage, which she also wrote about. Before she died in 1926, she closed her papers to scholars and historians, a ban that ended in the late 1960s. The diaries were ignored at first even by photo historians. Then in 1973, a well-known feminist novelist named Carol Chase Marino discovered the journals, excerpted them in *Ms.* magazine, and published an expanded version in a pink-jacketed paperback titled *The Love Diary of a San Francisco Lady*. Parker watching silently, I stepped over to my bookcase and searched the shelves until I found my copy.

According to Ellen, she and her lover had met briefly in childhood and used this connection in starting up a friendship after McFarland

married Ellen and brought her to San Francisco. The love affair probably got an added boost when McFarland hired Eng to make formal
photographs of himself and his new bride.

"Nineteenth-century kink," Parker said, though without his usual
verve. On his face was a look of surprise that lent him an unsettling
innocence. The affair, according to the diaries, lasted five months during the winter and spring of 1874. At first nothing but love mattered,
and it was only after some resistance that Ellen agreed to being photographed. "You tell me it is your act of love," she wrote, "& you blush
when I laugh."

> You look at me in a way I'm not sure is flattering, as if I'm merely
> alive to reflect precious light. The photographs never turn out as I
> imagine them. I never recognize myself. They seem the result of
> something other than sitting still while minutes of my life tick
> away. Always I feel like a fool waiting for nothing & I wonder why
> this is. "Who is meant to see them?" I ask & you answer only, "I
> am."

McFarland was away until June of that year, so Eng and Ellen managed to meet two or three times a week. They even fell into a kind of
routine. They usually made love first, and if there was time after their
picture-making sessions they made love again. Ellen wrote,

> In each other's arms we take catnaps of half an hour, no more. I
> wake with such confidence, with a feeling of well-being, even of
> rightness. I never sleep well here in this house.... Today I woke
> first & watched you for a time. Asleep, you do not seem to breathe,
> your face so peaceful, smooth & perfect, your lashes dark as a
> girl's. I sometimes think I could look at you forever. I could never
> give you up....

The affair was a refuge for them both. With Ellen, Eng let the outside world disappear in a way he never did again. Chinatown of the

1870s was an often violent, dangerous place and was destined to get worse. On the street one morning Eng was assaulted for no reason by a white man, and when Ellen arrived the same afternoon he was rigid with anger.

> I had never seen you like this, your face dark & your eyes full of hatred. You stared at me as if I were to blame. I felt the tears rise in my throat but pushed them down. I touched your face, then took you in my arms. Your body is always so supple but now it had turned to wood. I kissed your face, your neck & shoulders. You endured this gentle assault. The worst evil, you said, was being robbed of the chance to fight back. This thought made my heart quake but I said nothing. I unbuttoned your shirt & you let me slip it over your head. There was a bruise on your chest where this bully had struck you. I leaned down & brushed my lips across it, a darkening patch like a spreading stain. It looked as if your heart were bursting from your chest. I kissed it again & heard a breath leave you. A moment later I felt your fingers in my hair. . . .

This moment—and all the moments they spent together, since they were all as dangerous—drew Eng and Ellen closer, Eng losing himself in love, letting go in a way he most likely never did again.

When guilt and fear threatened to separate them it was the photography that kept them together. Exuberant, excited, he told her he wanted to photograph her in the summer, "your 'season of light,'" she called it. Ellen herself wanted only "to hide from the sun, to pull the curtains and draw you close." Over the months, in her way, she warmed to "the Box."

> You moved close & your warmth bathed my face. I brushed my foot along your calf. You moved your leg away which stung me. "Try to be good," you said. "I don't come to you to be good," I said & blushed. But you alone I can speak to this way without fear of being misunderstood. The idleness began to annoy me. I decided

to torment you with the story of Franz Lemke, my piano teacher of long ago. Mr. Lemke also spoke of discipline. The music lessons drove me mad with their dreary repetition, the futile hours poking at the notes. Scales went up only to come back down again like the tread of dead men. When I made mistakes Mr. Lemke gave my wrists smarting taps with his baton & once I tore it from his hand & threw it across the room. Papa scolded me for acting impulsively & I pleaded that I did not act on the impulse that was in my heart by cracking the baton over Mr. Lemke's bald head.

"They say," I told you, "that music stirs the soul."...

It occurred to me that Ellen had opened the lens for Eng's "self-portraits."

The possibility struck me dumb. Again I couldn't move or think, overwhelmed not just by the magnitude of the plates' very existence but by the fact that the story was already breaking free from decades of obscurity and denial. Now it would expand and begin to grow. Not only would this mythical love affair become real but dozens of theories would be proved or disproved. Old facts would slip into place, new hypotheses formed, new beliefs set in scholarly stone. I felt lightheaded and had to sit. Helplessly, I looked at Parker, who by now had gotten hold of himself.

"All the secrecy must have superheated the emotions," he said, "not to mention all the lies." He gave his version of a sly grin, then added, "We're also talking something like incest."

"McFarland was no saint," I said.

Though Eng was silent about Ellen in his ledgers—no doubt for his own protection and hers—every so often he complained about Joseph McFarland, who, when Eng was a boy, "treated me like an exotic, a trained monkey on a leash." The other staff in McFarland's house "despised me, called me 'the master's pet.'" I held out the paperback to Parker.

"They made a film from this sometime in the '70s."

At that time mainstream Hollywood still couldn't deal with anything ethnic and so changed the Eng character's name and made him white. The actress who played Ellen, fighting to rescue her career from the drudgery of soft porn, had brought a believable desperation to the role. But the script parted ways even with '70s trends toward realism and gave Ellen and Eng a happy ending when nothing like that was the case. The movie seemed to settle the matter in the minds of the scholarly community, and since there was no further proof than these diaries, which Ellen herself had denied were true, she was dropped from most serious discussions of Eng's life. Still, tremors from the brief popularity of the book and film had helped shake loose Eng's neglected reputation and caused a buying frenzy. Twenty years later, though the film was largely forgotten, Eng's stock was still on the rise. Parker gazed at the dog-eared paperback with photos of the actors on the cover. "Did you ever see it?" I asked. He shifted his gaze to me, holding his unreadable expression until it suddenly dawned on me what he was thinking.

"Jesus," I said. "We saw it together."

I went glassy-eyed, suddenly awash in the sensations of the long-forgotten moment. We'd seen *The Love Diary of a San Francisco Lady* in the gloomy Milburn Theater, long since demolished. I remembered glancing at Parker folded sedately next to me in the worn plush seat. Even back then I always seemed to be watching him, waiting to see what he would or wouldn't do and how I would react. Then, for a moment, my old self came sharply into focus. Back then all my worries were so petty and pure. I believed I was fighting the good fight for art's sake. I wouldn't have said so then, but I was freer and happier than I'd been before or since. I couldn't have dreamed that the Weston trouble was just around the corner. Yet now, as I sat in my Seattle apartment, that younger self looked forward to the present. From the young Robert Armour's perspective, the last decade of seclusion, wound-licking, and humility was the worst tragedy.

Now, as in the darkened theater, Parker seemed to be looking somewhere else, beyond the miniature images flickering in his eyes.

"If we can prove what you say," he said, "a lot of people will pay attention."

It was true. The stakes had just gone up. The supposed love affair of a famous photographer, proved after so many decades, would cause a stir outside the insular photo world. Suddenly it seemed as if I were on the verge of getting back a lot more than I'd ever lost. Parker drew silence to him like a magnet. I knew what he was going to say before he opened his mouth.

"Granted, we're not talking about original prints made by Eng himself," he said. "But once we prove the negatives are his—well, you tell me, you know best what modern prints go for. Think Eng's could fetch $500 apiece?"

They could. Easily. The idea of it made my insides quake with fear and greed. "You need serious money to even think about starting something like that," I said judiciously. "Not to mention serious balls."

Parker gave a look as much as to say he could take care of the balls part. "Leonard would go for something long-term like this," he said.

"Why?"

"Less capital outlay. He could give us a line of credit instead of paying you a lump sum. The beauty of it is we could keep it all in the family. You could even do the printing."

"I'd be rusty for something like that," I said.

But in fact the idea of it made me itch for a darkroom, for the mingling of experience and scholarship. Stepping inside Eng's eyes, seeing as he saw, staying true to the light as he would have used it with his lover a hundred years ago—it would be the high point of a career, the thrill of a lifetime. There would also be the delicious sense that each meticulous stroke of the retouching stump could be measured in dollars and cents. My heart hummed at the ease, the neatness. It was a way of making big money that relied on few outsiders—if, that is,

Parker and I didn't think of each other that way. I felt the pleasure sag some. Parker's "trust factor." That bank vault might not ensure it. And even if we managed somehow to do away with the petty uncertainties, the politics of negative-hoarding were full of pitfalls for the inexperienced. We'd be foreigners there. In international circles famous negatives were kept under lock and key, the scarcity and price of prints monitored as if they were in diamond markets. A lot of people didn't like this approach. A lot more people came to hate you just for your dumb luck. Parker knew all this as well as I did.

"The plates are public domain," he said. "No strings attached. The biggest mistake is trying to cash in too fast. It's desperation that kills most people," he said. "They lower the price and flood the market. With Leonard backing us we wouldn't have to worry about that. Also, if you were still feeling guilty, we could give the plates to the DeWitt when we were done."

"This works out better for you too, doesn't it," I said.

Hearing this doubtful tone, anyone else would have stood, maybe strolled to the window, a dramatic gesture to gain credibility. Not Parker. He stayed where he was in his chair, unmoving except for the discs of light on his lenses, quivering with his slow, steady pulse. Somehow it made him more believable. He wasn't pitching, he wasn't selling a bill of goods. He had a stake.

"I'll level with you, Robert. Maybe I *am* just a glorified gofer. I'd be lying to you if I said I didn't feel myself getting lucky. Think about doing something half-assed and what your life will be like afterwards. Think about watching someone else cash in. Think about the regret."

"Think about screwing up."

"This is too clean," he said. "Believe me, I've seen deals like this go down in war zones, and people still make money. A couple times I even got to squeeze the dollars myself."

A different Parker might have lost his composure at this point, bursting at the seams with plans, peppering his pitch with images of foolproof success and overstuffed bank accounts. He wouldn't bring himself to say something like, "You'll never have to worry again." Parker trusted that I knew what I knew, that Leonard knew the right people all over the world, that he could open almost any door. Instead of going overboard Parker grew practical, outlining the details. There would need to be a painstaking public process legitimizing the plates as Eng's. This would entail expert testimony, articles, magazine lay-outs—all of which, he said, we could easily handle together.

Then he stopped and stood suddenly in that frictionless way and walked out of the living room and back down the hall to my office. Following, I seemed to be somewhere else. I couldn't recognize this apartment as mine. It looked pathetic. I saw nothing but its shabbi-ness, the banged-up furniture, the dingy paint. Even the photos on the walls seemed like puzzle pieces that didn't fit, like fragments of a life that would never add up. In my office Parker sat down at the desk and switched on the calculator, his fingers flying over the keys. I stood there mesmerized, like a kid watching magic tricks. His fingers were nimble as an accountant's, the keys ticking like the pebble stream that started the avalanche. The little motor whirred and cleared its throat, each of its kick-start declarations inching the strip of paper across the desk top. Finally Parker snapped off the tape and looked up.

"We sell portfolios of all thirty-one for, say, $15,000. That's a steal. The beauty of it is we keep costs down by printing more or less on de-mand. Over the next five years we make maybe two hundred portfo-lios, also not unreasonable. That's over $3 million, gross, and that's conservative."

He didn't need to ask me to figure my cut. And that wasn't the end. Besides selling individual prints, we could maximize portfolio sales for a range of investors—the whole lot for groups and institutions as well as separate smaller sets of the best. Parker paused. It all sounded so reasonable, so *sane*. Still, I said, "Eng is known for landscapes."

He gave a look as much as to say, *Who are you kidding?* "A guy I knew in New York did the same thing with some Lartigue negatives five years ago."

"Billy Wrixton. I read about that."

"Wrixton didn't have half what we do. He had to pay off two estates and still had enough left over for a Tuscan villa."

I couldn't see myself going Italian exactly. But what *would* I do? What excess, what fantasy would I indulge? Diane had reminded me I was no high roller. Would I bury the money in a bank and gloat over the monthly statements? And then what? Would I grow impatient with scholarship, as I seemed to be doing already? With Weston, all those years ago, I had known exactly what I wanted—to expand my gallery, to mount more shows. Now I was at a loss. A month ago I would have said, "I don't want to scrimp and worry." Money might buy time for special research and travel. I might write a book. Was that *it?* Was that the end of the fantasies? Maybe I had never believed it would happen. Maybe I still didn't. Billy Wrixton had gotten himself on the cover of every trade magazine in the world. He sported a spade-shaped beard and a walking stick and took his pick of new projects. Is that what I wanted? Could that sort of freedom be purchased for any less than the sums Parker had calculated?

"Wrixton started out with money," I said.

"So will we."

"I'd be out of my league, Parker. So would you."

"Who isn't at first? And Wrixton didn't know money. You and I know money."

"Then there's Judith," I said. "What are we going to say to her now? This has gotten too big. There's no way she's going to just hand this whole thing over."

Parker said, "Maybe we'll cut her in."

But his look seemed to say, *Maybe we won't.* He might do anything, lie, cheat, even steal the Ellen plates outright. I shook my head. "This is crazy. I'm going to sell Leonard the five."

"You need *two* keys to open that vault."

I glared at him. "You'd do that, wouldn't you?"

"Your rules, Robert. I have to protect myself. Look. You sell Leonard the five and then what? Just keep quiet about the others? Could you do that? Walk by Judith's building every day, knowing what's sitting up there in her studio, knowing she might slip with a tube of paint or throw a fit because she's a failure and slam one of those doors?"

"Too much can go wrong," I said, quailing under the assault of Parker's logic. "Sills has too many other irons in the fire. He might not want the attention."

"In public he could say he didn't know a thing," Parker said. "We'd take all the risk and all the credit."

"And all the grief. How much will Leonard want?"

"Probably half."

"Like he needs the money."

"He'd know we couldn't do it without him," Parker said. "Anyway, how greedy do *you* want to get?"

"What if he wants it all? You said yourself that's the way rich people are. He could screw us both."

"If he did you could always go to the DeWitt," Parker said with languid sarcasm.

"I could do that right now," I said. "They might even make me a deal. I might end up with a nice piece of change."

"A bounty," Parker said. "It's possible." He stood. "But I'm guessing you'd settle for a pat on the head. You're right, Robert, you *are* out of your league."

He turned and started for the door.

"Where are you going?"

"I've wasted enough time and money on this."

I hadn't seen him take his vault key from his pocket. He might have been holding it the whole time or had it tucked up his sleeve. He tossed it on my desk.

"You want to play the choirboy, go ahead," he said. "But if you think the DeWitt Museum is a fucking cathedral you're worse off than I thought."

Then he walked out my office door. I followed him down the hall.

"You want me to believe you're just walking out on this?"

"Believe what you want," Parker said, heading for my front door.

"What about Leonard?"

"What about him?"

"What are you going to say?"

Parker stopped at the door and faced me. "I'll tell him the truth," he said. "That you folded up like a pup tent."

He gazed at me without malice. With Parker the absence of persuasion was itself a kind of persuasion, the worst kind. Lamely I said, "You're a real asshole."

"You know your trouble? You still believe your own press. Robert Armour, the savior of photography. The noble toiler among the hallowed dead. When somebody else cashes in, they're scum. When you start thinking about it, it's God's holy work. Maas told me that of all the people he could have screwed, he felt least bad that it was you. You've always been just that much better than the rest of us."

"It's not hard to be better than you."

"Does that make it easier for you, Robert? Well, try this: we're *both* assholes, I just don't bother with the smoke and mirrors."

He turned back to the door. I waited until he touched the handle. *"Wait."* He did, and I swallowed. "No one dying would say something like that."

"We all say things we don't mean," Parker said, though not to reassure me. Waiting, he stared at the door as if he could see through it, could see the unfolding and knew there was nothing in the world to worry about. "Fish or cut bait, Robert," he said with just the right mix of sternness and imploring. I remembered his line about groveling being aerobic, but this felt a lot worse. I couldn't bring myself to speak. Still, Parker sensed that I had come around. "I'm going to need something to take to Leonard if you're in."

"We can go together and take the five," I said.

He thought a moment, his expression studied, impenetrable. Then he said, "It's better if I see him alone."

"Why?"

Parker, I was beginning to think, was the Rasputin of intimate communication. With his near mystical shorthand for physical gestures, he made the air around him say, *Do you really want me to spell it out?* He said, "How to put it diplomatically?"

I sighed. "Armour screwed up once and can't be trusted." Parker affirmed this by raising his eyebrows an eighth of an inch. "One."

"All five, Robert. Look, the plates at Judy's are as good as locked up."

"Not if you're sleeping with her."

"Think it through. I slip out of her bed and pry the plates out of the doors. She calls Leonard and the cops and I'm through."

"Two."

"Leonard's going to want to keep them. His collateral."

"No deal. They come back here."

"That could be tough," Parker said. "But I'll see what I can do."

We drove to the bank then and came back with two of the plates, which I taped up in bubble wrap and packed carefully in my old briefcase. I offered Parker a ride to the airport, trying not to sound relieved at the idea of him not being around for a while. Judith was driving. Parker had come in on the redeye, but Judith had upgraded his return ticket to first class. They were taking the dinner flight that evening. "Chateaubriand and Mumm's," Parker said.

"Here," he added and handed me his vault key, which I'd given back to him. "I feel silly carrying this around."

When I took it he kept his hand out. Since he rarely made such gestures it took me a moment to see that he meant to shake. His grip was surprisingly firm.

May 2

You were still asleep when it came time for me to go so I rose &
dressed quickly, then leaned down to kiss you good-bye. Your head
had slipped from the pillow & I lifted it tenderly. How heavy it
was. I thought of my mother, whose head I often held this way
when she was ill. Hers weighed nothing at all, as if the wasting illness were unburdening her mind of the cares & needs of the
world. I wondered what she would think to see me holding my
lover's head. How she would despair of God Himself to know that
her many prayers & entreaties to Him had fallen on deaf ears. This
thought brought a wave of shame & sadness & several tears
dropped from my eyes onto the bed near your sleeping face. You
did not wake & I was happy for that, knowing how tears unsettle
you. I left you a note, then slipped out. The day was bright &
warm, a beautiful spring afternoon, but I was cold all the way
home. I am cold even now. Papa is due for dinner soon.

   Later. Papa has just left. It was just the two of us & so I had Mrs.
Dodd set a small table by the fire in the upstairs parlor. As we ate
he chatted warmly, but his cheer was somehow false. He is plagued
less by money problems, as he claims, than by plans that are
bound to go bad. He has now hatched a scheme for brewing ale &
when we'd finished eating he asked me to take his proposal to
Joseph. Papa has never asked such a thing before, believing that all
business matters should never be discussed with children &
women. I took it as a sign of his deep desperation. How he strug-
gles to fill himself, as if his spirit were punctured by disappointment & needed a constant stream of optimism to keep it full.
These years in California have not been the boon Papa expected

they would be. I wonder if he owes Joseph money, as he does to so
many of the people he knows. I told him of course I would talk to
my husband, just as soon as he was home. I would do anything I
could. He thanked me & when he looked down at his watch I saw
the fatigue & the shadows of worry & age in his face. He looked
up, smiling, & though he had not yet finished his port he said he
must be on his way. I sent down to have his horse brought around
& we stood & embraced. I was shocked at the weakness of his
arms. Yet there was a sensation I couldn't recognize, something beyond even weariness. The very air around my poor father seemed
to die, as if he had hung his life too long in a closet. I know that he
must die one day but the thought fills me with grief because he
will die with regret. I wonder now if I will too. He kissed me &
touched my face & I think it confused him to see his own suffering
mirrored in my eyes. "Are you happy, Ellic?" he asked. His question was a familiar one but I felt a sudden terror that my face
would give me—give us—away. This question always comes when
Papa is on the point of leaving so that he may quickly flee any
troubling answer. He only wants me to set his mind at ease. All answers are lies & so I only lowered my eyes to the floor. He repeated
that Joseph was a good provider, that I lived in such a fine house.
He paused, waiting for me to agree, & it came to me that he secretly believed his own arrangement of my life was wrong. "He's
away so much," Papa said. "Is his age a burden to you?" He
cringed, waiting for my answer. It both angered me & wrung my
heart. Finally he looked back to the fire. He shuffled his feet & put
his hands into his pockets. The firelight bathed his eyes, which
looked red & moist. He can never leave without my assurance &
yet this time I couldn't bring myself to give it to him, to forgive
those things caused by his own flaws which he would rather not

forgive in himself. But then I thought, "Who am I to talk of flaws?" I couldn't help myself & began to weep. Papa tried to comfort me & when he asked what was the matter I said, "I want to start a family."

The words surprised & terrified me. Was this a lie? Whose children do I want? I felt myself go rigid in my father's arms. He cleared his throat & patted my back awkwardly. "At McFarland's age companionship's the thing," he said. He cleared his throat. He addressed himself to the fire, even gesturing at it. "You should make yourself useful as his friend." He took out his watch again, his fingers fumbling at the chain. "I must be going," he said & gave my forehead a kiss. It was then that I had the most terrifying urge of all—to tell him everything & beg for his help. I couldn't, of course—for your sake but also for Papa's. It would kill him—I could kill him with what I have done. With this thought the bitter tears welled up again. I buried my face in my hands while Papa held me helplessly. He fumbled for words even as his unsteady hands tried to soothe me. "You're so grown up," he said as if he saw that I was growing beyond him. I took his hand to keep him near. "I'm sorry," I whispered, but even this was not completely true. He kissed my forehead again, forgetting that he already had—he might have meant to erase the last moments. I gave him the sort of smile he craved & told him I was fine. This lie is the same sort he tells himself to keep going, to keep taking the next step. What is the next step for me? I quaked at the thought & under false pretenses stole a last moment's comfort in my father's arms....

6

·················

At Shilshole Bay the clustered masts rocked, in Michael Mays' words, like hors d'oeuvres on a waterbed. Farther out on the Sound things didn't look so funny. A tug and barge struggled toward an isolated lake of light. Clouds moved on the horizon in mounting tiers.

Michael had just returned from his Uncle Sonny's funeral in Mississippi but was on his way back there again to be with his mother for a time. For once he was playing the dutiful son. He had offered Diane the use of his boat, *Rosanna,* while he was gone. She, Budge, and I were taking a long weekend cruise, and Michael had come to see us off.

Michael was tall and big-boned—huge but slack-looking. His chest was wide and shallow. When we first met I thought he had a cold until I found that he more or less always gave that impression. He and Diane had been together seven years, though married for less than one. Things had begun to go wrong just before Budge was born; Michael had left while the boy was in his cradle.

Only lately, according to Diane, had they started to grow close in a way they never had before. Michael was lightening up, or coming down to earth. He had grown his dark, silver-streaked hair long as if finally letting it down. He wore golf sweaters with bright striped shirts and fawn-colored Hush Puppies. His shoulders had a humble hunch, and his hands came out of his pockets only for broad, gracious gestures. He stopped talking when he smiled; such a smile deserved its own little moment of leisure.

Michael's eyes had the unnatural innocence of someone who got away with things. Even Diane admitted this had been true once upon a time. Now she said he'd changed. "I've never seen him trying so hard," she said. His recent attentions took the form of extravagant gifts to Budge and Diane. When they were a family, Michael had escaped by taking long baths. For hours in the evenings he'd sit in his tub surrounded by candles, listening to Mozart and rockabilly. He hadn't smiled much in those days. Now the smile was all Tupelo honey, sweet and tacky. You could get yourself stuck on a smile like that.

Once a fledgling filmmaker, Michael now owned a small but lucrative business producing courtroom videos. Since his second marriage he had dated only very young women, including Becky, the latest, the last.

In the parking lot Budge demanded the torpedo to show off for his dad. I lifted him reluctantly. We made a number of passes, and on the last I went a good way down the rows of parked cars to escape Michael's watchfulness. When we walked back he said, "That's clever, Sport," though it wasn't clear who he meant.

Aboard the boat with the first of our gear, Michael started filling out cards required by the Coast Guard. On mine he forgot the first "r" in Armour and corrected it, saying, "The lover or the soldier?" Diane laughed.

"Why don't you give Robert the tour?" she said.

Needless to say, Michael kept *Rosanna* in top shape. He claimed openly to love the old boat, though on board he looked cramped and uncomfortable. He might have counted on the low ceilings adding to his stoop and his vulnerability. In the bow quarters a small bookcase contained a set of Faulkner that looked untouched. There were signs here of a recent cleaning, vacuum tracks in the carpet and Endust in the air. To one side of the large bed was a vase of fresh flowers, to the other a narrow brass urn holding more of the unnautical peacock feathers. Michael explained that his fondness for the birds dated from early childhood memories of their presence in the same uncle's peach orchard. Death had consigned Sonny's memory to family legend. Michael didn't look like he was grieving. "Let me show you the diesels in case something goes wrong," he said. The gray eyes seemed to be saying something more. Aft, he opened the decking over the twin grease-blackened engines. For a long moment he stood silently as if it were up to me to say something, to explain what I would do in an emergency. Finally he pointed out the fire extinguisher with an apologetic nod. He unclasped it from the wall of the engine bay and showed me how to release the handle. His eyes glittered in their sockets. He held up the conical hose end and gave the handle a squeeze. The bottle gave off its hoarse breath, and Michael watched the plume raptly, as if it had nothing to do with fires. Budge, standing in the wheelhouse, saw the puff and naturally wanted a turn. The metal bottle was too heavy, so Michael held it. Budge struggled to press the handle and at the same time accidentally pointed the hose at me. "Be careful," I said. Michael didn't react. I imagined him hearing all manner of nuance and irony in those words. Budge said, "Sorry," aimed it away, and fired. The white jet shot out, and we watched it dissolve in the air.

When we were all back in the galley Budge told his father, "The new security lights really scared Robert."

"You don't say."

Diane, I thought, could have worked harder at covering her grin.

"He was distracted by his discovery," she said.

I flushed. It annoyed me that she had confided in Michael—had she also told him about my flight to California? She hadn't said another word about the negatives to me. Ever since that morning at my apartment, in fact, she had carefully sidestepped the matter, maybe to avoid exciting the regret I was supposed to be feeling. Diane assumed I was unhappy but resigned.

I had to force myself to remember that. That and a lot more.

Parker was back in California. When he left me that afternoon after the discovery of the Ellen plates, he went back to his hotel, where Judith later picked him up. The two of them flew to San Francisco, Parker with the two bubble-wrapped plates in my locked briefcase, which he took as carry-on luggage. It unsettled me to think of him holding this case on his knees right in front of unsuspecting Judith. Parker was made for long-distance pressure like that; anyone else would have been pumping adrenaline. In Parker's mind chaos was only an empty outline.

At three in the morning the day after they left I sneaked down the alley behind the Glorien Building. With a large nylon duffel slung over my back, I wrestled a garbage dumpster under the fire escape to reach the ladder. At the top, Judith's window was still unlocked. Lifting it, I thought I smelled dog and froze. A better burglar would have remembered to bring poisoned hamburger. But Pollock was not there; his potential presence was the only unforeseen obstacle. The rest of the night came off without a hitch.

Judith's storeroom had only one small window, so I felt safe working with the lights on. I'd brought pliers and a screwdriver. Removing each plate from the cabinet was tedious, and after an hour my hands were raw from prying out the glazier's points. Still, handling them was like cool sips to someone who'd been dying of thirst for a decade.

When Wilfred Eng made these plates, candles and oil lamps were the only forms of artificial light. For exposing prints he had only the sun, and a day-long exposure would have gathered into his prints the precise details my own crude renderings would lack. Besides tools I'd brought paper, chemicals, and rubber dish pans in the duffel. Judith's studio had a full bath, and I'd set up in there, putting the pans in the tub and exposing each plate with a droplight on the toilet seat. I did the nudes first. There were six altogether. In three of them Eng had left off with the technical tricks, substituting the faked, painterly light for ordinary sun falling over Ellen's form. When these positives came up I forgot myself for twenty minutes and just stared at them lined up on Judith's bathroom floor. Even crudely printed, they were powerful. Still, I might have thought so because it was now impossible not to see them generating huge amounts of money. In some ways they were clearly the erotic posturing of a young artist trying to find his way. In one Ellen's face clearly showed the impatience expressed in her diary. Eng had another agenda besides love—the number of plates made it plain. He was in love with light, with the care it took shaping the world. In a side view, white sun exploded against Ellen's naked, slightly plump shoulder, then feathered into shadow across her breasts.

By dawn I'd finished printing all twenty-four, and when I had the plates back in place I simply walked out Judith's front door, deeming this less suspect in the long run. I was determined to cover myself. These contact prints were my insurance, something to fall back on in case things went bad.

Home from this expedition, I opened up my copy of *The Love Diary of a San Francisco Lady.* In one of the nudes Ellen was draped in a shawl that bore faint markings I had taken for shadows in the negative, but which the positive turned into a distinctive pattern of lilies. In the book I found a passage in which she described not only this shawl but the pose itself. She also described other poses not among the twenty-four. In one of these she lay on the floor "in the grid formed by the many window-panes. The branches of the tree outside, with their tenderly budding leaves, cast shadows that moved gently on my skin...." I wondered again if there were more plates squirreled away in Judith's basement. More likely this picture hadn't worked. Maybe the movement of the branches had blurred, and the effect was lost. Maybe the effect had worked, but Eng had judged it too sentimental. Even in the daily portrait work at his studio he had written of countless failures after which he had scraped the glass clean and used it again. Ellen dryly told Eng she would not have to be very beautiful to be more appealing than "your true love, the Box." Elsewhere she referred to his camera as "the Cyclops" and "your three-legged princess who must be carried everywhere." "I know my place," she wrote. "You tell me, 'This is my act of adoration.' Uncertainty fills your eyes when I laugh…." All her protests rang a little false—any young woman in love would welcome so much adoring attention. And this love of his attention no doubt also blinded her to the fact that Eng was feeding another fire.

Now, in *Rosanna*'s galley, I chose my words carefully but stumbled under Michael's gaze, which he tuned up subtly.

"What happens now?" he asked.

Not looking at Diane, I said, "I don't know. I gave the plate back."

I was thankful when Budge intervened, tugging his dad's pant leg. When the two of them left, heading back to Michael's car, Diane kept me back in the galley for a kiss shaded, I thought miserably, with relief.

Lying even before we'd left the slip didn't bode well for the weekend. To make it worse, as Diane and I walked up the dock once more we heard a screech. In the parking lot Michael had hoisted Budge over his head, and the boy shrieked with laughter. Michael's theft was effortless. With the boy he always seemed to pull the right reactions out of a hat. My torpedo was suddenly the pirated version. Diane touched my back sympathetically, which only confirmed it.

Shaking hands with me at his car, Michael averted his eyes, as if the limits of my affection embarrassed him. Then he gave Budge one of his python hugs. And the kiss he gave Diane, though chaste, spoke of habit and familiarity, of intimacies that lingered and inhabited even parted lives in a way I wouldn't understand.

....

Strapped in a bright orange life jacket, Budge looked overstuffed but helped Diane cast us off. When we were under way the two of them stood in the wheelhouse, watching out the windscreen as we cleared the marina. Out in the open water Diane let Budge steer, lifting him onto the pilot's chair, where he knelt, gripping the wheel.

We hugged the shore for some time. Houses disappeared, and the shoreline turned rocky. Wilfred Eng had called the western coast of the United States "the facade of a country, a strip of alternating rock and beach with nothing beyond it…One could land again and again and step off and walk its unimaginable breadth. One could live in its cities and its countryside and still never be allowed *in*."

Over the years an Illinois dealer had sold me a number of early Seattle cityscapes that had trickled backward in the first years of this century: would-be adventurers had come to the end and turned back. The pioneers had gone home, which spoke to their evident disappointment.

Up in the wheelhouse Diane pointed out a freight train moving south along the shore. Smiling, she cut the engines and told Budge to turn, letting us drift near and watching our depth. When the locomotive drew close Budge blew the horn but got no answering blast. We were forgotten out here, alone. Under way again, Diane looked west at the clouds easing over us like something spilled. Though we cruised in broken sunlight, a squall moved toward us over the water.

Budge climbed down and went below, and Diane waved me forward.

"He probably wants to check out his gift," she said.

As part of his leave-taking act at the car, Michael had given Budge a Polaroid Land Camera, a ridiculous present for an eight-year-old. Like everything else about Michael, it implied deeper intentions and layers of meddlesomeness. "Robert can show him how to work it," he had said. Diane wasn't sure Budge could keep it, but I thought this attitude was just for show. She wouldn't let herself balk at Michael's new generosity. I felt a faint wave of hope that she would see the Eng plan in a better light if I could suddenly show her and the boy the same material generosity.

Now she sat me in the pilot's chair, then sat sideways on my lap and told me to steer while she shook out a chart of the waters. Her body hummed with pleasure. I felt I was falling behind again, lagging the way I had when I'd first met them, all movement mired as it was in bad dreams. Close quarters would put a magnifying glass to all our emotions. And it was just this effect—unhampered by lies, of course—that Diane was shooting for. A real family outing. The scenery passed slowly like a cyclorama. I thought of those pioneers reaching the end of the United States and peering over the edge, sighing, turning back. I wondered suddenly if I meant to stay put myself. If the Eng plan worked and the cash started rolling in, I could go anywhere in the world I wanted, back to San Francisco or New York or even Europe. Would I be going alone? Jesus Christ, was I looking for a way out? It came to me all at once that Diane might be a fluke among those women whom I'd let take only a temporary place in my life. She and Budge might be only a stopgap, an experiment in intimacy, a comfort indulged until what I really craved—vindication, acclaim—came along. Was I thinking to make my getaway with the negatives? I glanced guiltily at Diane, who smiled, then reached under her to give my cock a friendly prod. The motion of the boat moved us gently against each other, and I'd grown hard against her bottom. I put my arms around her suddenly and held her close, forcing out any thoughts of escape. Whatever good happened to me I wanted to happen to her as well. She sighed. I felt the muscles of her waist tense and release as the boat rocked. I thought how strange it must have been to push a child from her body during emotional upheaval, how hard to believe that such trouble could ever come right.

Half an hour later we headed away from shore toward Whidbey Island. Dead ahead, from around a point of land, a slender yacht tacked west into the Sound. Diane smoothed out another chart and pointed to where we were going, Useless Bay, at the southern end of the island. It was a favorite spot from old and not-so-old days—to promote mutual friendliness Diane had been back here a number of times with Michael and Budge. Around the point was a wide bay and at the southernmost end a cove with a hundred yards of rocky beach. The cove was surrounded by sheer rock cliff and inaccessible by land. We were alone there.

The squall hit just before lunch. In the galley Diane put on burgers, and I sat in the banquette feeling as useless as the bay. I looked out the port. To the northwest the sky was solid gray. Rain dulled the water's surface. It hissed gently all around us, a straight sound like a breeze through a parched crop. The rectangular port tilted out and deflected the *shh* inside. I felt suddenly smothered and panicky. I looked out the port. The surface of the water simmered but also looked solid, like a scalding was all you'd risk if you ran.

"What can I do to help?" I asked to shake off the uneasiness.

Diane handed me a bottle of wine and a corkscrew. By the time I got it open she had the burgers on the table and was sitting down across from me, spreading mayonnaise on Budge's bun.

"Smugglers used to hide out in this cove," she said. "Michael swears to this. Groups of them made a floating village of it, like a water version of those desperado towns in Old West movies."

The smugglers, Diane went on, lashed brush to log rafts and floated them across the entrance to hide it. The bottom of Useless Bay was littered with the hulls of little steamers and the skeletons of the unfortunate. Wilfred Eng once remarked that the dangers of his own travels decreased over time. He had explored these same waters himself. On the north end of this island he had photographed the inlet at Deception Pass and, later, the bridge that went across it. As water transport petered out he had begun hiring cars to take him to many of the spots he had previously visited by boat. He had taken care never to include himself in any of his landscapes; the images of these places, separated by time, would speak for him. "Ignorance of the future is a blessing," he had said. It was the one thing he'd claimed to feel grateful for.

As we ate, the rain slacked off. Now each time the boat rose the somber stripe of the distant peninsula eased over the port like an eyelid. When Budge had eaten all he was going to, he turned around and knelt on the banquette for a look out.

"It's starting to clear up," he said. "Can we go exploring?"

....

Beyond Useless Bay wind cleared off the squall and raised whitecaps on the waters of the Sound. Our cove, only partly protected, was alive with telescoping waves. We'd anchored *Rosanna* near the mouth of the cove, and now, as the three of us rowed the dinghy in, the fawn-colored walls seemed to grow taller, ready to tip over if we got too close. Scrub pine and brush twisted up from the fissures, and a dome of menacing silence pressed down. Parallel to the shore, we rocked sideways in waves that seemed too big for this small bay. Diane rowed confidently. I clung to the gunwales. I'd never had trouble on the water before. But here I felt cut off and closed in, like a jumper on a ledge who doesn't recognize the vastness and possibility around him, only the claustrophobia of his own second thoughts. Huge fallen chunks of rock sloped away under us in the piercingly clear water. *We're too high*, I kept thinking. I tried not to look down but couldn't help it.

When we landed Diane held the dinghy while Budge and I got out. "Michael usually builds a fire here at night," she said.

"Is that legal?"

We started down the beach—probably the wrong word, as the narrow strip of shore was covered with boulders the size of cantaloupes. Diane and Budge stepped over these familiarly while I followed, twisting my ankles. What was the attraction to this place? It reminded me of an abandoned quarry where prison crews with sledgehammers beat the walls into pea gravel. What drew Michael here? The outlaw past, maybe. Or maybe he reveled in the snow job, the challenge of convincing others that it was ideal. Could Diane be snowed? I might have been counting on it myself, and that panic might have come from knowing that she couldn't. Though I had no intention of leaving her for another life, the fact remained that I had already lied to her; at some future moment I would have to come up with a good reason for that. There was also Parker. The thought of explaining him to her made me shiver. Diane saw it, smiled, and asked, "Cold?"

"No, I'm fine."

She looked disappointed. I started to say I would build a fire if she wanted, that we could build it together, but she smiled again and said, "Come on," then took my hand.

At the far end of the beach was a small sand spit, a concession to the endless rock, tucked into a hollow dug out by tides and overhung with giant stone molars. Out of sight overhead, a seagull's cries twisted down around us, sharpened by the brittle acoustics of the rock. It was dim as dusk, probably never any brighter. The sand was cement-colored, peppered by the rain. Budge squatted and dug his hands into its aggregate chill as if glad to be embracing solid earth at last. But he'd seen something else and all at once unzipped the sand with a peach-colored bra. Before I could think I said, "Michael's been here all right."

Budge didn't know what to make of this but laughed because his mother frowned. Back at the dinghy he wanted to play "desert island."

"What's that?" I asked.

Diane let the boy explain: one person stayed ashore while the others rowed away; then the others came back and discovered the castaway and everyone was overcome with joy.

I didn't need to ask whose emotional erector set this game had come from.

Naturally, I couldn't get into it. Diane and Budge both did the two roles, each becoming the shipwrecked wretch and then the haggard voyager searching the world's four corners. I took each of them out, rowing only a short way in order to get it over more quickly. When the great moment came, recognition was at first dimmed by ceaselessly empty horizons, by hopelessness and repeated failure. "Is that…is that who I think it is?" each asked in a hoarse whisper swelling toward jubilation. Reunited, they fell into paroxysms of joy, beating their breasts and sending grateful oaths to the heavens.

When my turn came to be abandoned, Diane and the boy rowed far away, maybe to make me truly grateful. Or maybe Diane was just plain annoyed—at the crack about Michael, at my reluctance to pick up the cues when it came to uncomplicated fun. They went out even past *Rosanna* until they looked like Morse code on the rolling water, two dots of their heads and the dash of the blow-up dinghy. Beyond them the air over the Sound was gray-green. Whitecaps rose, wind lifting shrouds of spume in slow motion. Ten yards out on a sheer wall of rock, a heavy band of barnacles hissed, exposed by the snarling lip of the tide. Was the tide coming in? That gull cried. After a while it cried again, a sharp downward spiral, a screeching like a cork in a bottleneck. A keening. A warning. Would Crusoes take such things as dire signs in the struggle to survive? Or would they begin to anticipate any interruption in the fearful silence, the dread contemplation? Finally the two heads started taking shape again. Gradually I could make out individual numbers on the dinghy's bow. "Were you scared?" Budge asked as I climbed over the bow.

They'd been gone so long they'd forgotten the point.

....

We decided to spend the night in the cove. After dinner Diane tucked the boy into one of the narrow berths flanking the passageway to the bow quarters. She was determined to put the peevishness of the afternoon behind her. We finished off a bottle of zinfandel, and then she suggested we turn in early. She was longer than usual in the john. I was in bed by the time she finally came out in a white high-necked nightgown. Diane was not the nightgown type but gave a prancing half turn and asked, "What do you think?" Her face was flushed.

"It's great," I said, but the excess of enthusiasm made this sound unconvincing. Late in an old romance, one of those short-term lovers had started wearing this same style of gown. When I'd pointed it out she'd grown thoughtful and said, "Maybe I'm trying to tell us something." "Foreplay is dead, and this is its shroud," I'd offered. She'd laughed. Then she'd left. Now I wondered if Diane was trying to tell us something.

"It reminds me of my childhood," she said. "That's not completely true. I'm feeling a little shy," she said. "I've never made love to anyone else here. Hold me a minute, okay?" I held open the covers, and she got into my side of the bed. Settled, she whispered, "Do you think we should? I mean, he's right outside."

"He's as close as he usually is," I said. "Anyway, he probably knows more than you think."

I reached for a button on the high lacy collar, but she touched my hand.

"I need another minute. What about that camera?" she said after a pause. "Do you think I should let him keep it?"

"Hard to say," I said, thinking first this time.

She sighed. "It's so easy to feed kid-hunger. Michael doesn't always understand that."

"Maybe he does."

"I know what you're thinking, that he's doing it on purpose. It might have been true once."

"Is he making another play?"

She paused. She didn't guffaw as I wanted her to, only thought for a moment. Then she said, "He already did." She rolled over to face me. "I wasn't going to tell you."

Why did you? I wondered but asked, "When?"

"A few weeks ago."

"What did he say?"

She shrugged. "That if he had the chance he'd like to try again."

"Sounds a little vague, doesn't it? Are you sure that's what he was talking about?"

"More sure than I've ever been."

"So you believe him."

"Oh, Jesus, Robert, I don't know. I say I do. But how could he be serious?"

What if he is? I thought.

"There's so much water under the bridge," she added.

Then suddenly she burst into tears. She pulled me to her like a drowning woman, burying her face in my chest. She wept in long, shuddering drafts that seemed like relief. Why relief? Because my presence here had answered the matter of Michael's bid for a second chance? I felt the hull moving queasily under us. *Water under the bridge.* Finally Diane lifted her tear-streaked face and smiled sweetly through the redness. I felt depraved, accepting this gratitude. She gave me a soulful kiss and whispered, "We'll have to be quiet."

She pulled the nightgown over her hips and sat up. When she lifted it off, her breasts drew up in soft ovals. She tossed the gown on the floor and turned back, lowering her head and slowly fitting our mouths together. In the silence the water *tsk*ed against the hull. After a time I pulled away.

"It must be the wine," I said.

"It's okay," she said. "Let's just relax for a while."

But I fell asleep instead.

I woke late the next morning, alone. It was the first solid sleep I'd had in a week. The nightgown, well wrinkled, lay on the other side of the bed, where Diane had moved at some point. She and Budge were gone.

I was in the head when I heard voices, then Diane's laughter out over the water. When I opened the port I saw nothing but empty water. Then I heard their clambering feet through the hull as they came over the gunwale. *Rosanna* had shifted in the night, the stern now pointing toward shore. The water was calmer, and the air was cold and sweet. Beyond the mouth of the cove a faint mist hung over the bay, and above it a pale blue. By the time I'd dressed Diane had started breakfast.

"How did you sleep?" she asked but didn't wait for an answer. "You were snoring like a billy goat, Robert. You kept throwing your arm over me like you were trying to lasso something. You finally got it, and it pulled you over on top."

"I'm sorry," I said and added lamely, "It's the sea air, it's so enervating."

"It's that randy zinfandel," she said. "You kept breathing it in my face. I got drunk on your fumes."

Diane quickly finished eating, then went up with Budge to get us under way while I did the dishes. I was only half through by the time we were moving. The outside passed in unreal clarity, framed like a movie in the rectangular port. The thrum of those grease-blackened engines set a delicate pattern to the soapy water—Michael's dark machinery working out of sight, radiating influence beyond all the precautions.

By the time I came up the sun had burned off the last of the mist. The Olympics rose in a line the same blue as the sky, delineated by snowy peaks that seemed afloat by themselves. Budge was out on the bow in the bulky orange life jacket. Diane had put on sunglasses, and when I stepped up next to her she gave me a quick squeeze. We were headed for Port Townsend. I'd told her that Eng had gone there after the anti-Chinese riots in Seattle, and this had given her the idea—a kind of consolation prize. We cruised up the inlet, following the slow sweep of Admiralty Bay to a point just short of the Keystone ferry pier. There we headed west into the Sound. The wind picked up, and so did the swells. Now in place of feeling cooped up, all the open water left me exposed, teetering, with no land to hang on to. Diane stood up.

"I've got the worst headache. I need to take some aspirin."

She motioned me to take the seat, then called Budge back from the bow. The boy ignored her at first and turned angrily only when he knew she wasn't giving in.

"Robert can watch me," he complained.

She didn't answer, and after a futile moment of resistance the boy made his way back to the wheelhouse, sulking.

"Keep it headed for that mountain," she told me.

We were approaching the shipping lanes. To the south and north distant freighters the color of gunmetal only looked like they weren't moving. When I mentioned this Diane gave a quick smile and said, "Don't hit them."

For a time I gripped the wheel stiffly, keeping my eye on the ships. A smoke trail made one seem to bear down at a frantic cartoon pace. I pretended coolness by opening one of those charts over the wheel, moving the vessels on a memorized horizon, and trying not to look up too often. Budge watched with, I thought, a critical eye. Then all at once he asked, "Are you mad at me?"

"No. Why would I be?"

"I don't know." He shrugged. "You're not very lively."

Was I ever? Was I usually more lively than I was now? Or was the boy sounding a note of general impatience that I was *never* very lively?

"I'm steering," I explained and moved the wheel an inch or two. Budge stepped down to the stern, looking back at our fumbling, churning wake. The ships hadn't budged, and it annoyed me. *Make your move so I can make mine.* Ahead, the mountains hung in the air as if painted there, diaphanous, pale as watermarks. Our hull pushed into the waves, sending up mustaches of spray on either side. In his sixties Wilfred Eng had been caught in a storm in a small boat just off Kodiak Island in Alaska. The storm was so violent that some of his equipment washed overboard. His birth at sea, he claimed, had given him a seaman's legs and ease in rough water. "How the water dispels any urgency, even its own," he'd once said. I thought only someone deeply depressed could think so. I wondered if Eng thought of Ellen whenever he used words like "urgency."

The ships managed never to come near us, but the land ahead began to loom. Diane somehow knew. She came back up in the nick of time, taking the wheel and heading us north. Near shore the water grew calmer.

Just out of Oak Bay we neared a small boat with a lone fisherman. Diane gave him a wide berth, but the man stood. He looked robotlike in foul-weather gear. When he held up a large salmon by its gills Diane cut the engines. Drifting near, we heard soft country music. The fisherman called out good-morning and offered us the king.

"I just pulled him out," he said.

His face was heavily scarred, long white strokes on his forehead and left cheek. The scars were as studied as makeup, as if a terrible sort of care had been taken. One eye glittered falsely. He winked the other at Budge.

"How much?" Diane asked.

"Buck a pound sound right?"

Stripes of rosiness paralleled the scars like optimism pushing through. Scars aside, his features radiated warmth. When he called Diane "ma'am," she fought a grin. Or maybe she found this floating transaction odd. Since he was giving us such a deal the fisherman allowed himself to estimate the weight. He hefted the fish, then handed it up to me. His hands were huge, dream-sized. He said, "Six, maybe six and a half." Diane took $10 from her jeans pocket and handed it into the fake-looking palm, signaling that he should keep the rest. He folded his fingers stiffly around the bill, then pointed with the same hand.

"Up around the point there's a seal family," he offered with another wink at Budge. "I watched them part of the night."

"How long have you been out here?" Diane asked.

"I'm about to head in."

"Do you make your living this way?" She hesitated politely so he wouldn't think her pushy or condescending.

"I sell some to restaurants. Also, I do carpentry all over the county. There's a life there somewhere."

Diane laughed, and the fisherman grinned up at her. At the stern of his boat was a grease-shadowed metallic green engine, too small for the long aluminum hull. It was bulbous on its shaft like the head of a sickly child. There were two deep-sea rods, one in a grip with the line slanting out, also two tackle boxes and a small stained duffel between live wells under seats in the stern. More gear was packed into the con-tour of the bow under a bright blue plastic tarp, folded and neatly tucked under. On top of this a rope was coiled around a portable radio. Diane pointed at his thermos, wedged between the tackle boxes, and offered a refill. He thanked her but said no.

"Too much plays hell with my bladder," he said.

Diane smiled as if touchy bladders hardly mattered with the whole Sound to piss in. She asked about local beaches and landmarks she had visited before. I felt excluded by the fish and went below to put it in the refrigerator. From the galley I heard the man tell Budge, "No mistaking whose boy you are," and Diane laugh again. "What's your name?" he asked, and when Budge told him he said, "You're a good-looking kid, just like your ma."

When I came back up he was saying, "I got too close," talking about the seals again. He looked off in the direction he had pointed earlier, clearly pleased to have held our interest this long. His grin pulled the scars awry, making a delicate mesh of the wrinkles at the corner of the fake-looking eye.

"I heard them barking on this old raft and put my light on them. I got right up close. Then I got closer, and they lit out under water. I pointed the light down, and they looked like shadows going under the boat. Funny how they don't mind."

"Mind what?" Diane asked.

"Night. Double-dark water. Nothing scares them."

Budge asked, "What happened to your face?" and Diane said, "Sweetie, that's not polite."

"Vietnam," the man said. "You know what that was?"

"A war," Budge answered.

"Me and Vietnam didn't see eye to eye," he said.

Then he raised his hand and with a broad fingernail tapped shave-and-a-haircut on his false eye.

Diane gasped.

"Can you take it out?" Budge asked.

The man let go of *Rosanna*, bowing his face and raising his hands. Standing on the seat, he balanced himself like an acrobat, the boat moving under him like a ball and board. When he lifted his head the lid sagged. He wiped the eye with both hands and looked at it. Then he reached it over the side.

Budge hesitated, still looking at the socket, then cupped both hands, and the fisherman dropped the eye in. "It's warm," the boy said. Diane had also turned curious. She grasped the eye in Budge's hands and smiled. Then she took it for a closer look. After that she passed it to me. It was larger than I would have thought and lighter, hollow-seeming. A tiny dome of sky reflected wetly in the cornea. The pupil had an unnerving depth; it seemed alive.

"It's what they'll find in my coffin when they dig me up," the fisherman said, "a skull with one eye peeled. Maybe they'll think twice."

"About what?" I said.

It came out too loudly, and he looked at me as if I hadn't been there before. I gave him back his eye.

"Who's 'they'?" Budge asked.

The man turned away from us then, and when he turned back the socket was still empty. Then the real eye shut and the other blinked open in his mouth. The mouth-eye turned to me, bugged out, accus-

ing. Diane and Budge shrieked with laughter. This was the fisherman's cue. Grinning, he spat the glass into his palm. "Grave robbers,"
he answered and pushed off.

·················

"What would make scars like that?" Budge asked when we were under
way again.

"Lots of horrible things happen in war," Diane explained.

I said, "You bought all that?"

"Why shouldn't I?"

"An eye wasn't all that was phony about that guy."

"Do you say that because he was flirting?"

"What kind of jerk turns a war wound into a way to pick up
women?"

"One who can't deal with it any other way. It was harmless,
Robert."

"It was a cheap barroom gag."

"Budgie had a good laugh. Why are you getting so upset?"

"Vietnam my ass. Maybe a boyfriend made him see eye to eye with
the floor once when some other gag didn't work."

Diane looked at me, then glanced at Budge, who looked beyond us
both, quietly taking it all in.

It was early afternoon when we reached Port Townsend, idling past
the backs of the old buildings lining the shore. Though the wind was
still steady, the bluff above Water Street broke it far over our heads.
High up, gulls skied down the steady slope of wind, breaking underneath into still air, then rising again to the bluff, which cast a shadow
of stillness on the water a hundred yards into the bay.

When we docked I said I needed to take a walk, and Diane said that
was fine.

I climbed that bluff. Chinese laborers had moved part of it by hand
and dumped it into the bay. Some years back, workers renovating the

waterfront had unearthed hundred-year-old artifacts from the early Chinese settlement in Port Townsend. Combs, liquor bottles, and gambling tokens had been found buried deep in the sand. Most of the Chinese had come here on dangerous illegal boat trips from Vancouver. They could emigrate from Canada more easily than from China, though without so much hope of finding work. They had built their bars, restaurants, and whorehouses on stilts along the beach, dumping their garbage on the sand, where the tides took most of it away. Port Townsend, then a mill town, was untouched by racial hatred, at least to the degree that no Chinese were run out. Their labor was worth too much. Four generations later, white kids raised on this peninsula still told scatological jokes about them.

Eng had stayed here briefly in 1891, living in two tiny rooms above a restaurant. Everywhere he went he had trouble connecting with the Chinese. In Port Townsend he'd had no shortage of portrait customers. Poor laborers, queuing up to be made immortal, handed over their pennies, which Eng often did not take. Almost everywhere he went he was welcomed hesitantly, seen as different, suspect, a fish out of water among both races. In part he blamed the camera, which "makes me an interloper everywhere." Still, Eng often lashed out at anyone's attempt to accept him. At the Paris exhibition of his landscapes in 1922 he was wined and dined by admirers but ended his stay by publicly shouting in the face of the fashionable woman who was his hostess. In Ellen he had found total acceptance. What must that have meant to the rest of his life?

Back in the center of town, I wandered among the tourist shops but grew restless and headed back to the boat. Diane and Budge had gone exploring and left a note. In the bow I opened my bag and dug out *The Love Diary of a San Francisco Lady*. As much as I'd been looking forward to getting some distance on it all, I hadn't been able to resist sneaking the book along. If Diane happened to see it I could explain that it was just research. I took the paperback to the end of the dock and sat down on a piling to read. In the introduction Carol Chase Marino quoted a passage Ellen had written on her honeymoon to demonstrate Joseph McFarland's bullying. One afternoon in Florence, McFarland, Ellen, and a party of friends visited the Uffizi. Botticelli's *Annunciation,* Ellen wrote, "had a powerful effect on me—the wings, the fingers of the hands nearly transparent, yet communicating the full weight of the Virgin's fate." Trying to return to see it again, Ellen was turned away by an officious Italian guide. When McFarland heard of this incident he would not leave until a museum official was summoned and the guide, in tears, apologized. Ellen was taken aback by McFarland's humiliation of the guide but gamely took her husband's side: "A museum should be a place of freedom, it should not place strictures on its patrons who may never see such miraculous works again...." When McFarland trotted Eng out to make pictures of his friends at parties, Eng suffered slights from other staff members. But he also reveled in negative attention. Later, his social criticism seemed aimed at people like McFarland whose greed caused suffering. Clearly, some part of Eng longed for love, hungered for such a forbidden feast. But I wondered now if his affair with Ellen was meant to propel him away from McFarland's influence and into the sort of life he thought he needed.

I looked up. I'd been reading nearly an hour. Though the day was bright the wind had brought in the edges of a new front. Powdery cirrus now lifted straight up from the top of the bluff, easing over the sun. A breath of cold advanced the afternoon. It was only three o'-clock, but the day looked robbed, cheated of daylight as if dusk were approaching. Dusk, the hour of truth. I experienced a pang so deep that if Diane had been near I would have broken down and told her everything. I wondered if she were driving home a point by staying away so long, but just as I was about to go look for her someone behind me called out.

I turned and saw a woman kneeling at the side of the dock in the space between two boats. I stood and started running toward her,

thinking someone had fallen in. When I got to her I saw a white envelope floating just out of her reach. The woman wore glossy black leggings and a short leather jacket, which she now stripped off. Seeing
me, she tossed her hair out of her face and said, "I dropped my envelope." She was very pretty, and her alarm seemed strangely bland. As
she leaned back down to the water one leg rose to balance her, bitter-
green high heel cocked back like the hammer of a gun.

"Let me get a stick or something," I said.

"It's sinking."

She turned suddenly, reaching out with the same pointed shoe.
Then all at once she took the shoes off and lowered herself over the
side.

Not long ago I'd read that a stickup man, running from the police,
had dived off a pier here and been dragged out half dead from cold
ten minutes later. Twenty minutes in this water was tops, they said. I
bent down to the woman and caught hold of her arms. She smelled of
buttery lotion. "This really isn't a good idea," I said. She was in to her
waist but hadn't murmured a word of complaint, hadn't shivered or
shown any sign of shock. I felt the hard, narrow muscles of her arms
tense as she held herself, craning, looking around for the envelope.
She reached for it underwater with the same leg, her foot like a pale
fish. Then she looked up at me in frustration. Our faces were inches
apart. "Shit," she whispered. Her lips were turning blue. "You're going
to freeze," I said, and when I tried to pull her out I lost my footing.

Lost it? Or did I feel her arms flex, a subtle levering of her weight?
Falling forward, windmilling, I saw her look up at me innocently.

When I hit the water it hit back. I couldn't get my breath. It was less
scary than chastening. Death, I understood in an instant, was like the
world flicking lint from its sleeve. A lead vest clamped my ribs, and
behind my shut eyes I watched slow explosions of a deep, mortal blue.

When I broke the surface and looked up, the blond woman was
standing on the dock, only now she wore a dirndl dress and a squash-
ed-looking hat with a satin rose. I thought maybe the twenty-minutes

thing was a myth; it took only seconds for life to start offering its last hallucinatory scraps. I tried to speak but could only make clicks in the back of my throat.

"Get that envelope," she said without moving her lips.

Then the original, hidden by the bow of a boat, stood up. Behind them both Parker Lange appeared.

"You'll be glad you did, Robert," he said.

Parker's voice was untroubled, warm and round. Three days earlier he had called from San Francisco to say the meeting between Judith and Leonard Sills was set. I'd made the mistake of telling him my plans and even mentioned the name of Michael's boat. Now I managed to reach the sodden envelope, dog-paddled back to the dock, and handed it up. The twins, both of them incredibly strong, heaved me out face down on the dock, right at Parker's feet. I noticed for the first time that he hadn't lost his penchant for expensive shoes, these ones Italian, with finely woven uppers that would have creaked subtly if he'd squatted down to help. The twins also figured they'd done enough. I got up like a drunk from his own puddle. My ears roared, and my joints felt arthritic.

"What are you doing here?" I asked.

"It wouldn't wait."

Judith and Sills, Parker told me, had hit it off better than expected. Sills had taken her out for elegant meals with local media people and art mavens. He'd pumped her so full of praise, Parker said, that she would be like putty in our hands when it came time to make our deal for the plates.

Beaming openly for once, Parker now introduced Meagan and Christiana, and the two gave pale "Hi's" as if nothing had happened. I would find that the twins had a way of downshifting like athletes, cool when it counted. If genocide happened in front of their eyes their blood pressures would flicker up slightly, but later they'd sleep like mummies.

"I've got to get out of these clothes," I said, because no one else would. I turned, stiff as a statue, and started toward *Rosanna*.

"We'll wait," Parker said solicitously.

Christiana followed.

"This isn't a good idea either," I told her.

"My leggings are soaked," she said, but again the protest was blood-less. "Let me use the head," she said. "You've got a head on this thing, don't you?"

She vaulted the gunwale, holding her shoes in one hand. In the bow, as fast as I could, I got undressed and dried myself with a T-shirt. My heart felt panicky, the beats percolating, running together. I put on dry clothes, hid the wet ones, then walked down the passageway and saw Christiana inside the head with the door open, her back to me. She was naked from the waist down, blowing her leggings dry with Diane's hair dryer. She didn't hear me over the whir. For maybe fifteen seconds I stared dumbly at her buttocks, perfect as risen loaves, blue blush of cold under the flawless skin. She saw me in the medi-cine-chest mirror but gave no reaction except to flick the door shut with her foot. "Relax," she called. "It'll just take a second."

I then stepped out on the bow to keep a lookout for Diane and Budge. Parker smiled and gave the barest nod.

Christiana appeared, dressed again, and without a word jumped back over the gunwale, this time in her heels. She started back down the dock, and I scrambled from the bow to follow. I had known her less than ten minutes, didn't know her last name. A part of that panic, I realized, was out-and-out lust. I thought I must have dreamed the naked buttocks. Time itself was not the same since my swim: the erotic parade was running backward. But charges still came where they always would have—the still-damp leggings clung in the cleft of her bottom; her shoes showed toe cleavage.

When we reached the others, Meagan handed me the envelope. "It's yours," she said.

Inside, stuck together, were twenty new hundred-dollar bills. I shoved the damp bills in my pocket and looked nervously down the dock.

"We meant to surprise you," Parker said, as if they hadn't. "Well worth a little dip." The twins laughed tonelessly. Their mirth seemed bleached. "Don't get nervous, Robert, we won't disturb the family outing." He nodded up the dock. "Let's take a little ride."

On the street outside the marina was a rented Mercedes with smoked windows. Parker motioned me into the back, next to Christiana. He let Meagan take the wheel and turned back to us from the passenger side, nodding toward Christiana.

"I told her to put it in her pocket."

"I don't *have* any pockets."

This caused an erotic surge all its own. Christiana had no *interior,* no capacity or need for generating warmth. She didn't need the encumbrances of self-sufficiency. She had no keys, no purse, no wadded tissues with lipstick bites. What little makeup she wore might have been tattooed. She had nothing but shoes and three garments, no identification but *blond* and *body.* In freezing water or luxury cars she was pretty much the same. She was all readiness.

Meagan seemed made of the same stuff. Relaxed and confident behind the wheel, she soon had us on the same bluff where I'd walked earlier. Parker said, "The tap is open, Robert."

"Who all have you told?"

"Seattle's made you nervous," he said. "What a different guy you were on Chestnut Street. Remember the Indian?" He addressed the twins. "This drunk Indian wanders into an opening at Robert's gallery and starts doing a little chant. We all listen politely until we're stifling yawns. Then people start to leave. Robert tries to give him a five. The guy goes ballistic, so Robert starts wrestling him and ends up on his back on the sidewalk."

Christiana flicked her hair back and asked, "Is that true?"

"I was trying to shake his hand." Meagan seemed to be heading toward the highway, so I asked, "Where are we going?"

"Better turn around," Parker told her, rolling his eyes.

Back in the center of town Meagan parked, and she and Christiana got out and left us without a word. Parker turned in his seat.

"Are you going to tell the whole world?" I asked.

"Them? They couldn't care less. When they're around I have to remember to use short sentences. They want to shop. Let's get a drink."

"What did Leonard say?"

"'Yes.'"

"That's it?"

"You won't get handsprings from Leonard, Robert. He's into deals like this all the time. I talked more with Enfanta."

"Who?"

"Leonard's head accountant."

"His accountant's name is Enfanta?"

"From Paraguay via Harvard Business and Barney's of New York. Wears skirts made for a much smaller woman. She has nails yea long and writes checks like ink was blood."

Enfanta, Parker told me, had been instructed to give him cash to cover immediate expenses.

"Leonard wants to make sure Judith comes onboard," he said. "It's our job to convince her. That's what the money's for."

"Christ, we're giving her the shaft. What should we do, buy her flowers?"

"It might soften the blow. And who knows, she might invite us back to the gym."

"Where are the plates?" I asked, aware that this question came too late.

"Safe," Parker said.

"Safe where?"

"You just know I'm going to fuck you, don't you," Parker said.

"You would if you could."

He shook his head. "We're doing this by *your* book, Robert." Mockery pinched the corners of his mouth. "They're in the trunk."

"*This* trunk? Jesus, Parker. What if some drunk rear-ended you?"

"The plane could have crashed. Leonard could have sneezed. His office is all marble and leading edges. I thought you'd want them back right away."

"I do."

"They're yours."

I paused, then said, "I can't take them right now."

Parker gave me a look.

"Don't tell me you're still keeping the little family in the dark. 'Who all have you told?' Spare me this shit, Robert. You know, your paranoia is starting to make *me* nervous."

"I need to get back," I said.

On the way I spotted Diane and Budge walking along the sidewalk. They looked like strangers. Passing them, I fought the urge to slide down in my seat.

....

We decided to spend the night in our slip at the marina. Diane, maybe also feeling claustrophobic, wanted to eat in town, but I was afraid of running into Parker and the twins. We had the salmon, I reminded her. I even offered to cook.

The next day we recrossed the Sound and anchored once more in the same cove. Budge and Diane took a row while I stayed aboard, reading *The Love Diary* and working my way through most of a bottle of wine.

During dinner Diane drank a fair bit herself and turned magnanimous: Budge could keep his camera. I showed the boy how to open the accordion body and what button to press. When he took the first shot—of Diane and me in each other's sloppy embrace—the camera nearly covered his head. It felt dangerous, like giving him a Harley or a loaded gun. He loved the flash and the whine as the undeveloped shots spat out the front. I caught myself drumming my fingers as we watched them develop. Budge turned to me and said, "You're squinting in every one." Diane laughed a hard, barking laugh I hadn't heard before—a crack in her spirited resolve. "Do you think I could take pictures you could sell?" the boy asked, and I answered briskly, "Who knows?" Then I took the Polaroid from his hands and shut it, the black body collapsing with a mechanical sigh.

When he was in his berth for the night Diane said she had something to show me.

Among Michael's videos, stowed under the bed, she had found a cassette with a sticker that read, "Old stuff, 1976, V1." To get away from his family in his twenties Michael had moved to the Northwest with the idea of making serious short films. Seattle had been a good stopgap on the way to Los Angeles, a compromise that showed the sensitivity Diane claimed Michael usually hid from himself. In the interests of making a living he had long since given up the earlier aspirations, transferring all his old work to tape. Diane hadn't seen any of it in years.

Much of the cassette was a kind of running journal. Michael had taken his 16mm Bolex everywhere, roaming his subjects vérité style. He had even taken the camera to bed, harnessing the thing to his chest to capture the first true moments of sleep. There was also an early experiment with animation. In one segment objects appeared from a tub of mud, including some silk ties that lifted out spotlessly and rose like snakes' ghosts. Then came sixteen quick takes of those same ties slithering from a wire hanger. These were either slapstick or failed visual haiku; the burden of seriousness shifted to anyone who laughed, as I did. Diane didn't. She sat on the edge of the bed with one leg tucked under her. She gazed at the screen as if filling in the blanks, splicing together moments of the old life still surrounding these images. Michael reappeared, holding the camera to a mirror, meditating on his own face. He looked heavier, darker, easier to pin down. Then the picture cut to a slow pan of four warehouse windows glowing with a frosty light. "This is our little loft in Belltown," Diane said. "Developers bulldozed the building a few years ago." She grew still as if she knew what was coming. In a moment she herself appeared before those misty windows, naked, in a shy dance.

To keep in shape Diane swam three times a week, and once she'd invited me to do laps with her. I'd fallen way behind and sat on the edge of the pool, watching her body slip through the water in graceful quarter turns. Afterward, amused by the ogling, she'd told me that before having Budge her slightness had made her body seem senseless to her: "Maybe it was because everything birthwise worked so well while everything marriagewise didn't."

"Look at that hair," she murmured now.

She was twenty-three or -four. Her hair, now clipped short, was bushy and closed around her face. Her movements were quick but unsure, nervous. There were all the signs of a hesitancy I couldn't recognize now. In her decision to marry Michael, who had told her he never would, she had made a step toward the confidence and strength she would later need to agree with him when he wanted to move out. In front of the lens she forced casual abandon. But the soft light and the music—something grand and sentimental from the last century—could not disguise the sense of innocence breaking down. Even her body lacked the self-knowledge it had since acquired.

"God, I used to take myself so seriously," she said.

The dance aroused me powerfully, and maybe she had known it would. I stood and switched off the VCR, then turned to Diane and eased us back on the bed. Her eyes had grown misty and made mine prick. She went out of focus and doubled—two Dianes, younger and older, superimposed. Her kiss came from all that way back, from the woman who wasn't there anymore, who had once loved someone like Michael Mays. I couldn't help imagining what she might have become without Budge—ironic, discontented, early hopefulness yielding to impatience and inertia. I thought, *She might have become like me.* For ten years, maybe longer, I'd been holding out for the big prize, putting my life in neutral until my luck turned and my reward arrived. What difference had Weston made? What lesson had that experience taught? In the dance Diane had moved her arms like wings; raising a male child had taken this delicacy from her gestures. Whatever had changed me like that? What life eruption had ever done anything but make me think I was owed something for a wrong I couldn't admit was my own fault? Eng would pay off Weston. Did that sound like real life? Now Diane was pulling off her shirt and skirt, and I was falling behind again. As I struggled with my jeans, the damp wad of hundreds fell out of my pocket and dropped to the floor.

I still had one leg in my pants and stood like that, looking at the money as if for a way to disown it.

Naked, Diane picked up the bills and slowly sat back down on the bed. Conflicting emotions produced an unlikely calm. She said, "We saw you with your friends."

"His name is Parker Lange. I knew him in California."

"There I was trying to figure out something to tell Budgie, some reason why you'd want to get away from us. Much less why you'd be doing it in a black Mercedes with two strange women." She looked up. "Maybe they aren't strangers."

"They're *both* Parker's friends," I said, aware how absurd this sounded. "I was with them less than twenty minutes; we didn't do anything."

"No?" She tapped the folded bills, unaware how her nakedness gave a scary charge to her silence, though she hardly needed it.

"He's brokering the negatives."

Now I had to scramble backward to cover tracks I hadn't actually made, but that lies made it seem I had. When I told her Judith had handed over the other four self-portraits, it sounded ludicrous. "Then

I—we, Parker and I—found a lot more. We didn't tell Judith—we haven't told her yet. I lied to you."

"There's, what, a couple thousand here? Is that all you expected?" Her glare reinforced the irony.

"It's part of a loan," I said. But before this was out Diane slapped the side table with the flat of her hand. The blow shivered through her body.

"Don't make me drag it out, Robert. For Christ's sake, what are you up to?"

Then I told her everything, my voice cracking like a pubescent teen's. "I stand to make a lot more," I said. I pointed at the bills like money was my best excuse and felt suddenly, stupidly emboldened. "Am I supposed to give it up and stay at home like some fucking trained dog?"

She looked at me.

"It's not the money," she said. "Or the women or Parker Whoever or even the negatives. It's acting on your own and leaving us out." She shook her head. "How long were you going to keep us in the dark, Robert? Or are we even still part of the picture?"

"What's that supposed to mean?"

"All weekend you've been acting like you wanted to be somewhere else."

"If I have it's because you keep talking nonstop Michael."

I hadn't realized this was true until I said it. Still, Diane wouldn't bite. The olive tint of her face had blanched white. Her jaw flexed and her mouth narrowed, erasing its warming corners of shadow. Her face shut like the door of a vault. "What are you going to do?"

"I'm committed," I said.

"To *what*?"

"Look, you're overreacting. All you have to do is give this a chance."

"Give *what* a chance? You're not saying *what*."

"I'm not doing anything wrong," I said. "This kind of thing is done all the time."

"Are you talking about negatives or lying?" she said. "What else are you going to lie about down the road? You're not *with* us, Robert. Suddenly you're the High Plains Photo Dealer. When you left this afternoon I got scared and confused. I knew something wasn't right. Budgie even asked if you were coming back."

"Why, so *he* could throw more Michael stories in my face?"

She gave me a pitying look.

"That is so unbelievably cheap," she said. "And I haven't been talking about Michael the whole time."

She reached across the bed for the dreaded white nightgown and tugged it over her head. The intent here was clear—denial disguised by righteousness. I pulled my jeans back on.

"Michael gives you the word," I said, "and you start thinking you can put your old life back together again."

She laughed. "That wouldn't fly even on your home planet," she said, buttoning the lace at her neck. "That's what *you're* doing with Wilfred Eng."

"This has been one long stroll down memory lane for you," I said. "Michael's favorite spots, Michael's home movies."

"I was trying to show you my past," she said. She tossed the hundreds at my feet. "What were *you* trying to show?"

"You've been waiting for me to fall short," I said.

Then the door opened and Budge came in.

"Why are you guys yelling?"

"Come in and sleep with me, honey," Diane said.

It was beneath her to use the boy like this. I didn't say another word and stormed out, boiling mad with nowhere to go. In the galley I snatched another bottle of wine and went up on deck. There was nothing to do there but fume. Across the expanse of black a distant line of lights twinkled like Oz. I stayed up there drinking until it started to rain, the night's pointless reply.

Belowdecks again, I stumbled in the passageway. No sound came from the bow. I sat on Budge's berth. The rain beat down all around, drumming inches overhead like dropped BBs. I could hear it hissing along the hull at the undulating waterline. Blind elements moved against each other. Without undressing, I got under the blankets. Pushing my feet down, I felt a faint body of the boy's warmth lingering there. No, too late for that, I thought miserably. It must have been the wine.

May 14

A week has passed since I have written here. Many things have
happened. I have been ill with fever, delirious, I'm told. Also
Joseph came home. I have not seen him yet—he came while I was
quite ill & unaware. I should dread this meeting but am still too
weak to summon much emotion. This morning I felt strong
enough to stand & Mrs. Dodd took my arm & walked me to the
window where she pulled aside the curtain. The world looked so
harsh. I felt a rolling in my legs & remembered a dream of sailing.
You were there on the ship, though I could not see you....

May 15

This morning Mrs. Dodd told me something that froze my blood.
When I was delirious & Joseph standing near the bed, she said I
seized his hand & kissed it. Telling me this, Mrs. Dodd smiled,
thinking it a fitting gesture for a sick wife long separated from her
husband. Was it? Or did I think his hand was yours? She said I
spoke nonsense & I wonder if I said anything to give us away. The
thought terrifies me.

   Later. Joseph has just left. He took my hand & told me I was
looking much better & said how grateful he was to have come
home just when I was ill. Then he read to me for half an hour but I
did not hear a word, watching his face for signs of suspicion. What
would he do if he knew? The thought makes me sick with fear. You
& I have spoken little of my husband—shame & fear have kept us
from it. Once you told me, "He gave me my life." You would say
nothing more even when I pressed you. He gave me my life as well
but our lives do not come to us without a price. Joseph also
brought us together. His long absences even seemed to justify our

love. Whenever he returns from one of his trips it is always like meeting a stranger. And a stranger he remains, though only to me. He has been home four days after months away & already he has received a handful of dinner invitations. Tonight he was on his way out but asked if I wanted him to stay & keep me company. I told him I was tired & needed to sleep. He smiled & leaned down to kiss my forehead. I held my breath, my heart in tumult. His gentleness moved & shamed me....

May 17

I felt well enough to dress & ate breakfast downstairs. Joseph was already gone—out to a meeting with business partners. It is a beautiful day & I sat outside for a time wrapped in a blanket. Now I am back upstairs in my rooms. The clocks begin to chime through the house. The morning stretches out endlessly with nothing to occupy it. I can't sit still. I don't want to think & yet maybe that is what I am meant to do. I wander from room to room as if fleeing. Maybe the fever was sent to stop the way to disaster. Maybe I am meant to walk these halls & rooms until I love them as I once vowed to. The husband who is master here seems to haunt every room when he is gone. Even when he is home he occupies all the spaces of this house like a shadow & is felt in every corner.

How my heart aches to be near you. When will I see you again?

Just now I climbed the stairs to Joseph's study, where I am not allowed. It is another door shut upon friendship, which a wife is told to strive for & from which I am prohibited. When I first came to this house it was curiosity about Joseph that drove me to disobey. Now it is you. As a child you spent many happy hours in that room reading by the window. I sat there for a time as you once had & drew close to you. I imagined never seeing you again & the tears welled up in my eyes. I tried to pray for you, for us, & terrible pangs of guilt came over me. God must indeed be listening. You enliven the world for me, my love, you bring me all of its untouchable mysteries. Nothing else makes such perfect sense. I think I must pay for this love—pay, I hope, not by losing it but by losing something I care for much less. I try to pray again—Dear God, please help me. The words die on my lips....

7

· · · · · · · · · · · · · · · · · ·

"Can't it wait?" Parker asked over the phone from his hotel. On his earlier trip he'd stayed at the modest Northwesterner with the Buddy Squirrel candy shop in the lobby. Back from Port Townsend, he and the twins had checked into a suite at the Inn at the Market.

I was insisting on a research trip to New York. A private photo library, the Hagen-Mills in Brooklyn, had two of Eng's journals from the 1870s. I told him these would shed more light on the affair, though I wasn't convinced myself. Parker sensed that I wanted to get away. He didn't like the idea.

"Judy isn't a sure thing yet," he said. "You can't just run off." He paused. "She knows about Weston. Frankly, she's not impressed with your scruples."

"Would she know a scruple if she saw one?"

"A little schmoozing wouldn't hurt," Parker said. "Become her friend, Robert."

I said I wanted to lock up the two negatives I hadn't been able to take with me in Port Townsend, and he invited me up for a drink.

Parker's rooms were twice the size of my apartment. When I asked about the cost he said, "We'll compare receipts when you get back," eyeing me like a fellow profligate. He rubbed it in by ordering snacks and a pitcher of martinis from room service. While we talked the

twins got into a fight over the television remote. Meagan wanted a series about Hollywood rich kids, Christiana a Schwartzenegger film.
They started wrestling for the remote, and their cries soon turned to
spumes of cheerless laughter. Parker watched this fetching struggle as
if from the predatory perch of himself. He had no intention of stepping in. Meagan was fine as long as no one was winning. When she
lost, she stepped out onto the shallow balcony while Christiana lay on
her back, watching the screen through her raised knees. A hulking an-
droid was being shot to pieces, spraying blood and scattering mother-
boards but somehow keeping the trigger down on an outsized assault
weapon. It was all the same to Christiana. When the ads came on she
watched with the same stunned attention.

From the living room I could just see into the bedroom. As much
as I would object to Parker telling me, I was curious about sleeping
arrangements. I asked him if he'd seen Judith yet, and he answered
that they were meeting the next morning.

"We should make a plan and approach her together."

"You said it yourself," I said. "I'm a liability. It's better if I'm out of
sight."

"We need to make a move now," Parker said. "I can't stay here forever."

I wondered if the twins would be sad to leave, though perhaps the
novelty of the threesome wore off in time. To console Meagan, Parker
now pointed out her new outfits for me to admire, hanging on a door.

"*I* paid for them," she said, glaring in at me from the twilight of the
balcony.

Christiana had bought only an expensive watch with an enormous
face. Her interest lay in the purely functional. Her leggings and heels
were a kind of uniform. She wore burnt orange this time, with a
stretchy brown tank top. She turned toward me from the TV with its
stew of blood and fire and asked if I wanted to look at her luggage—
to prove, I could only guess, that she was less interested in clothes than
her sister. I didn't know how to refuse.

In the bedroom she slid her bag from under the bed—did that mean Meagan slept alone? Did they alternate? The bag itself had a fat black zipper. Christiana held the toothy sides apart, and I felt my neck flush. Shoes took up the most room. The multicolored leggings were shrunken, folded in long, wrinkly wads like bark chunks from endangered trees. She waited, as if expecting me to choose. "Nice," I said.

Then she excused herself to go to the bathroom, and when I came back out Parker said, "You've made a friend." Meagan, still outside, had turned away, watching a ferry's lights reflected on the water like strips of bright film. I looked at Parker. "Sills must have said more." This was old business. But I'd been left out, and the meetings didn't quite seem real.

"Truth to tell, Robert, if these were paintings he might take a keener interest. Or do you mean what did he say about you?"

It was easy to forget how deeply Parker's knowingness could penetrate. He didn't look incisive or even like much of a threat. In fact, sometimes he looked as passive as a wallflower at the Harvest Ball. He sat back on the pillowy sofa, moving only his finger on the remote as he surfed the channels. He was right, of course. I wanted sanctioning, to be taken seriously after my stumble. I wanted assurance that it *was* just a stumble. I wanted membership in the club.

"The bad-boy rep hurts only in squeaky-clean towns like Seattle," he said. I flushed again and felt Meagan's eyes on me. "With Leonard," Parker added, "sticking your neck out means you're in the game."

"I wasn't sticking my neck out with the Weston thing," I said. "Or I didn't think I was."

"Risk is always where you least expect it," he said and added with special emphasis, "So is trust."

Christiana came back now, and Parker closed the conversation with a flicker of his eyelids. I tried not to look at her. "I should probably go," I said. Parker stood.

"Don't forget this," he said, picking up the briefcase with the two plates inside. He looked like he wouldn't grin if somebody paid him.

Christiana took it from him and led me out.

The elevator had a mirrored ceiling, and as the two of us rode down a fantasy soared upward through my brain: Christiana looking at herself from the carpeted floor while I peeled her. On the first floor the doors opened and a cool breeze entered. Stepping out, I hesitated and thought she did too. Was she thinking the same thing? When our fantasies are near at hand and we don't act, real life becomes a mockery, and we walk through it with a kind of dreaming disappointment. At my car she held the door and stood in the dark on the busy street while I buckled up. Then she flicked her hair back and waved with just her fingertips.

I didn't surface for three blocks, then pulled over and opened the briefcase. The plates were safe inside.

....

"What happens now?" Diane asked.

We were eating dinner at the restaurant where we'd had our first date. It was the night after Christiana's enigmatic send-off. That afternoon I'd made reservations for New York. I was leaving at midnight.

The whole way back on our nightmare cruise I'd sat below in the galley pretending to read while Diane stayed up in the wheelhouse. Budge shuttled between us, asking annoying questions, knowing something was wrong and maybe trying to fix it. I was finally so short with him that he got the message and stayed up with his mother. I felt craven as a bully. When we docked at Shilshole I took a cab home, and Diane let me. Since then the pettiness and anger had ebbed, and I'd called her in a guilty panic. I was beginning to see that the upcoming months would be fraught and chaotic. Suddenly I couldn't face them without trying to sort things out with her.

She might have meant her question to hurt: Did she mean the plates or us? I felt a wave of discouragement, which made it harder to explain my plans with any sort of excitement. Still, I described the love affair and the diaries. I told her about printing and selling the negatives. I quoted numbers to make the plan sound well thought out, even practical. This was no flash in the pan, no quick killing. Profits, I told her, would be long term. A gift had been laid at my feet—surely it was obvious that all my years of study and denial had led to this moment when I would make it all pay off. Letting such a gift slip away was an outrage, like leaving a newborn on the stoop of the church where idiots worshiped. Diane asked about Judith.

"If she agrees," I said, "she'll get the career she's always wanted."

"What about you?"

Again I heard more than one question. "I have to start researching Eng's life."

"From what you've told me, his life doesn't sound all that appealing."

"Lives aren't always appealing."

Diane could have drawn the personal parallel with a tart reply. Instead she said nothing. Her indifference was disappointing. I'd never seen her like this. In as neutral a tone as possible, I said, "I'm trying to figure out why he brought these heavy negatives with him all the way to Seattle."

"His ball and chain," she said. "Hard proof of everything he didn't want out of life."

I had actually thought the same thing myself. Why not make one perfect set of prints and keep those instead? Maybe Eng needed a more lasting monument. Maybe he couldn't bring himself to destroy the plates but counted on innocence like Judith's to do it for him. Maybe a cluttered basement was what he'd had in mind, the images living on like the love they recorded, intact but unproclaimed.

Diane said, "Maybe he was planning to blackmail her down the road." She left a silence, letting me absorb her anger. Then she asked, "Why didn't he ever settle down with someone else, say, some nice Chinese woman?" It was possible that Eng had had other clandestine affairs and left no record. But something made me doubt it, and when I didn't answer Diane said, "If you ask me, I think Ellen found out that a little too much McFarland had rubbed off on Eng. Didn't he prove it later on? The constant trips, and always to the same places? Men like that are in love with chasing their own tails. They dare life not to change. Look at the pathetic way Eng died. It's right out of a dime novel."

She might have had a point. As the fire spread through the boarding house, Eng had appeared in an upper-story window, staring down calmly as if welcoming the end at last. Witnesses claimed he could have saved himself.

"It's as if he didn't believe his own death would really happen," she said.

"Does anyone? Do you?"

"He probably figured he could take pictures of it afterward and moon about it for eternity. Look, Robert, what's the point of all this? Are you trying to bring me around?"

"What if I am?"

"I'd say you were still missing the point."

"I'm being honest with you."

"Are you? Anyway, what's happening to us has almost nothing to do with Wilfred Eng or Parker or Judith."

Her anger had a great force of logic and rightness. But before she could go on, our dinners arrived. I tried a friendlier tack and asked about Budge. But Diane had dug her heels in. Budge was fine, she said, then shut her mouth. As we ate her silence became a kind of sidestepping farce meant, I was sure, to make me angry. I'd never seen her so close to vindictiveness. I couldn't eat. I kept looking at her, expecting this false face to crack. Finally, more bilious than scared, I said, "Look, forget about dinner. Let's go somewhere and make love." She didn't even blink and kept on eating.

"You're on your way to New York, remember?"

"I'm sorry," I said, "that was out of line. But you're so, I don't know what—aloof."

"Who does that sound like?"

"Why did you agree to dinner if you're not going to talk?"

"You and Eng," she said, shaking her head. "You're a pair. You both keep coming back to the same spot. I wonder if he watched the clock like you do."

"What?"

She nodded at my wrist. "You keep looking at your watch. Dinner *and* sex would have been a stretch, Robert. What was the plan, call for doggie bags, then stick it in me in the airport parking lot? And you say you don't understand."

This angered me as only an unwelcome truth could. Still, pettiness and nastiness were the poor cousins of hope, weren't they? She *had* come to dinner, after all. She hadn't given up.

"You know I love you," I said.

"I come with a son."

This was shallow and smug, a slap in the face. It was unbearable. Diane the Madonna. My belly flared hot. But her own anger eclipsed mine. It was a shock to see her like this, hard to see myself as the cause.

"What if I told you right now that I'd give up the whole thing?" I said. "What would you say?"

"It's the lone wolf I can't deal with. I can't live with a stranger."

"You could have told me to go to hell over the phone," I said. "Why drag us both down like this? You're not acting like yourself. What's wrong with you? What's happened?"

She shook her head again. "I must be blind. Michael said you didn't fit, and I didn't believe him."

"Michael again. It all comes back to fucking Michael."

"All but the screwing up," she said. "You did that all by yourself."

"Maybe the two of you planned it that way."

"Even if that were true, Robert, you did nothing to prove us wrong."

"All that shyness about making love in the bow—that was just an act."

"I've got a son to think about," she said. But now a crack did appear. She obviously heard it too and lowered her eyes to the table. "I came here tonight to tell you we can't see each other anymore. I've got to do what's best for Budgie."

"And Michael's what's best?" I looked at her again, but she wouldn't look up. "Jesus, you slept with him."

She didn't reply. A chill invaded my bowels. I dropped my fork on my plate and stared at her.

Then she was on her feet, jerking her coat and purse from the back of the chair. Tears had surprised her, and she blinked at them furiously. Without another word she turned and hurried out.

....

Facing each other near the middle of the Aperture *Wilfred Eng* were two images of Alcatraz. On the way from the restaurant I'd bought a pint of Scotch and now lay on my office couch sipping and staring at these pictures. At the time of the earlier one Alcatraz had been a fort, but Eng had photographed it from an angle that made it look uninhabited, bristling with fir and cedar trees. It was stony, primordial, the birthplace of heroes. Both the water and the sky were white, and the island seemed to emerge from the mouth of heaven. It was otherworldly and yet precise in its natural features—the craggy rock, the trees. The second image, taken much later, showed the prison. As an old man Eng had said of his famous *Return* landscapes, "Each one implies the next." The last implied the one he wouldn't live to take, and maybe this idea wasn't all bad. Heaven or prison? Life seemed to be forever proving Eng's point: bitterness and disappointment were everyone's ultimate legacy. "I have understood the shape of my life from an early age," he'd said, "and it has been a curse." He had not just grown up with photography but grown old with it; by the time he died photos had recorded maybe more of life than we could bear to see, much less remember. Bitter as he could get, Eng also knew what chance had put in his way, that photography was like nothing else in the world. When he was a boy it was a parlor fad; late in his life he wrote that photographs "carry on without sound, feel, smell, or taste, without the context or color of the life that made them. In time only purged & purified images remain. These grow potent and inscrutable, like objects the dead are buried with, trailing forward into their own vanished future."

I wondered what Eng made of his own future during those afternoons he spent in Ellen's arms. Clearly she trusted him with her life. Did he ever wonder what he would do with such a responsibility? In the end he must have seen that it was a mistake, maybe the biggest of his life—too momentous, too binding.

It was after ten when a knock came at my door. Parker had promised to drive me to the airport to catch the red-eye, but I was not surprised to find Christiana standing in the hall instead. She moved confidently past me, not waiting to be asked in.

"He's still with Judith," she said.

"You want a drink?" I asked.

She nodded, then followed me down the hall to my office, where I poured her some of the scotch in a coffee mug. She sipped like an old hand, turning to look at the photo-covered walls. The night was cool, and she wore a dark sweater and cinnamon tights patterned with what looked like Renaissance maps of the world. She looked softer, fitted with a subtler skin.

"You must know he's fucking her," I said.

"Meg and I aren't with him that way."

"That's not how he tells it."

"Parker's fun for a while," she said. "But he has to run the whole show, and then it's like we're a couple of trained monkeys." She sipped. "Meg slept with him once. She said he was a real corpse."

She turned and took a few casual steps toward the windows. She wore brown ankle boots and black socks with the tops rolled down.

She seemed warmer, less erotically imposing, than she had the night before. She stopped and faced me again. "He can fuck who he wants," she declared with a look that said, *So can I.* She wore a light, almost floral scent, more intimate than the buttery lotion I remembered from Port Townsend. She seemed less straightforward now, striking northerly tones. Maybe I was meant to think there would be no maneuvering, no sudden thrust to send me cartwheeling. Maybe none would be needed. I poured myself another drink, which was stupid before flying—seven miles up, I'd sleep for exactly thirty minutes, then sit awake for twenty-five hundred miles with cottonmouth, restless legs, and a jagged head. Christiana looked at a John C. H. Grabille. The print was of an Indian camp. It was made just after Wounded Knee, but the image was all somber peace, the velvety ponies standing in the creek at the bottom of the picture, tepees spreading out over misty hills.

"Is it worth a lot?" she asked, pointing.

"A lot," I conceded. "It's not mine. I'm selling it for someone."

I hadn't made any calls yet and knew that the client, a rich dabbler named Countryman, wouldn't like it if he knew I was waiting for some way to afford the print myself. That way seemed to be here. The two thousand had dried out. I could give it to Countryman as a down payment or a show of faith. But I'd hidden the hundreds in my bookcase, for some reason wanting the money out of sight. Was it because Parker had given it to me? I wondered if I would soon be sitting on tens of thousands I also couldn't bring myself to touch. I poured myself another splash. Christiana stared at the Grabille, maybe waiting for it to catch fire or bleed. I felt a sudden shuddering ache, as if all these images were threatened by any but a loving regard.

"Just what *are* you and your sister doing here?" I asked.

"Meg and I work with Leonard too," she said.

"Fancy that."

"Parker said not to tell you," she went on. "He wasn't wild about me coming here tonight."

"Why did you?"

She gave her head a languid toss and said, "I wanted to," then paused, waiting for me to say something. "He said you were paranoid enough already, and you'd think it was a plot or something."

"Is it?"

"We can call Leonard if you want to."

"What would Parker think of *that?*"

"Who cares?"

"Anyway, what will it prove? You know Leonard. So what?"

"You want to?" she said. "He stays up all night."

This was true, I recalled. I wondered if she knew from having stayed up with him. She paused again, and when I didn't answer she picked up the phone.

"What do you do for Leonard?" I asked as she punched in the number.

"It's a part-time thing," she said. "We work parties and openings, host exhibitions, you know. Hi, it's me," she said, presumably to Sills. She glanced at me then and tipped the receiver, inviting me to step near and listen.

It was Leonard all right—the confident inflection, the precision, the syllables weighted with consequence. He started right in telling her about Ferrari, the factory at Marinello near Modena. He wasn't always this open. He had to know you, and when he did he bathed you in the gift of his ideas. All conversations were only one big conversation Leonard was having with the world. If he liked you, you could stand in for a while. To someone who looked like Christiana, Leonard would give the benefit of the doubt. He would talk to her as if she really cared or understood. As I listened, my eye strayed up to the Grabille, then to the empty ceiling. Christiana touched her hip to mine. Despite the Scotch my dick started jumping like a teletype. My hand was suddenly on her waist, feeling the damp heat trapped in the fabric of her sweater. Abruptly she told Sills, "Gotta go, I'm on someone's phone." A blurred moment passed.

Then I was catching my breath and Christiana was walking toward the windows, leggings pulled down to the tops of her thighs. Had I done that? Her naked buttocks were getting to look like old friends, plump uncles red-faced from grasping. They tick-tocked musically, promising a jolly time. Christiana pulled the blinds, then turned back, slipping a condom from her sweater cuff. She no sooner had it on me than I pushed her onto my desk. I wrenched up her legs and stripped the mapped tights to her boots. Then with her smooth, muscular arms she pulled my head down to her crotch. My tongue seemed to have a mind of its own, probing her deeply. My eyes widened, reading the curves and scrolls of her pubic hair, sparse and waxed column-thin, each strand like a flourish, the path of something flying ass over teakettle. Christiana cried syllables so distinct they seemed charged with meaning. *Finally,* she seemed to say. I straightened, chin and cheeks wet. The leggings made a circle of her legs, and she hooked my neck hard, then spread her arms to steady herself as I pushed inside her, rocking her back and forth while the pictures stared silently down.

June 1

I took Joseph's niece, Annie Mowry, to lunch at Silverton's restaurant while Joseph was elsewhere on business. I did not care to go— all family responsibilities seem so empty to me now. Annie is to be married & her fiancé joined us. She is near thirty but vindictive as a child. Some years back she lived at Stockton Street at a time when her fortunes were low. She spent much time in certain "tea" rooms where other drinks are served. She has always seen in me a heaping-on of good fortune that unbalanced the scale on which her own prospects register less & less. She was always fractious & melancholy. Now she is transformed. Today she wore a pretty springtime dress of pale yellow linen & turned down the offer of sherry with a temperate look, even managing to blush. In this blush is the resolution of Annie's pain & desires—I feel myself indicted in it. Annie has compromised. She has always had impossibly high standards & I can't believe she thinks her fiancé suitable—he will not be able to provide her materially with all she has said she wants. Still, it is done. We ate salmon in cream with chunks of spiny lobster. I barely tasted it. I answered Annie's chatter with syllables of exclamation, agreement, & joy. There is a certain sharpness in her eye & voice as if she knows I am unhappy & means to make it worse. She seems to want to say that I should lay aside what can only be petty distresses & complaints & obstacles. Peace & contentment are just one decision away. I wonder if it is the bad example Annie senses in me that has forced her to make this sudden match. Does she see the future more clearly, more reasonably than I do? I almost wished she would shout & point her finger.

Then suddenly your name was on her lips. I felt my face blanch & struggled to hide my emotions.

Joseph was insisting she go to you for a wedding commemorative & Annie was insisting she never would. "I'd never go to that—" and she used the most awful epithet. The word stunned me. For a moment I could only stare at her. "I hated the way he looked at me," she said, "as if I wasn't human." "He is a most gifted individual," I said weakly & had to pray that my voice did not give me away. "None of the household staff could stand him," Annie said. "Does he still use the kitchen entrance?" She might have sensed some weakness in my manner & looked at me with her hard eyes, wanting an answer. I looked for help to her fiancé who out of solidarity with his future wife also pressed me with his gaze. They did not want an answer to this demeaning question so much as they wished to cut me down to size. I found myself explaining that you felt more comfortable entering the house as you did.

Then I managed to get us off the subject but by the time we left my head was splitting horribly. I ached to see you, to hold you until those awful words stopped ringing in my ears. But the risk was too great with Joseph home. The evening was turning foggy. I couldn't help myself & wept—for you, for the pain in my head. I felt caught & helpless & unfairly singled out. I came in quietly to avoid seeing Joseph. I felt disgusted, worthless, of no use to anyone. I came upstairs here to rest. Sleep would be welcome but sleep will not come. Somewhere outside there is a noise that grows ominous—a rhythmic sound like a knife on a whetstone or a scythe cutting wheat. Merciless, inexorable strokes. In the silences between I pray each stroke will be the last. I look out the window for the source. The fog has grown heavy, long wisps trail past the glass. In the yard the flowering pear glows like a snowstorm in the mist. Still the strokes will not stop. It is a torture.

June 3

Joseph will not speak, will not tell me where he has been or
where he plans to go & what he will be doing. He only smiles &
kisses my cheek. The only idleness he allows himself is a few
moments in the study taunting Tommy & Pig with a length of
string. "They miss the point," he says, smiling. He means, I suppose, that it isn't the string they should claw & bite. The cats
know as much about my husband as I do (What bitterness there
is in my heart when I think such things.) When he flies off to
one of his meetings they curl up to nap & forget their madness.
Joseph has told me he must leave San Francisco again soon.
For once I did not ask where he was going & this angered me,
though I don't know why—perhaps because he is indifferent to
my indifference. Or perhaps because both of us are now keeping
secrets.

   Later. Joseph & I had bitter words after dinner. I found myself arguing against his going away as if I wanted him to stay. Do
I? Do I want him to rescue me? I could never tell him the truth—
the danger to you would be too great. Could I compromise as
Annie has done & build a life on yet another lie? I could not
confess as duty binds me to. I will have to find another way—
earn Joseph's love & gratitude & let these take the place of forgiveness. But no, the lies will only complicate themselves: marital
duty does not bind my husband to do anything about his own
infidelities except commit more of them. As we spoke tonight
he controlled his anger, as always, which only made me lose
my temper. I held back the bitterest accusations. "You require
more than a little patience," he said. He smiled but grasped my
arms too tightly. Then he looked at his watch & told me good-
night.

June 4

I have no appetite. Mrs. Dodd served a lovely dinner but I ate nothing & only sipped a cup of beef tea. Joseph was out once more at a dinner he asked me to attend with him. I refused, giving no excuse. Mrs. Dodd sat up with me in the parlor. She seemed wary of telling any of her stories. She was at my side constantly during my fever—perhaps she is as tired of me as I am of myself. I feel spoiled & vile. Finally she fell silent & I felt her watching. As she said good-night she looked at me strangely & I thought with ter-ror that she knew, that she had somehow guessed at the truth. I sat up alone after she went upstairs & was suddenly overcome with the guilt & shame. These awful emotions appear as a warning to protect us. My loneliness gives rise to such dangerous thoughts. They appall & frighten me....

June 5

This afternoon I slipped away & came to you. I took such an awful risk. We had not planned this meeting & I surprised you in the midst of work. You made me wait out front & while I sat my heart grew so heavy I had to force away the tears. When you were free at last & we were alone you took my arms & shook me, demanding to know what I was doing there. I told you, "I can't live in that house any longer, I can't live apart from you." Your face darkened with rage. Then you shouted, saying all the risk was yours, that I was only diverting myself from petty unhappiness. I had never seen you so angry. I tried to tell you that I understood, that I knew you were more alone now than before & that I must bear the blame for that. But I was weeping before I could finish & you left the room in disgust.

In a moment I heard you in the work room. I followed you there & crept up behind you where you stood at your bench. I could not speak to say I was sorry & so touched your back & you jumped as if you'd forgotten me. It terrified me that you would forget so I touched you again & you turned. Your eyes were full of tears. I had never before seen you weep. I touched your face & the sobs leapt from you, grief heaving against everything in you that resisted grieving. I took you in my arms & we sank to the floor, where I held you for a long while, your face hidden in my neck. Finally, when you were calm again, you began to stroke the hair at my temple. This tenderness moved me beyond words. I could have held you that way forever, breathing in your sweet dampness. We were silent a long time. Then you raised your head & looked at me. I told you I had some money of my own from my mother's family. "We would never starve," I said. And suddenly all we have never spoken was before us, the wildest possibility we have kept hidden in our hearts. But is it so wild? Is it only anticipation that makes it seem impossible? Is it always so? And what a paltry few moments this anticipation might seem when we have spent a happy lifetime together. You raised your head & looked at me in a way no man ever has, as a beloved partner. With such a look I have always imagined two people could forge their lives together, each showing the other his courage & resourcefulness. Such a look might uphold us both forever. The afternoon light was gently falling away. The air around us seemed golden with resolve & even before you whispered, "We'll need a plan," I understood that we were of one mind....

8

· · · · · · · · · · · · · · · · · ·

The awful perspective I wasn't ready for was waiting somewhere over northern Montana. We would run into it like turbulence that would last the whole trip. The confidence of a scotch-addled fuck would unravel in palpitating despair. Hovering out there in the night were wrenching images of Diane and Michael and Budge peacefully asleep while the old house ticked and sighed around them.

When we'd taken off I ordered a large black coffee from the flight attendant and sneaked in a healthy splash from the pint. I knew that even trying to sleep was begging for trouble—remorse would ambush me if I wasn't careful. I'd brought along *The Love Diary* and settled in to read. Someone else's pangs of conscience might, after all, be an antidote to my own, but more likely I would find even more penetrating reminders of my own remorse and culpability.

The plan Eng had spoken of was to book passage on the steamship *Nethercutt,* which sailed regularly for Panama. The fare included the coach ride across the isthmus, which Ellen hoped would work as a decoy: she was convinced that McFarland would try to follow, so they would leave the ship early and head for Mexico City. "These may be the last words I write as a woman alone," Ellen wrote.

I am leaving not one life but two—my brief life as a wife & my
childhood as well. I look around this room & see so many familiar
things brought from home. They never seemed to belong here.
Still, I never imagined I would one day leave them behind. I give
them up gladly....

She then described a shelf full of beloved objects from her childhood, and I couldn't help thinking of Budge's shelves, his toy ambulances like talismans. I remembered meeting him for the first time,
picking Diane up for a date. On the way over I rehearsed my half of
different exchanges, all of them sounding like apologies for stealing
his mom. His neon-green sweatpants were muddied at the knees, but
his hair was wet and brushed down. He stepped onto the porch, saying my name, his hand out to shake. Diane had taught him well.
Budge was her messenger and her message. He announced that the
boundaries of her self had been enlarged and that I was being asked
inside.

The flight attendant came around with more coffee, which I again
dosed with scotch. With such a brew, I thought, I might drink my
way to a kind of clarity. All the unwanted images would seem to belong to ant-sized people in a deep valley, crystal clear but far away. I
got up to go to the bathroom, pissing powerfully in the cramped,
shuddering head. Twenty minutes later I had to go again. My neighbor sighed, shifting his knees as I squeezed back into my seat. He
wouldn't quite make eye contact, only glancing at the peaty, roasty
cloud around me and maybe wondering why I couldn't seem to decide between stimulants. I ignored him and settled back into *The
Love Diary*. It occurred to me that the idea of running away with
Ellen may have put Eng in mind of his mother's flight from China
and set up the eventual failure of his love. Despite the prejudice
prevalent in America, Eng's life to that point had been charmed. And
now he would be risking it all with this white woman whom he

maybe didn't want to love as much as he did. The film version had Ellen and the white photographer jumping ship in Mexico, true to the plan. Chasing them in this highly fictionalized version, McFarland came down with malaria and died mad as Ahab. In truth neither McFarland nor Ellen ever left San Francisco, at least not right away. Joseph McFarland died many years later in Portland, Oregon, in the home he had set up for his mistress, who had given him three sons. The movie left Ellen and the bowdlerized Eng poor but blissful on a small *rancho* high in the mountains in San Miguel de Allende. Nothing could have been further from the truth.

> Tears would help but they will not come. I am in shock. My heart is shattered. What am I to do?…

I looked at my watch. It was barely three. At this hour, I knew, Diane often made a trip to the bathroom. I saw her sitting up on her side of the bed, her sleeping space diminished by Michael's considerably larger bulk. Would he notice? Would he wake? Would they pass a sleepy word? In the bathroom, with its gentle, muted lighting, Diane might look at the tub and think of Michael escaping there in days when his life was still floundering and hers was just taking shape. Did she really believe Michael was the one? Maybe she did. Maybe he was. It was certain he would not show the same face to Diane that he showed to a rival. What made it all worse was that I trusted Diane to know what she needed; if that was Michael, then there was little hope for anyone else. On the way back down the hall she might pass Budge's room. Would she go in and sit for a time? She might not need to. The doubt and uneasiness that had driven her there in the first place might now have vanished. I'd done this much for her at least: I'd shown her the way she needed to go. I'd marked the end of a cycle in her life, one that would take her back to bed and carry her instantly into deep sleep. I emptied the pint into my cup. My neighbor finally looked over and said, "Haven't you had enough?"

Was I wrong? Could I have made a mistake? I have been over
everything a thousand times in my mind. I have not left my rooms
for two days now, I can't eat or sleep or think. I don't know where
you are or if you are safe. We were so clear, I did everything just as
we agreed. If we got too excited as we spoke, fear sobered us. We
repeated the words like words of love & indeed that is what they
were.

Late Tuesday night I slipped downstairs & took the buggy
horse. I felt the most awful exhilaration, with no hint of the nightmare to come.

You were gone.

Josh & I were half an hour getting to your door, my heart full of
terror & joy. I knocked & through the glass I saw your man Gee
Hock. You had said you would be alone, that no one would see us.
Gee was working late & answered the door with a lamp in one
hand & a pen in the other. This image, like a tableau, struck me
dumb with fear—the Light, the Word. Something was wrong. I
asked for you in an imperious tone hateful to me but one that dis-
guised my desperation. You were gone. That was all he knew, he
said, but his eyes said more. I couldn't help myself & said, "There
must be some mistake," & he answered, "No. Is that all?" When I
couldn't reply he shut the door & I watched him disappear down
the hallway.

I stood alone on the darkened street & shut my eyes. I prayed
that this was not happening. Could I have misunderstood? Could
you?

I decided that you had gone out & meant to come back. I knew
you sometimes walked down by the wharves late at night—it often
grieved me that you were sleepless, that I was the cause. I told myself that that was where you must be & so I rode toward the harbor. The way was slow & terrifying, a journey with an unknown
end. My mind teemed. Poor Josh is not used to riders & stopped
often to look back at me, to make sure this was really what I meant
to do. When I urged him on he slipped in the muddy streets & his

own slips frightened him. Again & again he stopped to look over his shoulder, his eye skittish & uneasy like another soul frightened in the night. The streets narrowed & lost their names. Between buildings the masts of ships loomed like black crosses against the violet sky, gnarled black ropes wrapped like sinews around the beams. There was distant music, shouts & whistles. Two women raised their skirts & shrieked, their faces blue in the night. An Indian tall as Josh, like a statue come to life, staggered on his stone legs into the muddy alley & collapsed so that Josh had to step around him. There was nowhere to go, no room, no way to turn back. What could you have been looking for down here? Was it escape? What else could drive you to such dismal streets, where there is nothing but despair? I prayed as I passed but the prayer stopped in my mouth. My cloak caught & pulled against my throat. I turned to see a woman with broken teeth holding the hem. She looked at me as if it were my flesh she held, the very edge of my life. Before I choked I loosened the knot & let the cloak slide free. Josh stopped. I thought I might never get out. I spoke your name aloud in as calm & clear a voice as I could. I told them I was looking for you, that it was important. There were others watching whom I had not seen at first. How quickly the eye adjusts to visions of hopelessness—one shadow gliding within another, a silhouette breathing on a sagging porch under which long black grass grew. My words stopped them all dead as if none of us spoke the same language. In the stony silence the woman's only answer was to whirl my cloak around her shoulders. I felt her cold & shame. I touched Josh's flanks & he stirred himself leadenly. He moved as if asleep, as if we had traveled from one world to another. I felt emptied. I felt I weighed nothing....

A day after this writing McFarland found the diaries and read them. Ellen protested that she'd invented the affair just to make him jealous, though now it was clear that she was trying to protect Eng. McFarland flew into a rage, and Ellen moved to her father's house.

When McFarland tried to force her to return, Thompson Danforth confronted him with his bigamy. Carol Chase Marino suggested that Danforth had known about the other woman from the start and was hoping to use his knowledge in some advantageous way. McFarland surprised everyone and fled. "I was to be the virgin wife," Ellen later said. "I was the Ideal, the other woman the Real." Shortly after McFarland's flight Thompson Danforth suffered a stroke. In her afterword to *The Love Diary* Marino speculated that Danforth's illness was brought on not by Ellen's marital troubles but by losing McFarland's financial backing. When he was well enough to travel Ellen took her father back East, where she cared for him until his death a year later. Eng stayed out of San Francisco for nearly two years, returning long after both Ellen and McFarland had left. McFarland managed to outrun his scandal and in Portland left a lasting mark. A downtown street was named for him. One of his great-grandsons, a philanthropist fiercely loyal to the family name, had tried to stop production of the film version of Eng and Ellen's story.

The engines changed pitch. Ahead of us was a gaseous dawn, and the plane now drifted down toward it. I felt a faint lightness, a lessening of the body maybe something like what Ellen had described, a slow version of the bottom dropping out. Forty minutes later we were on the ground.

It was nine A.M. My eyes were gritty, but I felt strangely light and alert. The shock of New York neutralized other shocks: at this hour Diane would just be getting up, perhaps kissing Michael, who would then roll over for a couple more hours. For now, at least, the pangs held themselves at bay.

Outside the terminal I hailed a cab. At my small midtown hotel I paid the driver and asked him to wait, then stepped out into New York's wearily effervescing air. This city was tireless the way vampires were undead. I felt I fit right in. I checked in and stashed my bag at the desk, and when I came back out we headed for Brooklyn and the Hagen-Mills.

The dregs of a Gulf storm had moved up the coast, torrential showers turning the smoggy sky pink. One of these hit as we drove, the cab's wipers laboring, pushing heavy sheets of water back and forth. Traffic slowed around us under the sudden weight of the rain. I opened *The Love Diary* to the end, to the last entries.

> I feel the loosening of the bonds that hold body & soul together,
> the bonds that keep us caring....

Many had speculated as to why Eng had had almost no other dealings with women in his life. It wasn't so much love as its absence that held the most compelling place in his art. I wondered now if the affair with Ellen was an unconscious way of propelling himself into the melancholy and regret he refined in his greatest work.

By the time we reached the Hagen-Mills the rain had stopped, but the clouds held the steaminess close. After a security check as thorough as the DeWitt's, I was allowed into the library and given the Eng ledger that covered the period of the love affair. Over the next two days I read this ledger cover to cover, searching for clues relating to the Ellen plates. Not surprisingly, there were none. It was as if Eng hadn't touched his camera the whole time he and Ellen were lovers. As far as Eng was concerned, she might not have existed at all. He related his turmoil only obliquely. Gee Hock, his studio assistant, came upon him sleeping at his work table one afternoon in early June. Eng wrote, "When Gee woke me I shouted at him to leave me alone. I would sleep when I chose, I told him, though this is not true since I can no longer sleep at night." He avoided saying why. I knew from the ledgers that two days before the planned rendezvous with Ellen he had left San Francisco, not on the *Nethercutt* but on a steamer heading north. No doubt he felt he was running for his life, but which life was that? The entries in these journals were brief, staccato images of a shoreline that would come to symbolize his life in America—here but not here, allowed in but invisible. The grief was there between the lines.

> Storm two days. We stopped as long as we could but were forced
> to go on in rough water. In the shallows we passed a wreck—
> named the *Sarah Mercy*—thrown high on the black rocks, her sails
> whipped to tatters by the freezing wind. It is July, but the world
> does not look bright....

For decades quotations like this had been passed over as having little more than a faint biographical interest. Now, with proof of the love affair, the real emotions reached through. The absence of any intimate mention of Ellen in Eng's writings proved that he consciously sought to protect himself, not just from being caught but from getting too close to love itself.

I didn't sleep much that night. The air was still muggy and the air conditioner broken. A night-shift crew was tearing up a parking lot under my window, and every time I drifted off someone started in with a jackhammer. By morning I felt leaden but got an early start.

The Hagen-Mills had some of Eng's later journals as well. I had little time and only skimmed these. I found a quotation relating to McFarland's study, where Eng had been allowed to read as a boy. It was there that McFarland, according to Eng, "introduced me to life." "I still dream of the study," he wrote some years after the affair.

> When anything troubled me, I would look out the window there
> and find comfort in the view. This picture, framed by the sashes,
> constantly recomposed itself, crossed by a seagull or the masts of a
> ship, or covered in veils of weather and light—the same and yet
> not the same, hidden by fog or disappearing in dark degrees.

In this paragraph Eng forecast his motivation for pursuing the *Return* landscapes. He always disparaged the landscapes, the work, as he put it, "done in periods of thoughtlessness, in a waking, dreamless sleep." I remembered what Diane had said about Eng's life running in predictable circles. It was true, there was a distinct pattern—the public attacks and impossible battles followed by retreats into the landscapes. By looking at the same scene over decades, was Eng trying to re-create the lost peace of mind he'd relished as a child while looking out a study window? "The changing pictures in the window," he said, "were like expressions on a familiar face." In my head I seemed to hear Ellen tell him, *Let me be your familiar face.* Eng later claimed there was no haven we could count on. In all his writings he seemed to be hiding love from himself, and his stubbornness began to annoy me. Finally I gave up reading and went downstairs to see some of the prints.

In Eng's case the Hagen-Mills made a point of collecting everything the DeWitt couldn't claim, mostly the odds and ends, the experiments, the flukes and mistakes. Periodically, to make money, Eng had indulged a photographic fad in which he posed hundreds of people in eye-tricking arrangements. In one, dated 1895, a convention of guild women stood in the shape of a giant Christmas tree. Another was of a 1914 regiment gathered into its eagle insignia on a dusty parade ground. Eng admitted that he enjoyed marshaling bodies for this sort of circus, calling out to assistants with a megaphone. In the ledger he'd written, "These images beg the eye to cross delicate borders: symbol or individuals? Life or the memory of life?" One of the guild women had been caught midsneeze, her head a blur, hand rising too late. There was an arrow in the eagle's claw, five men in the tip. The fierce glint in its eye was the lining of an upturned cap. Most scholars agreed this peculiar turn in his work was typical of the lengths Eng took to avoid facing the truer, gentler artist of the landscapes. Still, the experiment was not without a telling insight. Eng wrote,

> In square inches there is a shattering agglomeration: lips, nostrils, eyes, mustaches, flowered bonnets, spectacles, a pattern of folly

and choice, of bad marriages and mad uncles. We are all de-
scended from strangers, their luck reduced to essences that affect
our lives in ways we cannot guess at. In one hundred years these
individuals will all be gone. Our uniqueness, so intricate and
thorough, matters almost nothing to the litter we make of ourselves.

Despite this, Eng claimed it was foolish to take comfort in the avail-
able certainties, such as love; you died regardless of how long you
lasted. Anyone was drawn to photography for its trick of defying time.
And yet Eng's *Returns* derived their poignancy and tension from the
failure of art. They breathed of the fear and inevitability of change, of
the need for solidity and the knowledge that it didn't exist. Reading
these cryptic passages, I couldn't shake my annoyance, and I couldn't
figure out why right away.

Then it came to me: Wilfred Eng was bored. He showed all the
signs. He was restless. He lashed out like a shut-in. Misplaced emotion
undermined most of his social criticism. He was bored in the way cul-
pable people were, trying to outrun a life in which familiar disappointment kept mounting up. Maybe he belittled his landscapes
because he had plenty of time to and because he knew that rock and
sea and sand and trees changed more than he did. Diane was right: he
loved his own paralysis. His landscapes were meditations on his own
terrifying boredom, and he claimed to hate them because they
showed him the man he should have been.

....

That night Parker called my hotel.

I was glad to hear a familiar voice and felt an instant wave of reassurance—a delusion it was later painful to recall, since Parker had not
just arrived home in San Francisco as he claimed.

"Everything's set," he said after a pause meant to convey impatience at the uselessness of my trip. "Judy's in."

I swallowed. "She agreed?"

"No thanks to you."

"How much does she want?"

"She's being fair. I'm glad you're showing an interest, Robert."

"What's that supposed to mean?"

"Listen," he said, "this was a mistake."

"What happened? Is everything all right? Did Leonard pull out?"

"Nothing like that," Parker said. "It's your little field trip."

"You had your twins with you, for Christ's sake, and on our money."

"You're not the only one who gets itchy." He paused, letting the long distance drone portentously between us. Then he said, "I need you in San Francisco with the plates."

"I just got here."

"Judy is ready to hand them over right now. We need to move before something happens."

"Something *is* wrong."

"It's Meagan, but it's under control."

"What happened?"

"Leonard gives them work every once in a while," he said. "It's not hard to be nice to them, is it?" He paused again. "Meagan thinks she owes him something."

"Owes him what?"

"She thinks you're in New York making another deal."

"That's bullshit."

"I'm glad to hear it," Parker said.

"Did she tell him that?"

"Look. She's not going to be a problem. Just get back to Seattle and get the glass plates."

I hung up and sat there on the edge of my bed, wringing my hands and sweating in the mugginess. Nervous, uneasy, I picked up the phone again and dialed Leonard Sills. While the call went through I wondered what he would make of it. Would he think I was getting nervous? Would he sense that something was wrong and maybe back out? I hung up before anyone answered. Then I thought of calling Judith. But she was the last one I wanted to show weakness to. So I called home for my messages—but who did I hope would give me reassurance at this point? Was I hoping Diane had magically second-guessed herself? That she now wanted me back? There was nothing, only clicks followed by a whispering sound, like air passing over the receiver. Three thousand miles away I listened to this electronic breeze, my answering machine recording the rustle of its own works, a maundering, a dry digestion like ghost talk—the language of regret. What was I waiting for? Would Budge have called? Was his regard for me enough for him to defy his mother and call, regaling me with one of his adult voices? The thought of hearing his voice was suddenly unbearable. I remembered his greeting on the porch that first time, the air around us cool and fresh, his hand reaching up. I hung up.

I'd bought a deli sandwich at the corner and took a few bites now and chugged three beers. Then I managed a few hours' sleep despite the peppering jackhammer. Deep in the night I called out in my sleep and woke, panicked and sweating. Without thinking I reached for the phone and called the airline's twenty-four-hour reservations number. I had to get back. The woman I spoke to probably worked right downtown, but she sounded as if she were bathed in sunlight, untroubled by the vagaries and terrors of the night, by images that seemed to be dissolving as slowly as ice in the air around me. I didn't want to, but I had to go home—was it still "home"? Diane and Budge had made it that for a short time. In the dream that woke me Budge had spoken from the future. We had met in the street and he was grown, a stranger. He had used my own voice to tell me who he was.

I couldn't get a flight until noon, and yet when I woke the next morning I couldn't face the Hagen-Mills again—there would only be more of the same.

Instead, once I'd packed and checked out, I walked to the large brownstone near Schubert Alley where the Theater Guild of New York had its library and archives. Ellen Danforth McFarland had been on the board of the Guild for years and had left her diaries on deposit there. The Guild's librarian was a tall woman with a name tag that said, "Ms. Benning." Ms. Benning gave me a suspicious look, though her gaze was unfocused, refracted through the prism-thick lenses of her glasses. When I told her I was interested in looking over Ellen's later diaries she said, "Funny."

She cocked her head to one side and poked her graying hair with a pencil eraser, sizing me up, focusing her myopic gaze midway between us as if on some ghost Robert, some Robert aura she could read like a book. She didn't look ready to explain herself, so I said, "What's funny?"

"You writing a book too?"

"No. I'm doing research. I'm from Seattle," I added uselessly, as if this added honest sanctioning.

"Nobody's ever bothered with the later ones, not even that smarty-pants Marino," Ms. Benning said. "I take it you know who *she* is."

I took *The Love Diary* from my jacket pocket, and Ms. Benning grunted.

"Poor Ellen. Such a grand woman. Some people couldn't be bothered with the whole story."

"You've read all the diaries?" I asked, curious but also with a note of sarcasm.

Ms. Benning gave me a look of indignation softened by her watery gaze. "It's my *job*." She shook her head in disgust. "They dig up Ellen's bones, make a pile of money, then just dump her back in the grave."

Then she explained she could only give me one volume at a time, a "library policy" clearly of Ms. Benning's own invention. After a pause to let this statement sink in, she disappeared in the stacks behind her and returned with a thick journal covered in plain black leather.

When she handed it over I didn't notice right away that she didn't ask for ID like the DeWitt and the Hagen-Mills. There were a number of tables and oak library chairs, and I sat down with the volume in clear view of Ms. Benning behind her counter.

I had never seen Ellen's hand before. She was now in her sixties, and I wondered if her handwriting had evolved over the years or if at twenty, in a defining moment of her life, she had also managed this small, orderly script. In her introduction Carol Chase Marino said that the diary Ellen used when she and Eng were lovers was no bigger than a paperback and speculated that this made it easier to hide. Back in New York, Ellen used money from the sale of the San Francisco mansion—"that towering, turreted bird cage," as she later called it— to buy a small house that still stood on the east side. In this later diary the intensity had not disappeared but had merely changed pitch. Her sense of humor was still evident, but the desperation was missing, even when thinking about death. "I'm of a breed of women who die slowly in their thirties," I read.

> I'm a lifetime past due. Sometimes, when I don't have enough on my mind, my dying self seems to be choosing its place—"Find a comfortable spot," it says, "take care not to fall, you bruise easily." …Strange that the world has turned out as it has, that our minds & bodies are the way they are. Sometimes I think we're too complex, functional, even beautiful but far too much trouble. We're meant to put greed above love, selfishness above generosity & yet we almost never do.…

The summing up was like a reprimand, a hand reaching out from lost decades to slap my wrist. Once more I felt diminished before the dead. This woman was more real than I was, becoming more and more distinct; if I read on I might disappear completely.

"She's sixty-two years old," Ms. Benning called out in singsong, like a child reciting. "The 'L' she talks about is Linnea Outland. They met when Ellen was forty-four. They were housemates," she said, then paused before adding, "and lovers."

I looked at her. "What?"

"You heard me."

"Are you sure?"

"Of course I am."

"How do you know?"

"Ellen says so." She wagged her finger at the journal. "Read all the words," she said. "Don't be a Marino." She shook her head again. "Now *there* was a piece of work, with her tresses and her three names. Once I caught her moving her lips while she read. I almost offered Chapstick."

As I read it became clear that Ellen had lived a life with few regrets. She had not missed out on the sort of love she craved. She and Linnea Outland were an odd couple, Linnea robust and uncomplicated, Ellen introspective. It was not exactly what I wanted to read just now, someone succeeding at love. But the charm of their quiet clashes carried me halfway through this volume to the beginning of 1912, so that I'd completely forgotten that this was the year of Eng's New York show at Stieglitz's 291 Gallery.

April 1

A good day for foolish decisions. Driving home from dinner last night L insisted we detour past a gallery of some repute, where she pointed out the current artist's name in the window. My surprise was hard to hide. It was late, fortunately, & the place locked up or she'd have made us go in for a showdown.

This morning she asks again if I mean to go & gives a look when I say I see no point. L is always simplifying life & succeeding maybe better than I think.

Later. What I remember as warmth might only have been torrid heat blunted by uncomprehending youth. Must say I am compelled, though mostly curious, the way one is at a zoo. I want to

avoid the righteousness, also the temptation to ogle the disaster
this man & I avoided in each another. Perhaps I'll go just for the
pictures first....

I said, "Jesus Christ," out loud and looked up. Ms. Benning was inclined over a card file, benignly whorling her hair with the pencil
eraser. She didn't look up, only waved her hand and repeated impatiently, "*All* the words."

April 2
Decided going for the pictures was cowardly & so went to face the
man & ended up by making him ill!
   When I arrived the gallery was empty & he stood in a small
back office with his back to me. When he turned he recognized me
instantly. For a moment we stared—like apes in whom we recognize ourselves, like the apes time has turned us into. He turned
white as a ghost—I might have been Death itself staring back at
him. He put out his hand to steady himself but there was nothing
there & he stumbled. Instantly I came forward & took his elbow,
helping him into a chair. His color was truly alarming & I took his
other arm & turned to look for help. "Shall I go for a doctor?" I
asked & he just managed to shake his head, repeating that he was
fine. He was so weak it seemed he spoke sharply only to convince
himself. I fetched him a glass of water from a pitcher on a sideboard & he drank like a man in a desert. Coming back to himself
he seemed somewhat sheepish. For some reason I couldn't help
laughing & it was this he seemed to be waiting for. He took my
hand then—seized it in the old way. It almost seemed he would
touch his lips to it but then thought better & just as suddenly let
me go.
   In advance I'd scouted out a tea room around the corner & offered to take him there if he was feeling well enough. As we walked
I began to feel easier & just kept myself from saying that this was
the first time we had ever been in public together. I took the op-

portunity for a closer look. His jet-black hair—once such a
crop—is now as gray as my own & thinning across the whole top
of his head though still parted neatly in the center. He was not
oblivious to the looks people gave us. Seated with our tea, he told
me he thought age had made him look less Chinese. He said this
too loudly, like something he had said many times before. I remember thinking his dearness had derived from his having no
sense of humor about himself. And yet I wonder if he was being
completely serious when he then said, "Think what I could be if I
lived forever." I laughed again & he stared at me in that blank,
childlike way. He looked suddenly abashed, as if there were some
other meaning in these words that only he could hear. Then in the
same self-conscious voice he began to tell me about his aborted
trip to China, his stay in Hawaii & subsequent return to America.

In 1899, twenty-five years after the love affair, Eng had sailed for
Hong Kong, meaning to stay there for good. On the eve of this depar-
ture he had written to San Francisco photographer Horace Wilkes,
"On this trip I am tracing a route of despair." In the ledger entries
from this period he repeated the word "paralysis." It was the last year
of the century; he was fifty years old. He claimed he wanted to die in
the land of his parents. Instead, when he reached Hawaii an outbreak
of bubonic plague kept him quarantined there. Chinese on their way
to America had brought the disease with them to a section of
Honolulu known as the Native Quarter. To check the spread infected
shacks were set on fire and antiseptic baths erected, which Eng photographed. As if by accident he caught the same adrenal hysteria
found at cockfights. In these terrifying images seminaked men
shouted at others who cowered in a steaming pit. The images were
nightmares, the emotions for once unforced. There was nothing else
like them in his work. Eng also made portraits of poor Chinese coming from the opposite direction, as his mother had. "These poor
strangers and I have only one thing in common," he wrote ruefully,

"and that is that we are stranded. I share nothing with them, not even their courage." He needed a translator just to speak to them. In the end they might have changed his mind, though he claimed it was the spread of the disease in Asia that made him sail back to the States, never noting the irony at having made his own inevitable "return."

The vehemence was still intact. He apologized for the pictures on display, swearing that the land- & seascapes I saw had "no backbone." I smiled to myself at the delusion. If he truly despaired of these he would not submit them to galleries & to the competitions of which, almost in the same breath, he told me he has won many. I decided to tell him about my life, my theater work. Once more he looked surprised. Perhaps he was putting us together in his mind, imagining how different our lives might have been. But no, I don't think it was that. He did not so much resent what I had done with my life as he didn't seem to be paying attention. Frankly it annoyed me & so I turned the talk to lighter subjects. After close to an hour I told him I had to go.

Out in the street again he said, "I have thought of you often." He seemed to force the admission. There was a question in his eyes. He wasn't asking forgiveness but something more—something, maybe, to gauge the extent of his own delusion. Forgiveness I gave him decades ago. But his look, his lingering, angered me again as silent expectation often does. I managed to hide this with a smile, I think, & to assure him gave his cheek a kiss.

This had a most unbelievable effect.

Standing there on the sidewalk among the passersby, he gave a sudden cry & covered his mouth. His chest shuddered & his eyes filled with tears. I took his arm again. It startled & bewildered me that the past seemed to be so fresh in his mind. "I'm sorry," I told him. "I shouldn't have come." But he only shook his head. He looked ready to speak but said nothing. I offered to walk him back to the gallery but this too he refused. When he felt better he raised his eyes & looked at me with the same unaskable question. Then,

still shaky on his feet, he turned & I watched him until he disappeared around the corner....

When I finally surfaced and looked up, Ms. Benning was not at her
desk. Instead she had sneaked up behind me, and when she spoke I
jumped so that my wooden chair barked loudly against the linoleum
floor.

"You could have beaten Marino over the head with that." She
wagged at the journal again, at its startling revelations. "She wouldn't
have cared. Such a busy little bee and so smug, every five minutes
dashing off to meet editors and film producers at the Russian Tea
Room."

"So you didn't."

"Didn't what?" Ms. Benning poked innocently at her scalp.

"Beat her over the head with it." I held up the black journal. "You
didn't show her these later ones?"

She shrugged. "She never asked. Miss Moffet Marino got on my
nerves in a big way, pushing my face in her Ph.D. every chance she got.
If I'd had one iota what she was doing I'd have strangled her with her
fifty-dollar hairdo. She was a sex maniac, you can tell from those nov-
els she wrote. Is it any wonder nobody's heard a peep from her in ten
years?" She looked at her watch, bringing the face within inches of her
eyes. "Time for my espresso."

I looked at my own watch. "Christ, I'm late."

Ms. Benning's eyes narrowed. "Lunch at the RTR?"

Then she reached over and snatched the black book from my
hands.

"You people never understand. Life is moments, but it isn't *just* moments. Marino had a public orgasm all over Ellen Danforth and left the
whole world with the wrong idea. So you won't mind my asking what
your story is, Mr. Squeaky-Clean Seattle. What are *you* after? What
pretty mess are you going to make that nobody will ever forget?"

April 3

L's brother & family spent the afternoon with us here playing cards & having tea. All have just gone home & for once the quiet isn't welcome. All day I've wanted what's mine around me, to protect myself with home, friends, accomplishments. When I think of Wilf it's less by himself than as part of the larger picture of the past which is perhaps never that far away. Thought myself so solicitous today but Linnea's grandnieces (and L herself) caught me with my mind wandering....

Later. Spent two hours in the attic just now with early writings, my younger self purer in many ways, preferable in some. Strange what a jumble time is. After decades I felt blood in my cheek & remembered the uncertainty & gnawing fear, the thing that forced me along no longer recognizable as love or any other sane emotion. His face looked so old, I could almost read the hesitation there—he was always so sure of himself. Maybe it surprised him to learn that in some ways we are two sides of the same coin. Just this moment realized that in deciding whether I should see him at all I was also deciding whether to acknowledge to him that he also gave me my freedom for which I am very grateful. He was to have met me & he did not—that deep long-ago humiliation made my current life possible. My youth was shaped by strong men. Each was meant to be the solution to the last. Their strengths (including Papa's) were very different except in their pitch & blindness. At one point I'd thought to "remake myself on a foundation of pain," which is nothing more than what these men sought to do. Given enough time I wonder if my present belief—that yielding is the greatest strength—would not also make me blush....

9

....

"You son of a bitch!" Judith Lund screamed.

I'd come straight to her studio from the airport and stood at the door, which she blocked, feet apart, hands on her hips. Behind her, against the back wall of her studio, one of her huge canvases had been slashed to ribbons; wide paint-caked strips of it flopped on the floor. Now Judith backed up, gesturing like a punch-hungry boxer.

"Come on," she said. "Come on in. Make yourself comfortable while I call the cops!"

I broke past her for the storage room, not realizing that Pollock was strategically absent.

All the cupboard doors had been pried off. Caught in one of the cabinet hinges were dark fibers. Christiana. I remembered her gracefully unhooking her legs from my neck, then looking at her moon-faced watch. "We're late," she'd said, though we weren't. Faint roses in her cheeks were the only sign that anything had happened. For added insurance, when she'd dropped me at the airport there had been more grappling on the front seat of the Benz. It wasn't hard to picture Christiana with a crowbar, reaching and bracing her body as she had on my desk, going at it so hard she didn't notice her sweater catching. Parker might only have looked on, amused and fascinated by this show of agility and strength.

They'd broken one. The pieces lay on the floor in a corner. It was one of the nudes, Ellen lying in a long, warm slant of sun. I squatted down as if over something dead and wondered if Parker had blown his stack at last, totting up the lost dollars. But then I thought, no, they had done this on purpose. This was for me, a sucker's farewell. A wooden-nickel tip. I turned to see Judith staring at me from the door, the phone to her ear.

"When did this happen?"

"As if you didn't know."

"You think *I* did this?"

She lowered the phone but kept glaring. "I should have known you were up to something. Those negatives. They're worth something."

"They're Wilfred Eng's," I said. "Don't tell me Parker didn't tell you."

For a moment she looked as if she couldn't speak.

"We were going to cut you in," I said and stopped when I heard how absurd this sounded.

"He offered me a show, and that was it."

"He said you agreed to the whole thing."

"You're in up to your ass," Judith snarled. "You'd say anything."

But this anger was hollow. I looked at her, trying to get a fix on it. "Did you actually meet Leonard Sills in California?"

"He was out of town."

"I'll bet he was."

She looked suddenly bewildered, and I almost felt sorry for her.

"I knew that before we flew down there," she said. "Parker wanted me to see the show space."

"He told me Leonard wined and dined you," I said. Judith looked honestly confused, and I fell for it. "He's probably selling the negatives to Leonard right now. Did he have a key to your studio?"

Her gaze wavered, and she leaned back against the counter. "Shit."

"He set us both up."

"Not that it matters much to you." She looked suddenly drawn and put her hand to her face. But this too, I would shortly find out, was a masterful piece of acting. "You haven't just lost a fortune," she said.

Neither have you, I thought, then blanched when she looked up with blood in her eye.

"Somebody's going to pay big for all of this," she said, dialing the phone again. "I'm going to lock you two lying shits up and throw away the key."

"I didn't do it," I pleaded. "I was out of town." She put the phone to her ear and glared at me. "Look, I still have five."

She dropped the phone. "So you *did* steal them! You pilfering fuck!"

"No," I said, exasperated, suddenly scared. "Jesus. Listen to me. I'm talking about the ones of Eng you gave to Parker."

"I made it so easy for you, didn't I?"

"That was before we saw these." I pointed lamely at the wrecked cabinet. "We put them in a bank vault along with a broken one I took down to the basement."

"*My* basement."

"I tried to tell you that first day, but you wouldn't answer your door. Look, the five are going to be worth a lot. You can have them, they're yours."

"The man says I can have what's already mine. You thieving bastard. You've got one hour."

I got to the bank just before it closed. When I got back with the case in my arms, Pollock had appeared. With the hand not holding his leash, Judith pointed at a spot on the floor. As I passed, Pollock swiveled his muzzle like a howitzer, his barks all finding the mark. When I set down the case, that "WE" scrolled on its old lid looked mournful, pathetically out of place. *Coward*, I thought. I straightened up to face Judith.

"Does this square us?" I asked and heard the belittled desperation.

Judith's answer came between Pollock's barks, her words skipping like a voice on a scratched record. I got the gist of it: I'd be hearing from her.

Then I was back outside, walking down the street in an upright faint. This was worse than Weston. Even if I didn't get blamed for trashing Judith's painting, she could make my life miserable. I'd have to find another town, maybe another line of work. I stopped at the corner near the Glorien's next-door neighbor. A workman came out the front door, and I watched him move down the sidewalk, shadow spilling up his back, then peeling him—a sight gag, a practical joke played out right under all our noses. When I got to my apartment I found the joke was far from over.

Opening the door, I smelled smoke.

I ran down the hall to my office, quaking with terror. The photographs on the walls were all intact, though the office itself had been trashed. After our session on the desk Christiana had made sure the front door was unlocked. She and Parker had found the rough prints I'd made in Judith's bathroom and burned them in the metal wastebasket. All that remained were corners where they'd held the flaming pictures and a fragment showing just Ellen's hand. I may only have imagined it, but one large deliquescent flake of ash seemed to show her face outlined, weirdly preserved, a negative once more.

Stepping across the floor littered with files, books, and computer disks, I found my answering machine under the desk, its plastic top broken off. When I pressed the play button the tape spools tugged and loped, and I heard only the same clicks and hiss. While I listened the phone rang. It was Meagan.

"I've been calling you for two days," she said.

"Parker broke my machine. He trashed my office."

"He figured you were holding out."

Parker, she told me, was donating the plates to the DeWitt.

Rather than showing the two plates to Leonard, Parker had taken them to the DeWitt's photo curator, a man named Freer Donaldson.

Donaldson had said it was likely Eng in the negatives but wanted more proof. Parker said he had it. He told Donaldson he was going to open his own gallery in downtown San Francisco and wanted the DeWitt to help. Donaldson refused. When I recognized Ellen in Judith Lund's cabinet, Parker called Donaldson back and told him, and this time Donaldson capitulated—the DeWitt would open all the cultural doors for Parker, send him a list of fat clients, and even pull strings to help him find a prime location. Otherwise out of the running with his track record, Parker would be a shoo-in with such a donation. It would turn him into a saint and inspire trust and faith in his future patrons.

At this point Parker let Judith in.

In bed with Parker, Judith had confided in him, describing how the dreadful reaches of her desperation had left her lonely and friendless, had made people think she was an awful bitch. It was Parker she viewed as her potential savior, not the Eng plates. Wilfred Eng be damned. If Judith ended up out in the cold again, what did she care about a moldy old romance or, really, about the plates themselves, these panes of glass smeared with dirty egg whites? It was recognition she wanted, and recognition on her own terms. She'd confessed to Parker that she hated Seattle, that she was frustrated to the breaking point by living in the overwhelming shadow of the past and of her more colorful ancestors.

Capitalizing on contacts of Leonard's and his own boundless initiative, Parker had managed to do what no one else could: he sold one of Judith's paintings. Judith was ecstatic. If he could do it for one he could probably do it for her other orphan canvases. She agreed not only to turn over the plates but also to spot him money for start-up costs. Needless to say, Parker would hang her paintings regularly at his new gallery. Her work would always have a home. She would never be an outsider again.

"That bitch Judith still has the doors," Meagan said.

"What are you saying?"

"Oh, man, they really took you. The doors are still at her studio."

"You're crazy. Parker stole them. He trashed her place just like he trashed mine. He slashed one of her paintings."

"Judith agreed to that. The whole thing was a setup to get you to give up the five in the bank. You didn't, did you?"

I could answer only with a constricted silence. Meagan went on in a more subdued voice, with quiet awe for someone so trusting and stupid. "Parker's going to drive the glass to California in a van. He's waiting up there in a motel by the airport. He's fucking my sister over," she said. "He promised Chris and me a thousand each. I know that bitch Judith has given him money, but he told us he was broke. I bailed, but he promised Chris a job. She's going to get shit."

The $2,000 was my end of the whole deal, chump change for doing exactly what Parker wanted me to. Parker's sudden yen for independence and legitimacy shouldn't have been a surprise. A gallery of his own meant, most of all, the promise of many smaller payoffs. He was a salesman at heart. He'd never believed in the possibility of printing the plates. The negatives were an albatross if you did anything but get rid of them. Parker had recognized his limitations, something I had yet to do.

I hung up, now in a state something beyond rage. Outside again, I stalked back down the street and had just made it to the front of Judith's building when good sense or despair took over. If I went back up there I would have only Pollock to deal with. At the corner the same workman walked back up through the gauntlet of light and shadow. He nodded at me and went through the doors. Inside I heard saws and hammers. A condo conversion was in progress. Above the double doors a large sign listed the general contractor, the architect, and the structural consultant below the name "The Fourchen Partners." I stared at it for a long time. Then the blood drained out of my head.

....

The next evening Parker Lange showed up at my apartment. I'd been expecting him. He wouldn't come in, choosing instead to stay in the hall. He'd lost the glasses and glared at me nakedly.

"I'm thinking about some coffee," I said. "Do you want some?"

"You're so fucking bright."

I was bright because I'd figured out that Judith Lund, though ignorant of their value at the time, had stolen the plates herself.

When I called the number of the Fourchen Partners it was answered in the offices of a lawyer named Stanley Chen. The home on Maynard Street where Wilfred Eng had died had been owned by Tommy Chen, who was Eng's cousin and, in this case, heir.

Stanley Chen knew Judith well and had recently tangled with her when she refused to grant him easements for reinforcement work on the basement wall their two buildings shared. I lied, trying to make Judith sound innocent, telling Stanley that her side of the basement was crammed with ancient junk and that she honestly believed the plates had belonged to her family. He wasn't buying it. "Even if it were true that she didn't actually think she was stealing," Stanley said, "she knew who her neighbors were. *You* figured it out," he said. "Why couldn't she?" He said he was angry enough to bring charges against Judith, and I reflected miserably that if he did, she would never forget that I was the one who had tipped him off. When we hung up he thanked me profusely.

Parker's eyes bored into me. Then he blinked. "You have to admit I almost had you cold."

"You and Judith both," I said. "Slashing the painting was a convincing touch."

"I did that myself," Parker said with a faint grin. "Judy had to leave the room. I'm on the run," he added more soberly. Meagan had gone to Leonard, and Leonard had called the DeWitt, then fired Parker. "I have no cash," Parker added.

I'd put the whole New York trip on a credit card and still hadn't touched the $2,000. I got it now and gave it to him. He looked amused.

"Couldn't bring yourself to spend it, could you? Honest Armour. Maybe things will turn out all right for you, Robert," he said. "Getting tarred and feathered in this town might be like a warm bath anywhere else."

Then he turned and walked back down the hall.

....

Stanley Chen was the great-grandson of Tommy Chen. He and his father and two uncles were partners in various business ventures, including the conversion of the Glorien's neighbor. Judith Lund, snooping in the basement adjoining hers, had found the plates there, and she'd already decorated the doors of her new cabinet with the negatives of Ellen before it occurred to her that they might be worth something. When I told Stanley about the find, leaving out all the sordid parts, he was clearly excited. He knew Eng's work well; he even owned a number of Eng photographs. Over the phone I told him as little as I thought I could get away with, counting on his excitement and interest to keep him from digging too deeply right away. I convinced him to call Freer Donaldson at the DeWitt. This did what I'd hoped it would and derailed Parker's plan. Anxious to avoid the wrong sort of scandal and knowing something of Parker's past, Donaldson had disowned him.

The same afternoon I gave Parker back his money, I met with Stanley Chen. When I arrived Stanley's excitement and gratitude had vanished. He didn't offer his hand.

"I talked to this Donaldson again today," Stanley said. I would have felt relieved at this news except for Stanley's doubtful look. "He actually called *me*. You know him?"

"I know of him," I said and swallowed. "We've never actually met."

"He seems to *know of* you too. He's flying in tomorrow morning," Stanley added, then stared at me. Stanley Chen was a short, handsome man with dark eyes like afterthoughts, seamlessly placed in the calm planes of his face. His steady gaze seemed to go right through me. I answered, "Good," as calmly as I could. Stanley seemed to expect some other reaction, as if Donaldson, a stately though fractious man, might be bringing along my death warrant. I thought this might be a good time to confess. But Stanley stood suddenly and said, "The others are waiting," then led me down a hallway to a conference room.

Approaching the door, we heard raised voices. The three brothers were arguing in Chinese but stopped abruptly when Stanley and I entered. They stood to shake hands, a hopeful sign. Stanley's father, Ed, the oldest, introduced the middle brother, Patrick, and the youngest, Tony. I was offered coffee, which I refused. Then we all sat down.

The exchange was polite at first. The three brothers were thrilled by the discovery and praised Eng as a great artist. The talk shifted to their grandfather's boarding house, where the brothers had lived until the fire. Eng had used the house as a kind of way station since the 1890s, leaving many of his belongings in the basement. After the fire, undamaged items—the negatives among them—had been dispersed to various other buildings in the area that the Chen family also owned.

"Wilfred liked Grandpa a lot," Ed Chen said. "He kept thinking he might settle down here. I don't think the guy could make up his mind." Ed was in his late seventies and remembered Eng from the '30s, when he was a boy and Eng elderly but spry. Eng, he said, let Ed rifle the pockets of his billowing suits, where he kept tart hard candies. He allowed himself to be called "Grandpa Wilfred," though his movements were quick as a boy's. Ed had brought along a birthday postcard "Grandpa Wilfred" had sent him. He handed it across to me. The writing, though still upright, was spidery and frail. The ink had turned brown, each penstroke now like the tracks of two minute wheels, fading to white at the center. The card said, "Many happy returns." In later life Eng watched all his causes fade away unresolved. His artistry never made peace with his politics. The high points of his public life—the rallies, the invective—all sounded hollow and cosmetic in the end. In his seventies he attacked a prominent New Jersey chemical company then sponsoring individual photography projects and, Eng rightly claimed, excluding any but white photographers. Eng panicked at the idea of not making such statements—an effect, perhaps, of that profound boredom.

"I was there at the end," Ed Chen said. The room went quiet. "I watched him in the window. He carried these big fancy pocket hankies. There was smoke billowing around him, and he held this hanky to his nose."

"These crazy white people started it," the youngest explained. This brother was a man of about sixty-five and gestured with sharp, emphatic jabs. "The cops didn't give a damn. Patriotic zeal and all that. Blood lust for the Yellow Peril."

"There was a crowd of us," Ed went on. "Nobody said anything. It was weird, it was so quiet. He looked like he was looking for someone in the crowd. When he saw me he waved."

"Wait a minute," Tony said. "I never heard that."

"He *waved*," Ed insisted.

"Bull."

"You were there?"

Tony looked around at the rest of us. "I mean, is that what you'd do in a burning building? Stand there waving? Am I right or what?"

"Nobody knows what they'll do at the end," Patrick, the middle brother said and smiled at me.

Then a grim silence settled over the wide table. Stanley had clearly found out more about me, but I didn't know if he had filled the others in. Tony asked how I'd figured out that the negatives belonged to them. When I mentioned the "Fourchen" sign he said, "It's a pun—Fourchen, fortune."

Then after a silence Ed said, "Stan has told us everything he knows. He thinks you know a lot more."

My face flushed, then blanched. I felt Stanley looking at me and didn't dare look back. I cleared my throat and then plunged in.

When I finished, Ed fingered his old postcard and murmured, "Still screwing the yellow man."

"You say the right place for them is with this museum," Tony said. "How come?"

"Eng wanted it that way."

"They'll try to cash in too, won't they?" Stanley asked.

It wasn't really a question, and when I glanced at him he looked back as if to encourage any way I chose to hang myself.

"Look," I said. "I know this looks bad. It *is* bad."

"We know what you tell us, but we don't know much else," Stanley said. "Maybe you make a habit of taking risks. Maybe you're just another careless guy."

"If we manage to get the plates back and do what you say, we might be playing right into your hands," Ed said.

"You're repenting a little too fast," Tony put in bluntly. "If this guy Lange hadn't screwed you, you'd have gone ahead and made your money, right?"

"I would have donated the plates eventually."

"We have just your word for that."

"You managed to break one before you even got started," Stanley said.

"That wasn't me."

"What's the difference? How many would have been left at the end?"

"None of it went the way it was supposed to," I said and heard in my voice the shrill certainty that it never would have.

"Like the gallery you lost in San Francisco," Stanley said. "You left out that part."

"I don't see what that has to do with this."

"I'll bet you don't."

"That was years ago."

"Your buddy Lange was here to see me."

Stanley looked like he'd been waiting for a reason to be pleased, and the look on my face must have done it.

"He painted a pretty grim picture of you," Stanley said. "This Freer Donaldson agrees. It seems you have a rep."

"I sold my gallery to get out of debt," I said. "I was cheated."

"And now turnabout is fair play," Stanley said. He pointed at his father. "Dad's right. This could all still work out in your favor."

"That's the last thing I want at this point."

"You could get a lot of mileage for your business," Stanley said. "We donate the plates and then what? You're the one who found them. It's you they'll want to talk to." He leaned back in his chair, touching his steepled fingers to his lips. "The expert," he said. "I could probably figure a way to have your expert ass thrown in jail."

"Stan, is that really necessary?" Patrick asked.

Stanley said nothing and kept glaring at me. My spine felt like it wouldn't hold me upright. My brain did fever dances. When I opened my mouth again, either to defend myself or beg, Stanley interrupted. "My father and my uncles and I have a lot to talk about," he said and nodded toward the door. "We'll be in touch."

....

Leaving Stanley Chen's office, I felt dazed and raw and manifestly friendless, so on the way home I stopped at Kau Kau for ribs and beer to go. What Diane had once called "bachelor comfort food" would have its work cut out for it. As I headed for my apartment with the food, it came to me that my part in this fiasco might be over with quickly, if painfully. When Freer Donaldson got here the next morning I could tell him everything I knew and take the predictable abuse. The hard part would be living with the aftermath. Once more I thought about leaving, heading farther north, maybe, to some watery

Canadian province. I could find a cabin on a cool spit too small to show up on maps, a wan finger of land pointing nowhere. I was already feeling like a stranger here. My apartment, when I got back there, still had the unfamiliar look it had acquired that afternoon when Parker sat at my desk totting up all the money we would make. I pulled the shades. I planned to drink all six Tsing Taos, priming the pump for a marathon of self-pity. But I didn't get the chance. The phone rang.

Now it starts, I thought. Holed up during the Weston trouble, I used to pray to my telephone, hoping the next hate call would turn out to be salvation instead. The phone kept bringing the same bad news, but I couldn't bring myself to unplug it even after heaving it against the wall. Now I picked up the receiver. It was Budge.

"Where are you?" I asked. "Are you okay?"

"I'm still at school."

I looked at my watch. It was after four. Diane, he told me, had left that morning for Orcas Island on foundation business. "Daddy was supposed to pick me up." He was not so much nervous as tentative, which meant he knew I was the last person he should have called— knew, therefore, how completely I was out of the picture. "I was going to take the bus, but I couldn't remember how."

"No, don't do that. Stay right there," I said. "I'll come get you."

He said okay, and I hung up. The negatives had put distance between Budge and me. But the boy's call had suddenly tipped the whole picture, given it a new perspective from which Budge and I now *looked* like something. We had history. Discarded, a thing of the past, our relationship now showed a character of its own. Ignoring the beer and food, the consolations for a bad day, I picked up my keys and hurried out, feeling a faint elation. But if I believed for a moment that going after Budge was an escape from everything that had happened or raised me a notch above negligent Michael, I got a rude reminder when I reached my car.

"Mother of God."

Snitch. Fuckhead. Asshole on Board. Between the words spray-painted on the hood, fenders, and windows were lurid cocks-and-balls, mooning bums, and splayed vulvae—art imitating Parker Lange's anger.

I couldn't see out the sides and had to drive with the windows open. Pedestrians and other drivers gaped and leered. At such moments you longed for the protection of a society whose citizens had supposedly seen everything. At Budge's school I parked a block away.

I found him standing inside the school's front door with his Masters of the Universe backpack and a teacher named Mrs. Harmon. When Budge introduced us I gave her the sort of smile no one would trust. "I'm a friend of the family," I said.

"Of Michael's?" she asked hopefully. Apparently Michael had been making headway here too, snowing the whole PTA for all I knew. Clearly she didn't want to believe Michael Mays capable of forgetting something so important and looked at me as if I should now come up with a plausible excuse for him.

"Diane's," I said.

Mrs. Harmon thought about this, then turned to Budge. "Will you be all right?" she asked, and he answered, "Sure." But he was still tentative and formal as we walked down the block. Seeing the car broke the ice. At first he looked at the next car down, thinking his eyes were playing tricks on him. Then he let out a yelp that was half shock, half joy. This too seemed to fit an old pattern. He read the whole car at top volume. Never had there been so many words in one place he didn't have to sound out. He finished off at the trunk with *Pervert*—Parker, I guessed, had added this for Christiana. As we pulled away from the curb Budge asked, "Who did it?"

"What makes you think I'd know?"

The boy grew quiet. When I tried to soften my sharpness I heard the victim's whine and stopped. We drove on in silence. At a stoplight a group of older women in the next car made a concerted effort not to look at us. As we pulled away Budge said, "Mom says you guys aren't seeing each other anymore." He didn't mean it as reproof. His voice was unsure again, as if he wouldn't come out and say that his father had come home to stay. I felt a deep, quavering ache, as if I hadn't truly believed any of it until hearing it from his mouth. Suddenly I imagined him years from now, as in that New York dream, looking back on this moment. Who would he see driving him home? What would he think?

At Diane's it appeared that no one was home. I'd have to stay until Michael showed. Michael, the resurrected man of the house. Without Diane around he would show his true colors. He would savor his victory as if it were a cuckolding. But I didn't think about that right away. Instead, as Budge settled down in front of the TV, I went out to the kitchen. It was less like stepping back in time than visiting my own forfeited future. Just last month I had been part of this home, this kitchen with its lingering blend of smells, its cupboards exuding spice and order. There were even a few of my beers left in the refrigerator. I opened one and walked up the hall, stopping at the boy's bedroom. I remembered Diane telling me she had redone this room five years ago. She had steamed off one layer of wallpaper and found another, patterned with the same bluebells and Bo Peeps she'd had in her own room at age five. "A million kids probably had that paper," she'd said, showing me the scrap she'd saved. She'd done all the work herself. She hadn't run to another city. Instead she had shored herself against emotional carnage, resetting the time clock at zero. Beneath all the layers, less permanent than the old plaster itself, which she eventually tore out, Diane had found names and dates and scribbled messages to the future. She had made this discovery in the aftershock of a marriage this house was supposed to have saved. And now, years later, it had.

For me everything here had lost function and intimacy. The house was like a museum display showing how one woman had forged her own permanence over the tyranny of memory. I looked in the hall closet—my two shirts still hung there. In the bathroom my brush lay on the counter. My razor and shaving cream were in the medicine chest, where Diane had made still more room. I couldn't imagine moving these things, taking them away, using them again. They were part of a story I would affect in no other way. I sat down on the toilet seat. I saw all these items in a single box, saw myself holding it sheepishly at the front door. I would try different smiles, different looks of silent apology, appeals for understanding. I would become an artifact in all their minds, less real than the missing comb or sock they would find months later under the chair or behind the cushion. Where would I be when that happened? What would I be doing then? And when Diane thought of me, would there be a pang or a bad taste, or worse, relief? Would she feel, as Ellen Danforth McFarland had, that she'd been saved from a terrible mistake? The room seemed to swoon as in a dream, as if I were only remembering it, flutes in the shower curtain wavering as if my presence here were departing in a faint breeze.

Then the shower curtain shot aside like a scorched ghost, and a woman bolted out.

The woman was wrapped in one of Diane's bed sheets. Her hip grazed my nose, and before she disappeared out the door, blond hair flying, she snapped, "Excuse the fuck out of me."

For a moment I worried less about who she was than why, given other likelier possibilities, she seemed angry. When I came out into the hall, there was Michael—Duff himself—beckoning from Diane's bedroom, touching his finger to his lips. He had on Diane's robe, which barely covered him. Hesitating at first, I walked up the hallway and stepped inside, and he shut the door gingerly behind me. The woman sat on the bed, glaring at me boldly.

A faint grin played at the corners of Michael's mouth. "Becky, Robert. Robert, Becky."

With at best a watery righteousness I told Michael, "You were sup-posed to pick Budge up after school."

"I forgot, didn't I. I saw you pull up," he added. "What a relief, though your new paint job really threw me. Very '60s, Robert. I thought either the Smiths' kid was home from college or the neigh-borhood was going downhill."

He smiled radiantly.

"Look, I'm getting Budge out of here," I said, though then I thought, *Why bother? Let the kid see his old man for what he really is.*

"That sounds fine," Michael said, his tone calibrated to show nei-ther irony nor gratitude. He opened the door a foot and ushered me through like the help. At the last second he mouthed, "I'll call you."

Back in the living room, Budge gazed at the television. He hadn't heard a thing.

"What do you say we go back to my place?" I said, my voice tellingly loud, full of false confidence. I snatched up my jacket and his, then stood beside his chair, bouncing on my toes.

"We just got here," Budge said, not turning from the screen.

"It looks like your dad's a no-show."

"How do you know?"

"Come on, we'll order pizza."

"You don't have cable."

"I just got it," I lied.

"We should leave Daddy a note."

"I took care of it," I said and pulled him up by his sleeve.

....

"The woman said it's going to be a while," Budge said, hanging up my phone. I'd let him read my Visa number to the Pizza Hut clerk while I tried to straighten up my living room. Picking up food cartons and plates from the floor and making neat piles of magazines, I raged in-wardly at Michael, at the likelihood of his getting away with it all.

"There's a baseball game," Budge explained, watching me bustle angrily around the room. "They're kind of busy."

The Kingdome was three blocks down, though I largely ignored the crowds coming and going for sports events. Now through the open windows we could hear people three stories below, talking softly as they passed.

"Do you ever go to baseball games?" he asked.

"Almost never."

He thought about this. "Neither does my dad," he said, as if he had a right to be disappointed that fathers and former role models didn't act the way they were supposed to.

"What smells funny?" he asked.

"I had a little fire," I said, though suddenly it seemed that the air smelled less of smoke than regret. I went to the windows and opened one. Budge wouldn't quite look at me. Clearly he was pondering the wisdom of coming back here, and maybe of the larger picture as well—my errors, Michael's second chance. His eyes teemed with doubt. He gazed at the middle distance, playing idly with a stack of magazines, lifting the edges and letting them flop.

"Could you stop that, please?" I said.

"It sounds like farts," he answered in a challenging voice.

"That would be a good reason for stopping, and how about right now."

He held up a thumbful of pages and gave me a stare scarily like his dad's. "You don't have cable," he said.

"It must be broken."

"Cable can't break."

He looked at me as if this lie would be harder to bear than knowing his dad had screwed some bimbo in his mother's bed. I felt suddenly sorry for him: the grown boy of my dream would end up not with my voice but with Michael's. That was certain cause for despair.

"Let's get a movie," I said.

Down the street at the video store, Budge's spirits picked up. He roved the aisles, knowing exactly what he was looking for. Done, he handed me his choices and I shuffled through them.

"Diane lets you watch this stuff?"

"My dad does," he said, almost like an admonishment: if I'd stuck around and behaved, he'd have let me have a crack at breaking all his bad habits. I paid for the videos with the same Visa card, and we left.

Back at my apartment, the pizza arrived and I took it out to the kitchen and served it up on plates in a further effort at bringing some kind of order to the evening. When I brought dinner out to the living room Budge had already loaded a cassette. Amazons with breast jobs and buckskin bikinis were fighting orb-headed invaders whose planet needed slaves. Budge had ordered the pizza exactly to his liking and ate with surprising greed. No doubt he rarely saw food like this in his mother's kitchen. I could almost see his mind ranging ahead to his own bachelorhood with its peculiar brand of logic, its delayed necessities, its piggybacked vices. The movie was a send-up of Romeo and Juliet. When it came time for the kiss Juliet's whole head disappeared inside her lover's cranial orifice. Lubricious, pulsing moments passed, the camera zooming in tight. Finally she drew her head out and smiled tenderly through the slime. Budge belched, then glanced at me quickly before wiping his hands on his pants.

"Shouldn't you wash?" I said without much authority.

"You wash *before* dinner."

White men came with an electronic decapitator—"de-Capuleter," someone actually said. Romeo dispatched and the Orbs routed, the men picked one Amazon each and turned them into wives. Grateful at first, the women were soon deep in kids and dishwater and every so often looked longingly to the stars, to which Juliet had returned, grieving, with her new people.

When the credits rolled the boy went up the hall to the bathroom. He was gone for a long time, and when I went to find him I saw the light on in my office. I still hadn't cleaned up in there, and Budge now stood in the middle of the floor, taking in the mess. It was clear he was seeing me in a whole new light, with a pride that was wholly inappropriate. I felt my face flush. I stammered that the same guy who had painted my car was responsible for this and heard the same straining self-pity. He asked, "What did you do to make him so mad?" His avidity made me blanch. This whole evening was a bad impression that required correction. So why not tell him everything? The idea was suddenly compelling, though maybe because my sort of trouble would sound familiar to an eight-year-old. Stealing. Lying. Name-calling. Budge could relate. Or maybe in the long run whatever he knew about me wouldn't make much difference. So I started in, and all at once the words flowed as if they'd been waiting. I poured out everything to him—Judith, the plots, the plates, the greed. I heaped all blame on myself. Halfway through, Budge looked blank. But I hadn't so much lost him as that he seemed to be hearing something else. He seemed to know that this confession cost me nothing since I now had nothing to lose. I stopped midsentence, and the boy looked past me as if seeing the truth plain as spray-painted porn. Finally, with a kind of wincing apology, he asked, "Can we watch another movie?"

Halfway through the second film—a Kung Fu bloodfest—the boy fell sound asleep. Sitting next to me, he keeled over like a sapling in a hurricane, the crown of his head touching my sofa cushion. He looked like he'd snap in two if I left him like that. When I lifted him now, he was nowhere near torpedo-stiff. It was as if I were holding him together. His head lolled, and he moaned the way I'd heard him through the wall when Diane went in to him on her nighttime visits. I took him into my bedroom, and when I laid him down on the bed he forced his eyes open. I stood over him, looking down as if expecting his judgment. He didn't seem to see me. Then he turned on his side and gave in to sleep.

I got another beer and watched the rest of the movie, a kind of Eastern version of Valhalla in which sweet-spot haymakers had little effect and assassins, shot with machine pistols, still had enough juice for roundhouse kicks. It all seemed more like disappointed sport than dying. After a time I fell asleep too and woke to knuckle taps on my front door.

"Goddamn it."

The beer had spilled in my lap, giving up a barny odor and drying around the edges. I looked at my watch—twelve-thirty. I went to the door and opened it a crack. Michael peered through with mock politeness. He hadn't called first, as he had said he would. When he saw the beer stain he said, "Am I interrupting something?"

I motioned him in, remembering at the last minute not to slam the door. "Didn't you bring her along?"

"She has an early shoot tomorrow. Beck's a model. I told her all about you and your photography. She'd like to meet you again sometime."

"It's after midnight."

"God, is it?"

"He's sound asleep," I said. "You should have been here hours ago. What the hell kept you?" I asked and flushed again.

Michael lit up his smile, then doused it. "What would *you* do, Robert? It might be the last pussy I get for a while."

He gave me a meaningful look, and I knew I was in for it: Michael had come to deal. He would stand his own sins against mine and thereby gain my silence.

"I'm just back from home," he said, stepping into the living room and looking around. "Mama was in a bad way, so I stayed on longer," he added. I wondered if Michael felt that filial duty entitled him to a tumble with Becky. "Butch must have told you," he said. "Butch," I remembered, was Michael's endearment, which the boy had mispronounced at two. Michael now spoke the original distinctly, as if he would force it into prominence no matter what anyone else had gotten used to. "Diane told you about Sonny?" I didn't answer. Michael sniffed adenoidally, combing his fingers through his long, silvery hair. "Poor Uncle Sonny," Michael said. "It's hard to believe he's gone. Sonny used to say, 'Time cures, but does it cure like a pill or like a ham?'" There was a trace of accent in Michael's voice. He was coming into his own on all fronts. He looked at me, his eyes glittering in their sockets like oiled steelies, his sickle-shaped smile daring to expose you if you didn't smile back. He sat. Despite the beer stain, I stayed on my feet.

"After his car wreck Sonny took to losing like some people take to Jesus," Michael went on. "Once he told me, 'We're getting older, Mikey, if something don't break soon we'll be dead.' He taught me this pigeon call."

At any given moment Michael's life might suddenly re-create itself. He was quaint and Machiavellian, bridging the two with his smile the way TV preachers did, baptizing the gullible with puffs of breath and later paying hookers to sit nude on deep-dish pizzas. For Michael the past could be annihilated with sudden plunges into homespun innocence. He cupped his hands and raised them to his mouth. The pigeon call had a certain authority. It was the kind of thing you could imagine him practicing for hours on end, allowing it precedence over more useful personal improvements. Becky or his studio assistant or perfect strangers might come upon him mid-coo, but Michael, unembarrassed, would turn the moment into something charming, a little tale elucidating nothing.

"Rusty," he said, "but it's still there. The hands are important, Robert. Once you've got the hands, Sonny used to say, you just do your owl like it's clearing its throat."

He looked at me over the still cupped hands, all surprise and wonderment. Then he leaned back on my sofa.

"Any more news about your discovery?"

I just looked at him.

"It must be a blow for you," he said, purposefully vague. Sonny's last legacy to his nephew might have been an intimate understanding of loss. Michael's face shimmered like the skin of an octopus, showing glassy depths; a fainter, deeper expression mocked anyone who let something of value slip away. Michael was agile, touching all the sore spots at once. He chattered like a torturer, bereft of normal company but needing to talk all the same. He talked about Diane's house, outlining improvements he planned to make and lying about all the work he'd done. I wanted to invite him to leave. But his son was in the other room, and he knew he could stretch this out as long as he wanted. The elderly former owners, Michael said, had sold them the house on contract just to be sure of having someone there who loved the place as much as they had. "The husband was a banshee with a paintbrush," Michael said. "Once I actually calculated how much weight all the layers added. The old goats loved it that a family was moving in." He looked at the air beyond me as if future moments of his life were massed there like fragrant honeysuckle. He stretched his enormous legs to encourage a proprietary air: he owned not only Diane and Budge's lives but mine too.

"You're a despicable fuck," I said, but my voice faltered: we were a pair, and Michael knew it.

"Let me tell you a little story," he said. He gazed up at those blossoms and touched his cheek. "Sonny called up a year ago. He said, 'I ain't much time left.' He told me he'd lost all but two plots of land, one where he lived and the other up at the cemetery." Michael smiled sadly. "He said to tell him about my life. I did, and it didn't sound too good. When I finished, Sonny thought a minute, then he said, 'You finally got everything you only just thought you wanted.'"

"You took that to heart."

"Things come and they go, Robert. The pendulum swings, and now it's swinging my way. The idea being that Di won't believe a fucking word you say."

"Then why talk?"

"Just being sociable," he said, and with an almost biblical flourish he added, "before I take my son."

"Where are you taking him?"

"What do you care?"

"*Try.*"

Michael grinned, giving me time to think about this, to see how abstract my anger was. Maybe he was right. My righteousness was cobbled up from thin air, braced shakily against the very likely possibility of losing traction where I had no business and making a jackass of myself. Still, when Michael stood, I blocked the way to the bedroom.

"Leave him alone."

"Nice touch, Robert."

He tried to bump past me, bringing his chest close to my face. I grabbed him, then didn't know what to do and pulled close like I wanted a hug. He smelled of Becky's bitter perfume and something sweet of his own. And behind both of these was another odor—the persuasive musk of sex. Lots of it. The sort of young, lubricated sex men had midlife crises for but that always seemed to have the same effect: it turned you into a fool. This erotic essence, more than the fight, made me suddenly weak in the knees. But I had to do something. I thought if I let go to hit him I might get hit back. We did a little dance, Michael stumbling as if he also wondered if this were a real fight.

Then he started swinging me back and forth. There was the sound of popcorn, joints snapping and only a few of them his. My spine made undulating S's, like a line of ice skaters cracking the whip. Michael was a lot bigger, and the swinging wasn't all that hard for him. His ease was devastating, and it drained the last of the sap from my legs. But the swinging had an odd sort of affection behind it—he seemed to know he couldn't admonish me without also admonishing himself. In a way, I saw, he was trying to make himself angry.

Then it seemed it wasn't me but my apartment whipping back and forth, blurring, turning into the smear my life had become. It made me rage. So I let go, punched blindly, and hit something bony that hurt like hell. Michael, getting the picture, punched back, rueful but obliged. He missed, but I felt the wind. It was terrifying. He was so much bigger he could do damage almost without thinking, with desultory blows he assumed would do much less.

Then I blacked out for a second, and when I came to I was sitting on my carpet. He'd punched me in the chest. My sternum felt strangely good, like an opening, a tingling break in the clouds, capillaries fizzing around the hole-shape of Michael's reluctant fist. He looked down at me, surprised at himself, holding his hand like a lost pup. When I came off the floor his face fell open, and he held the uninjured hand in front of him.

"No more, no more."

It was the first thing he'd ever said that I thought I could trust. He was shaking and scared. A knob rose on his forehead. Hanks of his silver-threaded hair hung around it, falling down his face past his chin: all he needed was a cauldron and a pointed hat.

"Get out," I said. I didn't have to ask twice. Michael pointed his long, shaking finger at my face.

"What do you think she's going to make of *this?*" he shouted.

"Fair is foul and foul fair."

"You're crazy," Michael said.

When he was gone I paced around my apartment to work off the energy, feeling elated and wondering how long it would last. Finally I sat down and thought, *Now what?* I went to the bedroom door and opened it a crack. Inside I could hear the steady puffs of the boy's breath. What did all this mean? What would Budge make of me fighting with his dad, with Duff? What would he think I was doing? Whose side would he take?

....

Next morning over cereal Budge raised his finger and touched my cheek. "What's that from?"

There was a bruise there in the shape of a kiss.

"I must have slept on it funny," I said.

"Did my daddy come here last night?"

I thought about lying, then said, "Your daddy was late."

Budge touched the bruise again, pushing it like a button. "Did he do that?"

"You were out like a light," I said, wincing, pulling away. "We agreed to leave you alone."

I was running late. Stanley Chen had called earlier. As he'd predicted, Freer Donaldson wanted to talk to me. I was to meet them both in fifteen minutes at the Glorien Building, where Judith, through her battery of lawyers, had agreed to surrender the plates. The threat of legal troubles had never bothered her before, but now she seemed to cave in with ominous ease. I couldn't believe that destroying the plates, in Judith's mind, would be a payback for her lost show, nor that she felt, as her attorneys claimed, that Stanley's threats were more than she could handle. She had even granted Stanley those construction easements he was after. I wondered if he suspected, as I did, that she was up to something.

Budge clearly didn't want to go, but his mother wasn't due back until the evening. When he finished his cereal, dawdling over the last soggy scrap, I put his coat on him and led him quickly outside and down the street.

Half a block from the Glorien, I spotted Freer Donaldson on the sidewalk. I recognized him from pictures in trade journals. Freer, a fervid documenter, was pointing a camera at the top of the building—for a kind of anthropological detail, I thought, the place where the Wilfred Eng plates had been found. But as Budge and I approached I saw a number of other people looking up, and when I reached Freer and introduced myself he said, "There's a woman screaming on the roof."

My blood froze. Before I could ask more he turned his camera on a fire truck wheeling around the corner. The truck was followed by a police cruiser.

Now a crowd began to form. Then Stanley Chen appeared, coming out the Glorien's front door. He walked slowly toward us, glancing up at the top of the building. When he reached us he said in a dry, unsurprised voice, "She locked herself in."

Then Judith appeared on the roof, her head darting over the fire wall. She wore a ball cap pulled low over her eyes. The cap had a long bill that gave her the beaky look of a bird of prey picking out a meal. She looked down as if gauging whether the crowd was big enough. When she dipped down below the wall someone murmured, "She's going to fly." Suddenly the cops were shouting, pushing us all out into the street. Then Judith reappeared with one of the cabinet doors and, with another darting look at us all, held it out over the edge.

When she let go the door sliced downward, the air moving it gracefully, a dreamlike wavering cut short by what seemed the upward slap of the pavement. I felt it tingle in my feet. I needed to run or shout, but I couldn't move. Judith's certainty pervaded the street. I stared at the pulverized glass on the sidewalk, blinking through a mask of disbelief and denial. Judith disappeared, and I thought, *That's it, she's finished now, she just wants us to know she's serious so she can make a deal for herself.* But she reappeared with another door and dropped it too. This was the worse shock, like a lover who slaps you twice, the second time studied, clarifying, cruel. Between each pair she disappeared, and when she came into view again holding another, the look on her face was absorbed, workmanlike. I wondered remotely if she looked this way when she painted, creating disaster after disaster with the same detachment. All her movements had the sanity of routine, like the drill of a seasoned artillery team whose shots killed hundreds in the unimagined distance. It was like some dreadful and instructive punishment we were being forced to watch, a laying on of lashes, the inexorable rhythm, the aching pauses, prescribed but unfair, brutal but no surprise at all, most wrenching for everyone allied with the inciting crime. Beside me I heard the click and slip of Freer's shutter, and I felt a moment of false relief that he didn't appear upset: at least one person who should have been anguished wasn't. For a deluded instant I thought the whole affair wasn't as bad as it seemed—it wouldn't matter that the plates had surfaced for a moment in time. This instant would have the same brief intensity as a film whose vivid characters dissipated in the air outside the theater. After this distressing episode passed, Eng and Ellen would go back to being legends. But to my right I felt Stanley Chen's accusing presence. Stanley might have been staring at me even as the glass rained down. And Freer's snapshots were reflex, a way of delaying shock. The precious images were dribbling out of existence like grains of gold, real to no one in the world but the few of us who had seen and touched them. From now on they would be what they had always been, but their existence would always be linked with this bitter end, and that end would always be linked with me.

Finished with the twelve doors, Judith lifted the five self-portraits. She had kept them in the case—but the case was something else now, simplified, expendable. Now it was garbage, and it dropped with that certainty, exploding with the short thump of a mortar. With that the ordeal should have been over. I had been counting senselessly to myself, like someone besieged who knows the date of his liberation. But now that the end had come, the horror wouldn't stop. Plates kept falling. It was as if some greater power had seized control, absurdity run amok, tragedy turning to torture. Singly now, the negatives knifed through the air. One struck a window ledge halfway down and shattered, spraying a fan of glass fine as ice. Others turned, flattening out, kiting, fluttering like butterflies' wings, their smudged surfaces frozen for a moment, then vanishing in that upward smack. I lost count.

Then, finally, Judith disappeared for good behind the fire wall, and silence rose like mist over the pool of shattered glass.

Without knowing it I had pulled Budge close. My hand clutched his shoulder, and in the silence I thought, *This is why he is here.* Alert to his own excitement, maybe waiting for more, Budge both sensed and didn't sense my shock. He was suddenly huge, he could absorb all I needed him to. And if I couldn't seem to let him go, he would find some way to accept it without a word and lead us out, through the averted eyes and the growing press of bodies, through the stark illogic of a moment that belonged to a nightmare.

10 June 1912

Dear Ellen Danforth,

I am back in the West after an arduous train trip across Canada. This country, which I have often visited, might have seemed more blessedly empty than the United States except that for the whole journey I could not put our meeting out of my mind. Some months after it, you are still in my thoughts and I have decided to write. Let me apologize in advance if this letter is presumptuous or painful. There is pain in approaching what I must tell you, albeit at this late date. It is a burden I do not wish to carry any longer. It is something you deserve to hear. It was clear from our meeting that your late husband never spoke of the matter.

I am certain you never knew that McFarland had made an allowance for me in his will. No doubt it did not at all surprise you to find that my name did not appear in that document at the time of his death. Its absence—its excision—was not like that of a blood relation. What was I to this man? His employee? Minion? Marionette? It is a question that haunts me still. Was I his son? Since his immense wealth was brought about in part from the sweat of "coolie" labor, could any "yellow" son of his take a share in good conscience? Perhaps you are thinking that by taking me under his wing McFarland sought to make at least a gesture of reparation to a people he had wronged. I do not expect that it will in any way explain or excuse my behavior toward you so many decades ago if I tell you that your late husband, before he was your husband, had relations with my mother, also his employee, that might easily have produced an even more compromised "son" than I must appear to you now. When she fell ill my mother begged him to take care of me. To his credit, he was true to his word. Please forgive me if this causes you suffering. You and I talked of many things in our short time together but could never speak of McFarland's infidelities without casting blame on ourselves. Still, I am sure you were painfully aware of his wandering, though perhaps unaware of its extent. I remember speaking to you of the "cat-and-mouse" games he made of his relations with most of the people whose lives he touched. Though I wish it were otherwise, his machinations live in me yet.

Perhaps you are thinking it unseemly to speak ill of the dead. I will be dead one day myself and can truthfully tell you I care nothing for what people may think of me—or at least most people. And this is why I am compelled to speak up now. Our last days together (you did not know they were our last) compel my mind to shame, though not for the reasons you might think.

Before I left you in San Francisco I wrote to McFarland. You have only to assume the worst to know what was in that letter. This is how he came to "discover" and read your little book. How do I know this? I will explain in time. I was saving myself. In such desperate light even acts of cowardice make sense, though at twenty-two years of age one is often blind to longer-lasting consequences. Still, I could see no other way out for myself.

Before sending that letter to your husband I drank myself into a stupor without thinking that false good always results from false courage. Afterward I saddled my horse and rode through the city for hours and at midnight ended up at the wharves, where I stumbled to the end of a dock. Here stevedores had made a pile of old rope, and I confess to you that, overcome with remorse and shame, I fell on this rotting heap with my feet and fists. A moment passed, which I do not remember, and when I woke face down on the stinking hemp my coat was torn and my hands bruised. A packet lay at rest at the dock and was due to sail at dawn. When it left I was on board.

When I think of you in those days, it wrings my heart. It is worse when I recall your generosity of spirit, when I imagine you making excuses for me until the truth became plain. No one who is white can understand the humiliation, the danger, the terror. Still, I do not call upon any of these facts to excuse me.

I knew you knew nothing of what I had done because McFarland later told me so himself.

I stayed away from San Francisco for quite some time, and when I finally returned you had gone back to Manhattan. McFarland had moved north. Some years later I heard he was ill. Needless to say, I'd had no contact with him. I felt equal reluctance to see him and to stay away. I decided to write. I must say I was not surprised to learn of his newly adopted city, and even less to hear of the reason that took him there. He answered my letter and invited me to his home, which he shared with his common-law wife and his sons. I arrived in the evening shortly after supper. He answered the door himself. This surprised me, as I had heard he was bedridden. I was shocked to find what had once been the great gust of his will so reduced by illness. He looked weary, resigned, even weak. He would live only a few months more. It took a great deal of his strength to shake my hand with anything like his former vigor. He led me into his study, where I recognized many books and pictures and other objects from Stockton Street. It was a balmy night, and the windows of the study were open. Sick as he was, he still inspired the old feeling in me, one that until now I wouldn't have called fear, also a desire to please him that I had felt as a boy and that was all the more troubling in light of his relations with my mother.

But my intentions in going to see him this last time were so tainted that for many years afterwards I came to doubt whether my intentions about anything could be pure. I had not meant just to tell him good-bye, or even to have him refuse me his forgiveness. We managed some small talk for several minutes. But gradually a welter of emotion rose in my heart, and I fell silent. My brow began to sweat. McFarland looked at me steadily, knowingly. Behind him out the windows the breeze in the chestnuts sounded like the ocean. With some effort he stood and turned away from me slowly. At the sideboard he poured us each a glass of whiskey. By that time in my life I had learned that one should be judicious even with one's pity. Still, I felt a strange collapsing in my chest. "We're so much alike, you and I," he said at last. "Neither of us knows what life is." I was flushed and upset, full of remorse but also anger. His words were challenging. I tried to tell him he didn't know what it was to be "yellow," and he asked, "Do you?" When I could only look at him, he raised his brows. "You probably blame me for that." He sipped, staring at me over the rim of his glass. His head trembled slightly, though from weakness rather than emotion. The curtains at the window billowed inward, a river of air pouring through as if the room could never be filled. He came near and handed me my drink and asked, "Why did you come?" When I still could not answer he downed his whiskey in a single gulp, then nodded toward mine in my hand. "Drink up," he said. "It's the last thing we'll ever share."

The moment gave him back his old strength. His smile alone might have undone me.

But then an even stranger thing happened. He brought his head close to mine, and without a word he did what he had never done before—he kissed my cheek.

The kiss stunned me like a shot. I had come for revenge, and I would leave with only this. I felt it on my cheek even after he left me in that study, amid the remnants of our mingled past. Even as I let myself out his front door, his kiss would not leave me—I feel it still sometimes. Outside I walked a short way, then fell on a grassy bank and in the warm darkness succumbed to bitter tears, though they would offer no comfort ultimately. McFarland knew that I could forgive myself only in the imperfect way he himself had always done, by a majority of exactly one.

By your lights, I daresay, Joseph McFarland and I may well have been cut from the same cloth—we are among those who "use" the world. Do I have the right to expect you to understand—you who also suffered under the yoke of an unyielding and inescapable will? You may believe that I used your love to exact a larger revenge. I denied this to myself for many years. I deny it no longer, nor do I deny that for a time I truly loved you. I wonder if you can believe me, Ellen. I never loved anyone else so well.

Yours Sincerely,
Wilfred Eng

10

....

The hours flying west passed as in a child's drawing. The world conformed to a limited palette. Above and below were miles of lulling blues. Solitary clouds drifted by, trailing their tiny shadows on the water.

Climbing after takeoff, the captain assured us of clear weather all the way. But half an hour out of Honolulu a turbulent hole opened in the air, and the plane plunged from under us. Drinks and magazines jumped a foot, briefcases and notebook computers toppled to the cabin floor. The fuselage bucked like a circus ride, shuddering and heaving as if about to fly apart. A flight attendant shouted for two startled men to sit down and buckle up. I had been chatting politely with the woman next to me, and now we suddenly grasped each other's hands with disbelieving looks. It was December, but she wore a bright floral dress and I thought, *No one can die dressed like that.*

Then just as suddenly the shaking stopped, and as we leveled off and cruised into calmer air my seatmate took her hands back with a shaky smile. The captain said nothing, as if some would blame him no matter what. Instead the plane banked gently left, as if to show us where the violence had come from. Then it banked right, making a lazy S, an aeronautic shrug. We could look forever and never see where danger lay.

It was Christmas Eve. I'd laid over a night in San Francisco after flying in from Chicago, where there had been an ugly episode with a student at the Art Institute. This Hawaii trip had been planned for two months. Despite holiday volume all the connections had gone smoothly, though the ease made it seem like escape: the turbulence was the long hand of Chicago taking a last swipe.

For months now, since the events of the spring, I had made a point of not running away. The days after the destruction of the Wilfred Eng negatives were like those following a senseless death in the family, unfocused, anxious, drearily long. Neglected work had piled up in my still wrecked office. At first all attempts at doing anything started with a spark of panic, then rolled to a dead stop. I would work furiously for fifteen minutes, then find myself staring out the window. At night the downward soaring dominated.

The carnage had made it into a thirty-second segment near the end of the CBS Nightly News with Dan Rather. A tourist passing the Glorien that morning had shot video footage of the whole thing. This man's film looked and sounded nothing like what I had experienced. I remembered only a galvanic silence, but his microphone picked up singular shouts echoing against the buildings, also a background of ordinary hubbub, strangers murmuring theories to other strangers. Only four people there knew what was really happening. To the rest, some psycho was cleaning house on a rooftop. Most of the crowd was chatty and bemused, relieved—or maybe disappointed—that Judith was not going to jump. At one point the cameraman panned shakily to a woman who shouted up to oblivious Judith, "Give him hell, honey!"—apparently thinking this was the culmination of some domestic dispute. Laughter bubbled up. I remembered none of this, and yet as I watched the footage I wished it could have been as most there had seen it. On tape the plates looked innocuous, inconsequential, less the point than the people watching. And yet each time the camera followed one down, there was the back of my head, also following the descent, then stopping suddenly with a kind of stunned, innocent hope, as if each time I believed gravity might do something different.

The local news clips showed police leading Judith away in hand-cuffs while the voice-over described her pioneer ancestors as eccentrics and drew inferences about Judith's mental health. But Judith looked neither eccentric nor crazy. Even in her beaky hat she looked sedate, in control, the perpetrator of some sleeker, subtler crime. When the crowds cleared, Freer Donaldson had the shards crated up and shipped back to San Francisco. Afterward the pulverized residue, fine as sugar, was hosed away.

Freer, though he wouldn't admit it to me, had convinced the DeWitt to purchase the tape.

Two weeks later I learned that the museum was planning to use an edited version of it as the centerpiece for an exhibit scheduled to open in August. These were poor scraps for making gravy, but the DeWitt was doing its best. When I heard about the show my bowels froze—I would be blamed publicly. I tried to prepare for the worst and buried myself in all that neglected work. Even here there was no escape—word was getting around. Colleagues, associates, and friends wrote or called, expressing shock, disappointment, outrage. This would be the last I heard from many of them. It was the beginning of the end.

Then, to my surprise, Freer called in early May. Though the reason wasn't clear right away, he was besieged. He needed details he didn't have time to research himself. The press was hounding him, and the requests for interviews, articles, and speaking dates were pouring in. He was also under the gun to get maximum exposure for the DeWitt. The museum was sifting through its Eng prints and borrowing what rare early photographs it could on such short notice. The show would start with a viewing of that tape, followed by a talk and slide show. The plates themselves, the heap of rubble, would be on view, laid in state under an enormous glass display box. On impulse I offered to ghostwrite, for free, the essay for the official show catalog.

"I can't keep your name out, if you're thinking I can do you any favors," Freer said. "Sad to say, Robert, you're a pivotal part of the story, and the story's just about all we've got left."

Then he said yes, but that we would coauthor the essay. He would tell me which parts he wanted me to write. It became clear that Freer was being used as a whipping boy by members of the museum board who were outraged less by the destruction of the plates themselves than by the loss of prestige and money. One sign of their fierce indignation was that Freer was forced to approach Judith for details, since she was the only one who had seen some of the plates. Judith refused. Stanley Chen had leveled charges of grand larceny and willful destruction against her, and when Freer suggested to one of her attorneys that he might try to intercede with Stanley on her behalf, the attorney reported her reply: "Mind your own fucking business!"

I was relieved to have this catalog work and went at it with an energy that surprised me. After Weston there had been nothing but bill-paying for reparation. This work felt better. It drew me out of the deepening funk. While there was more relief than joy in writing the story and doing the research, it was closer to comfort than I would ever have believed such work could be. As I faxed Freer notes and drafts, we both began to see the gaps that couldn't be filled without more travel. I thought he would do this himself. But he was buried. Every day brought more calls and mail from all over the world. Freer liked my work. As the spring and early summer wore on he grew less reluctant. Still, when a travel budget was arranged for me he tried to dismiss it as "routine."

I went back to New York for two weeks. Ms. Benning took pity and saved me time by guiding me to crucial passages. At first when I asked her if the DeWitt could borrow several of Ellen's diaries she refused. Then Carol Chase Marino showed up again, asking questions, thinking Ellen might hurdle her over her decade-old writer's block. Not wanting to let Marino near Ellen again, Ms. Benning agreed to avert her myopic eyes while I made off with a number of key volumes. Through another librarian friend Ms. Benning dug up the privately published memoir of a Mrs. Elizabeth Harold, who had been Thompson Danforth's housekeeper in Manhattan. Ms. Benning found a passage that described McFarland's visit in 1862, when he first met ten-year-old Ellen.

> All the adults had gone for a picnic in the park, determined not to waste such a magnificent spring day. Mr. Danforth left me word, asking if I wouldn't mind keeping an eye on his guest's "man"—a boy, actually, who acts as valet, fetching his master's clothes and toilet articles and the like. I found this boy upstairs with my Ellie in the nursery. I don't remember seeing a more beautiful child, unless it was Ellie herself. He almost never smiled and was so silent and formal, with a secret in his eyes that made me not want to trust him.
>
> And I had cause for not trusting him, for the two of them had got into my sewing scraps and covered the entire floor with them. I found them kneeling head to head, their noses nearly touching the floor.
>
> I blamed the boy for the mess, though I knew Ellie to be the culprit, as she had committed this crime many times before. She loved to throw the scraps high and stand under them as they fell, and I could see her coaxing a smile from the silent boy with this bit of wickedness, the two of them in their innocence standing in the bright storm. But when I came into the room I shouted at him, "Just see what you've done!" I felt bad later, for they told me he was an orphan. The boy might have known nothing of simple fun. It could well have accounted for his bewildering look, neither defiant nor penitent, only curious. Ellie looked up at me and touched her lips. "Come look," she said, nearly whispering. I did, bending over the spot where they knelt. I could make out nothing but the pain in my back that would come of clearing it all up. The boy kept the same look on his face, and for some reason it made me all

the angrier. "Time to clean up this mess!" I said, then I swiped my
hand down between them at the scraps.

Lo and behold, one bright piece of plush flew right up into my
face and beat itself against my eyes! I gave a shout and nearly fell
over backward from the shock. It was a butterfly! The creature
must have drifted in, drunk on the spring air and thinking the
scraps were its brothers and sisters. Ellie, the wicked dear, rolled
on the floor laughing at me, as any normal child would. The boy
was unmoved. I set them to help me clean their mess and looked
up at one point to find him staring up into the corner where the
lovely creature had lighted. I felt ashamed of my outburst then,
and in the morning when he was to leave I put my arms around
him to show there were no hard feelings. He went stiff as a tree
trunk in my embrace, and when I let him go he only gave the same
peculiar stare. . . .

Ms. Benning faxed me the passage with a note that said, "'Is it rarity that gives anything its radiance?' (E. Danforth)."

....

Over the spring and early summer I spent seven weeks in San
Francisco on three separate trips, consulting with Freer and sleeping
on his couch. By this time Freer Donaldson was giving an average of
one interview a day, some with art world luminaries such as Robert
Hughes of *Time*. I was often on hand, in person or by phone, to fill in
the blanks. On one trip I visited the McFarland mansion. The house
had been moved from Stockton Street and barged across the water to
the Marin County town of Tiburon. Before it was moved, in 1905, it
was renovated in a later Victorian style that suited the cloying use it
had since been put to. Now on the tree-lined main street of downtown Tiburon, it was home to three floors of expensive boutiques.
Ellen's room was a travel agency painted aqua and canary. A bath shop
occupied the front parlor where Eng, as a boy, had made some of the
first images of his life. And McFarland's study, much beloved by

young Wilfred, was now a shop that sold naughty lingerie to Marin County women. The bay window that had once looked out on the changeable face of the harbor had been divided into three doll-sized mullioned panes that gave onto a cramped back parking lot and a rising hillside of fern and eucalyptus.

Home from one of these trips, I got a call from Patrick Chen.

Patrick said he had something important to show me and asked if he could come to my apartment. On a hunch, he had been sifting through crates of old family memorabilia and had found Eng's 1912 letter to Ellen. He showed me a photocopy. The letter was written on three of the distinctively large sheets Eng favored; I had seen other of his writings on this same paper at both the Hagen-Mills and the DeWitt. The text was heavily reworked, words, phrases, even whole sentences scratched out or rephrased. Patrick wondered how it had ended up back on this coast, and I told him it might have been a draft. But when I called Ms. Benning in New York, she assured me in an admonishing tone that Ellen had made no mention of receiving such a letter. It was a good bet that she would have.

Whether from shame, embarrassment, or the fear of committing still another "sin," Eng had never sent it.

Perhaps he wanted to save Ellen suffering or was embarrassed that he'd hung on to the memories decades longer than she had. Or maybe he thought he was not telling her anything that she hadn't already figured out. One sentence he crossed out read, "You no doubt think this a diabolical thing to do to a dying man." Cutting this might have meant that Eng had already begun forgiving himself in that "imperfect" way.

"Stanley says it's not Wilfred's," Patrick said.

"Stanley's probably wrong." I explained about the paper, then added, "A handwriting expert could say for sure."

Stanley, Patrick said, thought it bad enough that Eng had indulged in a pointless love affair with a rich white woman. He insisted the letter showed Eng in a cowardly light.

"He wants to burn it," Patrick said. "He can't, now that I've told you."

"So I'm being used."

Patrick said, "That's about the size of it," with, I thought, a shade of a smile.

"As if your nephew needed another excuse to hate me."

Then he looked at me calmly as if he weren't about to ask something extraordinary. He, Patrick, had called a meeting to decide what to do and wanted me to attend.

"You must be joking," I told him. "You heard what Stanley said— he'd put me in jail if he could."

"Nothing's going to happen to you," Patrick said.

I told him that my having read the letter might be more incentive for Stanley to destroy it. But Patrick wasn't having any of it and wouldn't leave until I agreed to go.

Predictably, Stanley was furious. He wanted to burn the pages on the spot. Patrick remained calm. Of the four Chens Patrick was the mediator, the peacemaker. He was the least combative during meetings, the most sensible, the one least inclined to fly off the handle. He looked levelly at Stanley and said, "There's been enough destruction." For once Stanley looked surprised; he wouldn't quite look at me after that. "It shows Wilfred was human," Patrick added. "Just like Mr. Armour. Just like all of us." Patrick insisted that there'd been enough destruction, then suggested that they put the letter away for now and decide its fate at a later time. The others agreed, though Stanley reluctantly so. "What about Armour?" he asked and gave me a sour glance. "How do we know he'll keep his mouth shut?" It was no good making promises, so I just kept quiet. "Nobody'd believe you anyway," he said. I acknowledged this remark with another silence. Then, to ease the discomfort in the silent room, and also to show myself in a better light, I began telling them about my research, the work I had done on Eng's behalf. Freer and I had determined that the plates had come to

Seattle in 1896, when Eng thought he might try to settle here again. In all there had been four of the wooden cases. Each must have weighed thirty pounds fully loaded. I explained to the Chens that by moving them here from San Francisco Eng had saved them from the fire that destroyed most of his early plates and prints. "Fire seemed to dog the guy," Ed, the eldest brother, said. "Fire is light. And in the end it did him in. Literally."

"Of all his work to that point," I said, "why would he drag these unwieldy cases to Seattle twenty years after the affair?"

The answer to this might have had less to do with love than with those impure intentions Eng spoke of in his unsent letter. If he was afraid of compromising Ellen, he would surely have destroyed the negatives immediately. He didn't. This almost certainly meant he was still carrying a torch for her—I felt certain his admission of love at the end of his letter proved as much. Clearly he was guilty, remorseful, perhaps so keenly aware of the lasting effect of Ellen on his life that he needed to preserve the plates, to know they were safe, maybe even to look at them from time to time and remember, to revisit them like the beloved and hallowed places he preserved in his landscapes. Prints were too frail; the plates were a more lasting monument. They also preserved a negative image, so perhaps Eng could look at them and see something else, imagine some other, opposite life for himself.

But instead of speculating any further I told the Chens I thought it enough that he'd admitted fault to himself and tried to emphasize these words to reflect my own mistakes in a more compassionate light. By that time, though, Stanley was shifting in his chair and looking at his watch.

Later Patrick told me the letter had been put in a safe-deposit box.

....

As the date of the show drew close, Freer scrambled to finish his part of the essay. I offered to take charge of designing and printing the catalog. The show was put together at a feverish pace but opened on time. The DeWitt was determined to make hay while the disaster was still fresh in people's minds. I was not invited and wouldn't have gone anyway. The mayor of San Francisco attended the opening-night party, at which it was announced that the show would begin touring after it closed at the DeWitt in late August. Two days later Freer called, saying I was to accompany him on this tour.

"Why not ask me to face a firing squad?" I said.

"Things must be thin for you right now," he said. He was right. To make ends meet I'd started selling pictures off my walls. Even this was difficult: once potential buyers heard my name they backed off, and over the summer I'd gotten desperate enough to sell way low. "This might be a way to salvage something of your reputation," Freer went on. "I went to bat for you with the board. Still," he added slyly, "if you refuse, I'll understand."

"You think I'm scared," I said, "and you know what? You're right."

"We could set up a wire screen like they have in honky-tonks so the flying beer bottles don't get through."

"That's cute, Freer. But I'll pay my dues in the wings."

Still, he knew he had me over a barrel. No amount of free legwork would make up for my part in the smashed plates.

"I could describe what you did," he explained, drolly implying that this description would be at the expense of whatever was left of my reputation. "It would be better if they heard it from you. Who knows, it might be the making of you yet."

He could have used a better example than Judith Lund. Judith herself had called the police and fire departments to the Glorien that morning as well as all the media, including a stringer for the Associated Press wire service. Judith had a Plan B. When this AP man later interviewed her at her bail hearing, Judith claimed that her destruction of the Eng plates was not motivated by malice or money, as many believed, but was instead a piece of performance art.

Careerwise, it was her greatest move. An infamous New York art out-law who called himself "Zane Something" heard the story and imme-diately offered Judith a show.

A hustler of an order that made Parker Lange look like Minny Mouse, Something was noted for his sensation-causing shows and tabloid-style promotions. In his overcooked press release he openly promoted Judith as the destroyer of the Eng negatives, praising her "courageous and symbolic ode to the destruction of solipsism and the Western pipe dream that love is still possible." (I wondered how Ron Rizer, the *Yes*-man, was handling that one.) In case anyone might forget who Judith was, the entire floor of the gallery was covered with broken glass, and as patrons viewed paintings such as *Wall*, *Gray Construction #3*, and *Berlin 1989*, the enormous slashed canvas with its heavy ribbons flopping on the gallery floor, the shards crunched under their feet. At one point city health officials threatened to close the show down if the glass wasn't removed; Judith and Something, fanning the flames, began encouraging patrons to take pieces of the glass as a souvenirs. Hearing about the incident, a famous shock jock invited them to appear on his radio show, and both Something and Judith, according to a *New York Times* reporter covering the unfold-ing story of the exhibit, "seemed to thrive on the verbal assaults of particularly small-brained listeners." The same article showed a photo of Judith at the gallery in her long-billed cap, shaking hands with art lovers through a phalanx of security guards. Every painting sold.

The only gaps left now, Freer said, were Parker and me. He added that he was having trouble maintaining discreet silences when the subject came up, which it did more often as time went on. Then, pre-tending not to back me into a corner, he started pitching the idea of my touring with the show. The sordid parts would seem less sordid if I explained them soberly. Uneasy as I was at the time, I thought he might have a point. We had become a society that deplored shameful acts much less when they were turned into public spectacles; a good freak show could sedate our lust for scandal, if not exactly ease our minds.

"You could answer everyone and make yourself a piece of change as well," he said. "The museum is prepared to put you under contract."

"The board feeling flush, are they?"

Freer didn't answer. I wondered how much more the DeWitt would be making if there were no scandal, if the plates were still intact. It was a question I never asked.

We started off at college campuses, and the response was terrific if not always welcome. For part of the display the museum's conservator had cut open a number of the pasteboard sleeves that had held some of the negatives for decades. On the insides of these a fine layer of albumen had bonded to the paper, making what one reviewer called a "double negative." This same critic somewhat breathlessly added that this accident was "solemn and poignant, an image like the shroud of Turin, a physical memory of someone who is gone but lingers mysteriously."

At our first presentation, the University of New Mexico, Freer wrote out jokes for me. I thought he was crazy but got laughs even when I read them off his file cards. By virtue of this not always pleasant public contact, a persona began to emerge that Diane Mays called "your Ollie North."

"You're like one of these crooked politicians stumping their unrepentant selves after their jail terms."

I was in her living room showing her a videotape of our Florida State talk when she made this crack. She had a point. Momentum built with each success, with each audience won over by contrition. Diane meant I could start ignoring danger signs as devotedly as I had with the plates themselves and with the Weston debacle. I shouldn't be too quick to pin a medal on myself because things might start to come right. Nothing should rival the stinging fact that the plates were lost. The DeWitt might be willing to make it all a legitimate circus, but I should know where to draw the line.

Diane extended the political analogy to Parker, who, she said, had worked the situation like a ward-heeler. "He showed you the noose, then guided your head through the loop." But behind the humor was dry introspection: I wasn't the only one who could delude himself. Michael had proved this to her.

By autumn attacks began to appear and were gradually more difficult to defend against. *Print* magazine devoted a whole issue to Eng. One of the articles in it called Parker and me "members of that profession that is even older than the oldest one. That the DeWitt Museum associates itself with such reprobates outrages all who work in a more honest vein or pay more for their lapses, past and present." *Ms.* magazine published a scathing essay about how the art world's old-boy network had "for decades colluded to dismiss Ellen Danforth's account as the fantasy of a hysterical female." More often than not I was recognized as an "old boy" in good standing.

Audience members began quoting these articles, sometimes before I'd seen them myself. In Chicago, Freer and I had to be escorted by security guards through an angry group of Asian students boycotting our talk. As Freer and I stood at the podium, one older student shouted from the back, "What gives you the right to stand up there after what you did?"

"You asked me here," I told him, applying Freer's maxim that the simplest answer was best as long as it wasn't smart-assed.

"Some of us didn't," this student called back.

"I've studied old photography for a long time," I told him levelly. "I held the plates in my hands. No one else ever will, and I'm sorry for that. Like it or not, I'm afraid I'm all you've got."

"You fucking trashed priceless works of art," the student insisted. Murmurs rippled through the crowd, some in agreement. Freer put in, "It wasn't Mr. Armour who did the trashing."

"Same difference."

"Mr. Armour recognized the plates in the first place when no one else would have. It is because of his devotion and knowledge that this love affair is now acknowledged as real. Whether we think we owe him anything else, we at least owe him that."

"You're having your way with the dead," the student shouted. "You're preying on the oppressed. You're squeezing your dollars out of colored hides just like the white man always has."

Freer, who wouldn't point out that this student was himself white, calmly explained, "I'm on salary. Mr. Armour is taking something less than that."

Then he scanned the audience for the next question. The student, shushed by others who wanted the story more than the fireworks, got up to leave but lobbed a final insult with an almost merry grin.

"*You,*" he shouted, pointing at Freer, "are a museum organ grinder, and *Mr. Armour* there is your fucking monkey."

Outside he surprised us, knocking Freer to the freezing pavement. His friends helped me wrestle him away, and my face came within inches of his. He radiated outrage and something deeper that reason couldn't touch. The man was obviously unbalanced. This realization rendered a flash of triumph for the truth I'd meant to peddle. But whatever was wrong with him was also reflected in the faces of those pulling him gently away—not apology but uneasiness. They were not helping us but protecting someone whose version of the truth they couldn't quite dismiss.

·················

On the plane to San Francisco from Chicago I told Freer I was finished.

He had sprained his wrist in the scuffle but sipped wine calmly. "We're booked through February," he said.

"I don't have the stomach for it anymore."

"It means you won't be there to defend yourself, Robert."

"Only until this whole thing blows over."

He glanced over at me. "You think that's going to happen? You're always going to be dealing with people who know," he said, then asked practically, "What are you going to do?"

In Seattle a position had opened up with the maverick but chronically strapped Washington Historical Alliance. Maybe they were notoriety-hungry themselves. Or maybe they wanted the public nosethumbing of having someone like me on staff. There was a basement full of old prints and negatives that needed cataloging, and they might even have thought that with my luck I'd fish out something big. At any rate the Alliance had made an offer, and I was thinking it over. Freer sipped, clearly thinking this a step down.

"I'm taking the show to Europe next year," he said. "I need help getting ready. First stop is London. You could bring your girlfriend. The whole continent," he said. "Think about it."

But I didn't have to.

....

At the Honolulu airport I was still shaking from the turbulence when I stepped from the plane into the blanket of moist, welcoming heat. Outside the terminal I hailed a cab and headed for the hotel. The early-afternoon traffic moved slowly along a boulevard lined with palms that gave upward toward that blameless sky.

I'd been here last August researching Eng's failed trip to China. Over the months I had accumulated enough frequent-flier miles to get Diane and Budge free rides. They'd been here two days already.

The tendency when I hadn't seen the two of them in weeks was to carry over something of that performing penitent, which I had done this time by bringing too-lavish Christmas gifts from Marshall Field in Chicago. When I'd brought Budge home to Diane's that awful day last spring, she'd offered me the couch as she used to with Michael. I was in no shape to refuse. At first she seemed uncertain about extending even

such a simple kindness except that Budge followed his recounting of
the smashed negatives by telling her Michael had forgotten to pick him
up at school. Still angry with me, she couldn't press for details.

But an even more important question was soon answered when
she found Becky's panties stuffed under her mattress. After working
so hard to win Diane back, it almost seemed Michael was begging to
get caught. Months later, when Diane had cooled off some, she admitted as much. "All he wants is to mess with people's lives."
Afterwards, away so much, I was out of range of the damage I had
caused us. I began to call her from other cities. She grew uneasy in the
silences because in them I identified myself as someone who needed
to be sorry. My apologies meant nothing and began to annoy her;
when I told her I was sorry I became Robert again, the schemer, the
liar. So gradually I began to focus on the neutral third party of the distance itself, like a filter purifying her accusations, her ironies, her
angry vows to have nothing more to do with men.

"If you hadn't gone overboard with this thing," she told me one
night, "I never would have made such an ass of myself."

The logic here was forced, and I said nothing. Diane knew, as I did,
that there was no spectrum, no scale when it came to being a fool. You
either were one or you weren't.

On the bed in our hotel room she had left a note saying she and
Budge were on the beach. I'd had my mail forwarded to the hotel, and
Diane had set it on the bed, putting one letter on top so I would see it
first thing.

It was from Parker Lange.

The envelope was postmarked Amsterdam—I thought all the
trouble must have been more painful than his glibness let on.
Typically he started in without a greeting.

> How unlike Parker, you must be saying to yourself, to return to a
> scene of past wound-licking. How Parker must be hurting, you
> say. The Netherlands are very soothing. Christiana's here too and

says hello—she supports us by selling jewelry at a tony canal-side shop. All the locals think she's a spy.

Parker went on to say that he and Leonard were too much like birds of a feather for any long-term grudge-holding. He claimed that Leonard firing him was "all for show" and that Leonard had already recruited Parker to represent his interests in two small overseas deals.

Then Parker came to the main point of his letter. After I'd told him about the Ellen negatives, he confessed, he'd gone to Judith, who had shown him the rest. Counting the five portraits of Eng, there were a total of thirty-nine. For insurance, Parker had stolen one. But that wasn't all. "A friend saw you 'perform' last month in Arizona," he wrote.

> When I talked to this woman, she said you were brave but belea-
> guered. To my surprise, she said there was no mention of me as
> anything but this total art Nazi. Let me set the record straight.
> Even at this late date I figure you deserve to know that all is, or
> was, not lost. All this time I assumed that Stanley Chen had filled
> you in and that you were just too much of a tight-ass to hunt me
> down and thank me. What a dreamer! I should have figured out
> that Stanley is enough of an asshole to keep the news to himself.
> Like all emotional bean-counters, he'd rather keep you believing
> the worst. Anyway, to get him off my ass months ago, I sent him
> the plate. So you're not as evil as you think, though don't take my
> word for it.
>   C. just walked in the door, which means it's time for "lunch."
> Take care, Robert, until the next time—don't laugh, it could hap-
> pen. Cheers.
>
> P.S. Sorry about your car.

It crossed my mind that there may in fact have been no surviving plate, Parker merely pulling the chain one last time. But why would he at this point? Parker was the sort to pout and take what revenge the moment offered, but then he moved on. I was certain Patrick Chen would have told me about the surviving plate. But maybe he didn't know. The idea of Stanley keeping the negative from his loving family was hard to imagine—hard, but certainly not impossible. Freer Donaldson would certainly want to pursue the matter with Stanley himself. Depending on how that turned out, Freer might also be interested in having Parker fill in for me on the European leg of the tour.

I folded the letter and slipped it into the bottom of my suitcase. Then I changed and went down to the beach.

I crossed the warm sand in my bare feet. The beach was crowded, but I soon spotted Diane sitting on a towel I'd brought from San Antonio for her birthday. She smiled when she saw me and reached out her arm, drawing me down beside her. She asked how the flight was, and I told her about the hole in the sky. I decided not to tell her about Parker's letter—there was time for that later.

Then Budge appeared from nowhere, spattering water like a puppy.

I couldn't see Budge now without remembering that awful morning. Clearly he'd known something terrible had happened, and yet throughout the afternoon as we waited for Diane he'd asked no questions. He left me alone without leaving me. He watched TV and fixed himself a sandwich and dragged his Lego set from under the sofa, presenting me with a picture of a normal life in progress.

Now he came close for our hug. The "torpedo" had gone by the wayside. Our hugs, especially when I returned after several weeks, may have reminded him of Michael's "desert island" game, played on our disastrous cruise: sometimes he turned the embrace into high, humorous drama. But it didn't matter. Each one marked my own relief, reminded me of the unassuming power of his presence.

Now I let him go and he said, "We went to Pearl Harbor." Then he described the sunken destroyers, oil still bubbling up from their engines. Sailors' bones were trapped inside the hulls. From above, one battleship had the shape of a ghostly shoeprint, its conning tower rising like a warning finger at low tide. Finished, the boy ran off and Diane said, "It's weird. The sun and the green make the harbor look like a movie set. It's like it all never really happened."

"You're getting pink," I said.

She made a face, looking at her shoulders, then handed me the sunscreen and hummed when the cool ointment touched. Her suit was still damp from a swim, her hair swept back and opening dark fissures as it dried. Rubbing her shoulders, I watched the boy, who had stopped his breakneck run toward the water and now looked out at a distant cruise ship moving along the seam between two more shades of blue. The sky was empty and calm. Budge shaded his eyes, watching it all, the world's simple parts—beach, water, sky. The perfect fit. Then he turned to make sure we were watching, and when we waved he plunged in, arms wide, embracing it all as if he'd been lost a long time and just been found.